BR

Suncoast Society

Tymber Dalton

SIREN SENSATIONS

Siren Publishing, Inc.
www.SirenPublishing.com

A SIREN PUBLISHING BOOK
IMPRINT: Siren Sensations

BROKEN TOY
Copyright © 2014 by Tymber Dalton

ISBN: 978-1-62741-630-6

First Printing: August 2014

Cover design by Harris Channing
All art and logo copyright © 2014 by Siren Publishing, Inc.

ALL RIGHTS RESERVED: This literary work may not be reproduced or transmitted in any form or by any means, including electronic or photographic reproduction, in whole or in part, without express written permission.

All characters and events in this book are fictitious. Any resemblance to actual persons living or dead is strictly coincidental.

Printed in the U.S.A.

PUBLISHER
Siren Publishing, Inc.
www.SirenPublishing.com

DEDICATION

For Sir, who keeps insisting I'm not a broken toy. Thank you for putting up with me.

AUTHOR'S NOTE

While the books in the Suncoast Society series are stand-alone works that may be read independently of each other, the recommended reading order to avoid spoilers is as follows:

1. *Safe Harbor*
2. *Cardinal's Rule*
3. *Domme by Default*
4. *The Reluctant Dom*
5. *The Denim Dom*
6. *Pinch Me*
7. *Broken Toy*

Many of the minor characters who appear in this book also make appearances in—or are featured in—other books in the Suncoast Society series. All titles are available from Siren-BookStrand.

BROKEN TOY

Suncoast Society

TYMBER DALTON
Copyright © 2014

Chapter One

"So that must be a really cool job, huh? You know, I *totally* love watching *CSI*. That is *such* a great show."

Oh, my god. Kill. Me. Now.

Detective William Thomas forced a smile as his date, Cassie, took a sip of her Diet Coke, her dramatically overdone smoky eyes intently staring at him from across the table. "It's not like it is on TV at all, believe me," he assured her.

"Yeah, you don't have commercials in real life."

He'd started to laugh when he realized with dawning horror that she was totally serious.

Like, totally.

Thank god we didn't go to Marelli's. I'd be embarrassed to death right now. "Uh, yeah."

Scratch killing myself, I'm going to fucking kill Al for letting Sue set me up.

Normally, he wasn't a fan of blind dates. As in he didn't go on them.

At all.

Detective Albert Ogilvy, friend—*former* friend if this date dragged on too much longer—and coworker, had managed to catch him at a weak moment. It'd been two years since his last date, five years since the last second date he'd had with someone…

And nine years since Ella died.

By the time he walked Cassie out to her car an hour later, he'd tried to adopt a Zen attitude about it. It wasn't like he had to endure a second date with her, much less spend the rest of his life with the woman. He'd gotten out of the house for the evening, which had kept his mind occupied.

And now I'll have something to freaking guilt-trip Al over.

Totally.

* * * *

The next morning, Al's smile lasted from when he walked into the conference room until he got a look at Bill's face.

"Uh-oh."

Bill just glared.

"Um, I was going to ask you how your date went last night, but I can tell you're not wanting to talk about it."

Bill sat back and tossed his pen onto the conference table. He pretended to twirl his hair. "Wrong. I sooo *totally* want to talk about it. Um, I so totally think what you cops do is sooo cool. I mean, *CSI* and everything. Ohmagurd."

Al froze before letting out a snort. "Wow. That bad?"

Bill glared in reply.

His face fell. "Man, I'm so sorry. I owe you. Sue was driving me crazy to ask you to go out with that woman."

"What the *hell*, dude? I thought we were friends."

Al sat next to him. Their morning briefing would start in a few minutes. They could see through the windows overlooking the hallway that other detectives and officers were already making their way to the conference room.

"She's Sue's best friend's niece or something," Al explained. "I'd never met her before, I swear, or I wouldn't have agreed to it."

"Yeah, well, tell Sue thanks but no thanks if she comes up with any other dates for me," he muttered, his voice dropping off as two other detectives walked into the conference room.

"Ten-four," Al muttered back.

Hell, he was only forty-six. It wasn't like he was in danger of dying alone as a crazy old man with twenty cats or something.

He hadn't even adopted a cat.

Yet.

Although the last time he was in the neighborhood of the Humane Society over in Englewood, he had given serious thought to stopping by, just to take a look.

* * * *

Al stopped by Bill's desk at lunchtime. "Want to go grab a bite to eat, or are you still pissed off at me?"

Bill's first inclination was to say no, except he wanted to get out of the office and the only other option was a bag of chips out of the vending machine, or walking across the street for fast food at the Golden Arches.

Again.

Bill logged out of his computer. "I'm still pissed at you, so you're buying."

"Deal."

"And driving."

"Deal. Again."

"And that still doesn't get you off the hook."

"Roger that."

They drove a couple of miles south down US 41, to a small Greek restaurant they both liked. "Will this do?" Al asked.

"It's a start."

"You're going to bust my balls over this forever, aren't you?"

Bill grinned. "What do you think?"

"Oh, boy. I'm fucked."

Once they were seated at the table and had menus, Al asked. "So, give me the deets. What happened?"

Bill gave his friend credit. Al tried not to laugh. Tried damned hard. But by the time Bill finished the story, Al finally had to let out a chuckle. "Uh, wow."

Bill nodded. "Wow is right. Not the good kind of wow, either."

"So, okay, serious question here. What *is* your type of woman? Or are you into guys, because man, I've got a cousin in Sarasota who's single and he's not bad looking, according to Sue."

Bill scowled at him, earning another laugh.

"Come on, I had to yank your chain."

"I don't have a type. I'm not saying I don't appreciate an attractive woman, but there's got to be something under the hood to spark my interest. The chassis is irrelevant if there's not much more than a hamster and a rusty wheel inside."

"Such a romantic. I can see why ladies are flocking to you."

"I'm serious. You asked, I'm answering."

"Yeah, yeah." He put his menu down. "So tell me. I'm listening."

"Smart. A sense of humor. Someone who won't be terrified being with a cop. Someone independent enough to stand on her own."

"We talking Mensa-smart?"

Bill gave him "the look" again.

"Sorry."

"You know what I mean." Bill lowered his voice. He tried not to delve into his memories and make comparisons, but he couldn't help it. "You knew Ella. She was curious and loved to try new things. She was laid back."

The blanket of melancholy settled over him once more. "If I woke up on a day off and said, 'Hey, let's go to a car show,' or whatever, she'd be game. She had a fun side. She had a playful side." Bill rearranged his silverware on the table. "She was vulnerable and strong at the same time. She didn't cling to me, but when we were together, she knew when I needed her."

Al stared at him. "You just described a golden retriever."

Al was the only person he'd tolerate that kind of crap from because they'd been friends for so long. Still, he gave Al "the look" once more.

His friend's tone turned serious. "I'm sorry. I'm trying to help."

"I know you are, and I appreciate it. Whenever it's meant to be, it is. If it's not…" He shrugged. "I was lucky enough to have the love of my life once. I'm not naive enough to think I'll have that kind of luck a second time."

* * * *

Bill spent the afternoon working on a case involving counterfeit prescription slips and took a man into custody for that. Then a burned car, reported stolen the night before, was found over near the mall.

Fortunately, that rounded out his day. By the time he was ready to go home a little before seven that night, he breathed a sigh of relief he hadn't caught any disturbing cases. Not that they had a lot of those in their sleepy part of southwest Florida, fortunately, but it was always a good day when the worst complaint he had was getting a little soot on his pants while trying to read the VIN number stamped on a burned-out car.

"Did you want to come over for dinner tonight?" Al asked him on the way out.

Bill shook his head. "Nope. Look, don't make Sue feel bad. Just tell her I said thanks, but it didn't work out. For me, at least."

"Will do."

He didn't feel like cooking, so he stopped at his usual haunt, Marelli's, a small family-run Italian restaurant not far off US 41. The same family had owned and operated it for over three decades. A few years earlier, it had been leveled by Hurricane Charley. The owners had rebuilt it better than ever while still retaining the homey, cozy feel of the old place.

Fortunately they weren't very busy since it was a weeknight. Dori, one of the owner's granddaughters, smiled when she spotted him walking in. "Anywhere you want, Bill," she said to him.

He nodded and grabbed a menu and a set of silverware from the hostess stand as he headed toward the back, to a small two-person table right next to the kitchen. In this restaurant, he loved sitting near the kitchen. He enjoyed listening to the family's banter, getting a few extra minutes to chat with the staff and owners, and he could even lean over and refill his own water and tea from one of the waitress stations without bothering anyone.

They made him feel like family, including to the point of insisting that he come to their homes to celebrate holidays for the past several years after they found out he was a widower.

At least they hadn't tried fixing him up on dates with anyone.

Yet.

After Dori finished with the table she was serving, she poured glasses of water and iced tea for Bill before walking over and setting them in front of him.

She flashed him a friendly smile. "I was beginning to think we weren't going to see you tonight."

"And miss spaghetti Tuesday on a Wednesday? Are you nuts?"

She cracked up over *The Walking Dead* references every time. "You're too much. And it's Thursday. The special?"

He nodded and handed her the menu. "Yep. Don't know why I bothered grabbing a menu."

She took it from him. "Just to make work for me." Her grin made him smile in return. She stepped over to the pass-through window to the kitchen. "Bill's here," she called out. "Usual," she said by way of giving them his order. Then she carried the menu back to the hostess station and greeted an older couple who'd just walked in.

The kitchen door swung open and an elderly man swept through, dressed in checked chef's pants, a black shirt, and a kitchen towel draped over his shoulder. He wore a beaming smile on his face, his hand already extended for a shake. "There he is. How are you tonight, my friend? We missed you last night."

Bill stood to give him a hug. "Good enough, Papa Tom. How are you?"

"Eh, no complaints." He planted himself in the chair on the other side of the table. "I see you brought no work with you tonight. Must have been a good day?"

Bill shrugged. "Not the worst." Everyone called Tom Marelli, the family patriarch and head chef, "Papa Tom" if they were considered part of the family. The eighty-two-year-old had been born in Italy, but emigrated to New York with his parents and siblings when he was two.

When Hurricane Charley had hit several years earlier, Bill had gone out of his way to track down the family and make sure they were all safe when he found out the restaurant had been destroyed by the storm. Much to his relief, they'd all been safely hunkered down at one of the daughter's homes in North Port.

Dori called from the other side of the dining room. "Papa Tom!" She waved at him, motioning him over to the table.

The old man threw up his hands. "My apologies, it seems I'm wanted."

Bill smiled. "You have a big fan base."

He stood. "It could be worse. It could still be snowbird season."

Bill watched, amused, as the man crossed the dining room, quickly leaning in to hug the couple who'd requested his presence. Now that it was May, the winter tourists and seasonal residents had mostly returned home. Even in the dead of summer, sometimes the worst time of the year for local eateries, Marelli's always did a brisk business with locals.

When snowbird season hit, locals wanting to eat had to call ahead and make a reservation.

The food was good, better than average, and everything was prepared in-house. The prices were reasonable. But it was Papa Tom and the rest of the Marelli family who drew in the business.

The community had banded together after Charley to come help clear the property, salvage what they could of the kitchen equipment, and then get the rebuilding started. Even during the rebuild they served a limited menu of takeout in the parking lot, under tents donated by a local businessman who was a frequent customer.

Dedication. And that was why Bill usually ate there four or five nights a week, sometimes even more often.

It was also why he had to do a minimum of three miles on the treadmill every morning before work, to keep from gaining weight.

A small price to pay for the company and the food.

Tonight's special, eggplant parm. They knew he liked a larger salad and smaller portion of pasta on the side to help counteract the stomach-spreading effects of their delicious food.

By the time he arrived home nearly an hour later, he felt physically stuffed. As he switched on lights on his way through the house, he tried to ignore how lonely and empty the house felt.

Nine years, and I still can't get used to it. Maybe I should *get a cat.*

At least then he wouldn't have to worry about not getting home on time to walk it, like he would a dog.

After a shower, setting the coffeepot up to start automatically in the morning, and checking his e-mail, he finally slid into bed. It was something he always put off as long as he could.

The lonely minutes between hitting the sheets and sleep taking him were always the most agonizing part of his day.

Chapter Two

FDLE Special Agent Gabriella Villalobos took a deep breath and walked into the conference room. Currently, the four interview rooms they had were full, with people waiting. This would have to do.

In her hand she carried a file folder, but the truth was she knew the contents inside and out. Jorge Martinez was a piece of shit, of that there was no doubt. This wasn't his first bust, but this one would put him away for the rest of his life, if she had anything to say about it.

This time, instead of a penny ante drug bust, it was for human trafficking, child endangerment, kidnapping, child abuse, aggravated child sexual assault—the list went on, growing more sickening with each charge.

The vanload of young girls they'd rescued from an industrial park in Hialeah before dawn that Thursday morning appeared to be from all over, including Haiti, Mexico, the Dominican Republic, Guatemala, Columbia, and Nicaragua.

He was, it would seem, a multinational scumbag. It also meant a paperwork and jurisdictional nightmare involving people from Immigration and Customs Enforcement, Florida Department of Children and Families—since all but one of the girls was a minor—and a whole slew of alphabet-soup law enforcement agencies, local, state, and federal.

He sat manacled at the ankles, his hands cuffed to a chain around his waist, another chain locking his ankles to the table. Currently, his seven cohorts and a shit-ton of johns were being booked and processed and interviewed.

"So, Jorge. How are we doing today?"

He grinned. "*No hablo.*"

She grinned back and sat down, and in Spanish said, "Well, aren't you in luck, asshole?" She switched to English. "I do *hablo*. In fact, I *hablo* quite fucking well."

His smile faded a little, but he didn't respond.

It wasn't professional, and she knew it, but there wasn't a recording device in this room. She intended to stretch the boundaries a little to soften him up before anyone else got to him.

She continued in Spanish. "I want to talk to you about the girls we rescued from the storage unit this morning."

The smiled faded the rest of the way off his face, leaving the scar running at an angle across his right cheek, from the corner of his eye to his nose, a deep furrow in his flesh.

"One of them," she continued, "her name is Luisa Gutierrez, and she says she's only eleven and you raped her before you pimped her out."

"She lies. I didn't rape her. And she's older than that."

"Um, not according to the records we obtained from the Mexican embassy twenty minutes ago. Her parents reported her abducted six months ago. We were sent a copy of her birth certificate."

He glared at her, his eyes reminding her of something dark and dangerous, like a Komodo dragon.

Only uglier.

"She lies."

"Really? *That's* what you're going with?" She nodded. "All righty then." She flipped to another page in her folder. "Maria Hondo. Thirteen. Guatemala. She lying, too?"

He nodded.

He'd been Mirandized, and they had that on video, but she knew what the fucker was doing. He had someone he worked for, someone who fronted the money that supported the operation, probably a drug lord, and wouldn't lawyer up because he wouldn't give up the next rung of the shitty ladder he clung to.

Fuckers like him didn't say anything. They knew if they ratted out their bosses, someone would take them out their first week in general population, if not sooner. They considered doing their time a badge of honor and the price of doing business.

What he didn't know was two of his guys, lower level shits she'd already mindfucked into thinking they were going to jail for life and a future filled with assrape and giving blowjobs—if they lived that long—had already rolled over on him and were asking to cut deals with the prosecution before they'd even been arraigned.

Goes to show what happens when you hire cheap help.

She slowly closed the file and stood, walking around behind him. "You know, Jorge," she said, switching back to English, "it's not nice to lie."

She knew damn well he spoke English. They had over twenty hours of surveillance video of him speaking it just fine. He'd been born in Opa-locka, for chrissake.

"No *hab*—"

Before he could finish the sentence, she grabbed a fistful of his hair in her hand and slammed his forehead against the conference table.

He let out a howl. "What the fuck's your problem, lady?" he screamed in perfectly spoken English.

She knelt down. She'd split the skin over his left eye and blood trickled down his face. "Aw, wow, looky there. Amazing. A blow to the head, and listen to you *hablo*, asshole. It's a medical miracle. Let's put you on Dr. flippin' Oz."

The door burst open, her boss storming in first. "Villalobos, wait in my office, please."

She snatched the folder off the conference table and leaned in close to Martinez to whisper, "Just think what your buddies will say when they learn a woman made you *her* bitch, huh?" She blew him a kiss.

The sneer fell from his face, giving her some satisfaction as she walked out the door and left him to the care of two other agents.

She sat in front of her boss' desk and waited for him to follow her in a few minutes later. He shut the door and rounded his desk before sitting.

"You're damn lucky, Gabe," he said in the low, growly tone that told her she'd pushed her luck right up to the edge and was teetering on it, looking over into an abyss on the other side. "He said he tripped and hit the table earlier. That you didn't have anything to do with it."

"Clumsy, isn't he?"

Walker glared at her.

"Look, I knew the asshole wouldn't file a complaint. It's too big a hit to his machismo."

He continued glaring at her. "You have two choices. Take three weeks' paid vacation time, right now, starting today, or face an IA investigation. Your choice."

"I'll take my chances with IA."

He slapped his desk with his palm, making her jump. "Dammit, Gabe! You're one of my best agents. I need you in the field. I cannot risk losing you because you blow your damn gasket over some scumbag."

"A child raping, child pimping scumbag who didn't lawyer up."

"We have too much riding on too many ongoing investigations to have some goddamned public defender their first year out of Stetson getting these guys off on technicalities because of alleged improprieties."

She knew he was right and decided it was time to keep her mouth shut. She'd never seen him look this angry.

And there were plenty of times over the years she'd seen him angry.

Some of those times *at* her.

He pointed his finger at her. "You have eight weeks of paid vacation time on the books you haven't taken yet, some of it rolled over from last year. I know, because I just checked. Don't make me force you to use it all at once. And not this bullshit you usually pull of you taking vacation days and coming in to work anyway while you're not supposed to be in the office."

Her jaw clenched. She wouldn't be able to talk her way out of this one. Although, to be fair, this was the first time she'd ever crossed the line so far with a suspect. She hadn't planned on doing it, but indelibly seared in her mind was the terror those girls wore when the team burst into the storage unit and rescued them.

The screams.

The scene would forever haunt her, along with the myriad horrors she'd witnessed in her ten years with the Florida Department of Law Enforcement working these kinds of cases. Child sex stings, child trafficking, child pornography rings, investigating the worst of the worst crimes and criminals, to protect the weakest and bring scum like Martinez to justice.

She deflated as she sat back in the chair.

Apparently, Travis Walker read the defeat in her manner. He opened a desk drawer and pulled something out. When he slid it across his desk, she realized it was a set of three keys and one of his business cards, with a Sarasota address written on the back, along with a four-digit number.

"What is this?"

"Your three weeks' vacation. Those are the keys to my vacation condo there, and that's the alarm code. My wife and I aren't using it anytime soon. When you set it, hold the away button if you're leaving, and the stay button if you're staying so it deactivates the motion detectors. It'll beep and start a sixty-second countdown. When you come in you have sixty seconds to disarm it with that code. The alarm pad's on the wall just inside the door, on the left. You can't miss it. And it's a second floor unit. One of those keys is the front door, one is the garage and storage down below, and the last one is the mailbox."

She stared at the keys and the card for a moment as his words sank in. "You're forcing me to stay at your condo for three weeks?"

He smirked. "I can access the alarm logs online. I can see if you're there or not." His smile faded. "I'm serious. If I see you set foot in this office before three weeks are up, and I'm talking three weeks of workdays, *not* including weekends, I *will* call IA and file the report myself. You need some downtime. You're wound tighter than a freaking cheap watch. If you snap, you're not only going to take down your career, but a whole bunch of investigations that dozens of agents have spent thousands of man-hours working on. Think about that, Miss Dedication to Duty."

* * * *

How serious Travis Walker was showed a few minutes later when, after she grabbed her stuff, he personally walked her down to her car and stood there while she got in. She didn't crank it yet, ignoring the blistering waves of sunny Miami heat pulsing from the car's interior.

He leaned in, arms braced on the door and roof. "Look, Gabe. You're dedicated. I get that. We're all dedicated. I wouldn't have someone working for me if I didn't think they would give one hundred percent to this job. But you take it to an unhealthy level. You're going to be forty in a couple of months. You need to relax and get away from this shit for a while. You *will* burn out if you keep this pace up. You've lasted longer than most agents doing this work. Usually, people transfer out or request different kinds of assignments by now. I am very worried about you."

She wrapped her fingers around her steering wheel and nodded. "Thanks, boss. I appreciate that." She wouldn't look up and meet his gaze.

"Gabe, go up to Sarasota. Walk on the beach. Eat good food. Read a freaking book. Go see a play at the Asolo. Meet people. Anything. Something other than…this. Something not horrific, okay? There's even a community pool and hot tub at the complex. Use them. Lay out in the sun."

"Why are you insisting I get out of town? Why isn't staying out of the office enough?"

"Frankly? I'm worried Martinez, or the people he works for, might try to send someone after you."

She snorted. "They can try."

"You aren't bulletproof. Besides, I know you. The temptation will be too great for you to try to do something resembling work if you're in Miami. Twenty-one working days, Gabe. You set foot in this building before then, you're gone. You know I'll do it. Please, do *not* make me do it. It'd kill me to lose you, but I can't and won't risk our other cases."

Yes, she knew he would do it. He was a man of his word. She finally looked up at him and recognized his serious expression.

He definitely wasn't kidding.

"Fine."

"Enjoy yourself. I'll e-mail you the WiFi password and anything else I think of that you might need." He smiled. "To your *personal* e-mail account. And feel free to use the master bedroom. It's got a newer mattress in it anyway, so it's more comfortable." He closed the door for her and stepped away from the car while she cranked the ignition.

When she pulled out of the lot a moment later, she glanced in the rearview mirror and spotted him still standing there, ensuring she really left.

She focused on the traffic. In his haste to get her out of the building, he didn't seem to notice that she grabbed her work laptop and some files in the process.

At least *that* was something she could smile about.

Chapter Three

Gabe dumped her stuff on the kitchen counter when she walked into her condo. She set the thermostat down to seventy-three and walked through to her bedroom.

She undressed, locked her sidearm in the small gun safe hidden in her closet, plugged her personal and work cell phones into their chargers, and started the shower. When she turned, she looked away from the vanity over the sink so as not to catch a glimpse of her back in the mirror.

An ingrained habit, one she never thought about anymore.

She didn't really need a shower, because she'd just taken one that morning. But the soothing white noise of the running water was the only luxury she'd indulge in to relax herself.

That, and she wanted to attempt to wash off the mental stink of the morning. Not that it would work, but she'd feel better freshly showered before climbing into the car for a drive to Sarasota.

Not to mention it was one of the few times the ghost of Maria's voice couldn't pierce through her brain and interrupt her thoughts.

She grabbed her brush and removed the elastic band from the end of the braid in her hair. As steam filled the bathroom, she brushed out her long, dark brown hair. She had some grey coming in here and there, but she didn't care. She damn sure wasn't about to start coloring her hair.

That would be a waste of time and money.

She kept it long because Maria always made her cut it short when she was a child, and Gabe had hated it. She could trim the ends herself and only go to a salon a couple of times a year. And she'd found it easier to care for when it was long, able to quickly bind and braid it as needed instead of fussing with it with a hair dryer or curling iron.

With that done, she stepped into the shower and turned her face into the spray. The last thing she wanted to do was take time off. She'd rather spend twenty-one working days stuck in a witness holding area at the courthouse, waiting to testify.

Work *was* her life. What the hell was she supposed to do with twenty-one days of forced downtime? Not like she had any home improvement projects. The condo association took care of the building's maintenance and landscaping. Any repairs she needed, she had people to call if it was something she couldn't take care of herself.

Fortunately, the one-bedroom unit rarely required repairs. It was small, and it was all she needed. More than she needed, actually, but she couldn't find any studio units for purchase in decent buildings.

She wouldn't waste her money on rent when she could buy and possibly resell it later at some point.

As she bumped the water temperature to just short of something boiling up out of the bowels of Mordor, she started creating a list in her mind. If she was banished to Sarasota for what would actually be four weeks, when she figured in weekends, she'd make sure she took what she needed with her.

Lil Lobo, her stuffed wolf given to her by one of the kids in a case several years earlier, topped the list. No matter what, it always went with her. Followed by her personal laptop, a MacBook Air with a dodgy charger. She hadn't made herself buy a new charger yet because, technically, the old one still worked.

Well, I could crochet.

It was the only thing coming close to a hobby that she allowed herself. She crocheted hats, blankets, stuffed animals, and various things to donate to the local children's hospital and other charities. Unfortunately, she usually didn't have a lot of time over the course of the average week to indulge in it. She could rationalize it as a valid pastime because it was creating something helpful and productive.

One of the few things Maria had allowed her to do for "fun" as a kid, and just about the only thing left over from her childhood that she didn't resent. She liked helping people, being useful. It was one of the reasons why she went into law enforcement in the first place.

And it was one of the few things, besides long, hot showers, that allowed her to totally clear her mind and zone out, focused only on the soothing, repetitive movements of the hook through the yarn, and not hear Maria's voice.

The only other thing that gave her such mind-numbing solace was going to the range and burning through a couple of boxes of ammunition.

By the time she stepped out of the shower, she'd adjusted her attitude and completed her list. If Walker was going to make her go, well, she'd go. It didn't matter that she disagreed with his assessment of her mental state. She knew it wasn't uncommon for law enforcement officers who specialized in her field to end up with alcoholism or other issues due to the extreme stresses of the job. She'd read the literature and talked to her fair share of department psychologists as part of routine personnel reviews.

She wasn't, however, typical. She didn't *need* downtime.

She didn't *want* downtime.

If anything, work was the only thing that kept her sane no matter how crazy it got.

It was the only thing she lived for.

* * * *

When she got dressed, she donned, as she always did, a gun. Since she wasn't going to work, she put on the .380 Bersa she liked to carry. Tucked into a built-in elasticized holster in a pair of stretchy undershorts she could wear beneath her jeans, it saved her from having to keep a special holster hooked to her belt or under her shirt. It was a much lighter and simpler rig than what she wore for work to carry one of her two 9mm Glocks.

One of the Glocks, however, would make the trip with her as well. *I'm sure I can find a local range and get some time in that way. He didn't forbid that, at least.*

By the time three o'clock rolled around, she was packed and ready to go. She didn't have much in the way of perishables to clear out of her fridge, and would, hopefully, beat the worst of rush hour traffic to get out of the Miami area.

Her personal cell phone rang just as she was getting ready to leave the condo.

Walker.

"You on the road yet?"

"I would have been in my car if a nosy somebody hadn't just called me to check on me."

He chuckled. "Sorry. But I know you."

Not as well as he thought he did, or he wouldn't be ordering her gone. "I should be in Sarasota in a few hours, depending on traffic. You going to put a BOLO out on me if I don't disarm the alarm by a certain time?"

That chuckle again. "Nope." His tone turned serious. "But I do appreciate you not fighting me on this, Gabe. This is for your own good."

How many times had she heard *that* growing up? "Yeah, if you say so."

She got on the road and, fortunately, made the northern turn off Alligator Alley before the sun got too low in the sky and she had to drive directly into it. She hadn't been this way too many times, and even then always for work, with no time to sightsee.

Not that she was into sightseeing. That was an unproductive waste of time.

She stopped for dinner on the road, hit a Publix for a couple of things so she wouldn't have to leave the condo first thing in the morning to find breakfast, and finally made it to the condo a little before nine that night. The sun had already set and the last purple light still struggled to hold on to the landscape.

From what she could tell in the darkness, the condo complex looked tidy and well kept, with her twelve-year-old Honda apparently the oldest and least expensive car parked anywhere.

She unlocked and opened the door before punching in the code on the alarm pad. Her nerves felt unsettled for a few minutes while she quickly walked through the condo and checked it out. Nothing apparently out of place. It was neat and tidy, albeit the air feeling a little on the stale side. She found the AC thermostat and bumped it down a smidge, noting how it immediately rumbled to life.

Two bedrooms, two baths, the kitchen opening into the living and dining room area. A closet off the kitchen held the washer and dryer units. A small, private screened balcony looked off into a large swath of darkness she suspected would prove to be a golf course in the light of day.

Not bad.

Unfortunately, it grated at her.

Admittedly, the condo felt homier than her own did. She'd never been to Walker's home despite several invitations, but suspected the vacation unit was an extended reflection of both his and his wife's personalities. It felt comfortable and casual, with IKEA furniture and warm photographs on the walls.

When she examined one of the prints, a beach at sunset, she realized it was a mate to a smaller one hanging in his office, along with several others. Now she wondered if he or his wife were the photographer.

The flat-screen TV looked huge compared to the tiny one she had at home, and they had a full cable package, including all the premium movie channels. A DVD player and stereo rounded out the electronic ensemble, with the wireless cable modem set up located there as well.

The kitchen was fully stocked with dishes, cookware, and cutlery, but the spotless refrigerator sat empty. She rinsed and filled the ice cube trays and set them back in the freezer. She wondered at the expense of a glass-topped oven in a property they didn't use all the time before she caught herself.

Stop it. Not everyone's as cheap as you.

You don't have to be cheap. Not like Maria's looking over your shoulder. You can afford to treat yourself better than you do. You deserve it.

No, you don't.

Stop it. Just stop it.

She blinked and looked up, trying to kill the inner voices holding an all-too-common verbal jousting match in her brain.

Heading downstairs to get her things from the car, she resigned herself to making the best of the situation.

Besides, she had her work laptop.

Walker hadn't explicitly said anything about her not doing work online.

It was on that thought she smiled as she set to work getting her things unloaded and unpacked.

Chapter Four

Friday morning, Bill started his day with a cup of coffee and the morning news on TV as he suffered through his treadmill time. A shower, banana, granola bar, another cup of coffee, and he was good to go.

For a change, he got out of work a little early on a Friday afternoon. He'd had to talk to a witness over in west county, and decided to make a quick stop along the Cape Haze peninsula to check in with Laura Carlton.

The dive shop looked relatively unchanged since the last time he'd seen it the previous summer. He'd bumped into her county EMS paramedic husband, Rob Carlton, a couple of times in the course of his duties since Laura's attack, but hadn't had the time to check in on her.

When he walked in, he found her standing behind the counter, a sleeping baby cradled in her arms as she talked with a customer. Laura's beaming smile lit the room when she spotted him. She waved him over while handing the customer off to one of her employees.

She hustled him into the shop's office behind the counter and threw a one-armed hug around his neck, being careful not to jostle the infant. "It's so good to see you!"

He looked down at the baby in her arms. "I'm glad to see everything turned out well. How old is she now?"

She laughed. "Four and a half months. Yeah, she's healthy and happy and running us ragged, which everyone assures us is totally normal." She gently settled the baby into a portable crib taking up a corner of the office before turning to give him a better hug. "So how are you doing?" She indicated for him to take a seat.

"I had to be in the area and wanted to stop by for a visit. When I last saw Rob a few weeks ago, he was flashing everyone baby pics on his phone."

"He's a proud dad." She reached up and fingered her necklace, the heart-shaped locket there. It was a replacement for the one her attacker had taken from her, the same one they'd recovered from Don Kern's home after his death. That, and quite a few other mementos from his other victims, some as of yet not matched up to cold cases. It likely meant the victims might go unnamed, possibly forever.

The best investigators could figure, Don Kern had raped and murdered over forty women. Laura had been the first to escape him, and the reason they'd been able to break the case and piece together his cross-country trail of death.

"So. How are *you* doing?" he gently asked.

Her expression faltered a little, but she nodded. "I'm doing okay. Getting my memories back really helped." She shrugged. "I didn't start having nightmares until after Molly was born." She let out a snort. "They're better now, though. My psychiatrist said that was normal because of everything I went through."

"I'm glad everything's going so well."

"You know how it is. I have all I need. A healthy daughter, a good husband, and good friends…" Her voice faltered. "I'm sorry. Rob told me about your wife. I didn't mean to sound insensitive."

He shrugged. "You weren't, and it's fine. She's been gone nine years now. I've adjusted."

"Look, stay for dinner tonight. Please? We were going to grill burgers at home. Rob should be here any minute to get us. It'd be so nice to catch up with you."

"You mean to spend some unofficial time with me?"

"Yeah. Please?"

"Okay. Sure. I'd like that, thank you."

Actually, maybe that wasn't a bad thing. Something that had rolled through his mind many times since the case was the relationship dynamic between Rob and Laura. He knew from text message records he'd had pulled from their cell phones during the investigation that they had a Master and slave dynamic. It turned out to be irrelevant to the case. He'd managed to successfully keep that evidence out of the official case file, saving the couple and their friends in the lifestyle potential embarrassment, as well as possibly preserving Rob's job as a paramedic with the county's fire department.

Maybe my problem is that I need to fish in the right pond. Bill knew he wasn't sadistic by any stretch of the imagination, but one of the most precious things about his relationship with Ella, what he couldn't talk about with most people, and one of the things he missed the most, had been their non-vanilla relationship in bed, and sometimes out of it when the mood struck them. He never would have tried to boss her around all the time, or spank her, and it wasn't something she was interested in, either. But behind closed doors, she'd been more than happy to turn herself over to him in every way.

He'd been happy to have that control. He also probably wasn't the first cop to keep a pair of regulation handcuffs in his bedside table that got a lot of use.

Just never on suspects.

That wasn't exactly a topic you talked about on a first date with someone. *Hey, by the way, are you kinky?*

They chatted for a few more minutes when Rob arrived. Bill stood to shake hands with him before Rob pulled him in for a full hug. "Long time, no see, Detective," Rob said with a smile.

"I'm off the clock. Just Bill."

"I invited him over for dinner tonight," Laura told him.

"Ah, I see. Hope you like burgers."

"I do. Firemen are notoriously great cooks."

"You got that right," Laura said.

* * * *

Bill followed them to their house even though he remembered the way. He was glad to see the couple apparently doing so well emotionally, that their life had kept moving forward and the events of the previous summer hadn't irrevocably scarred them in ways that would harm their relationship.

Laura was inside with the baby and getting the rest of dinner ready while Bill stood on the back deck with Rob, manning the grill, each of them with a bottle of beer in their hands. Doogie, Rob and Laura's enormous black Lab, patiently lay on the deck, likely hoping for one of the burgers to make a suicidal leap from the grill and into his mouth.

"Let me guess," Rob said. "This is more than a courtesy visit."

Bill took a swallow of his beer. "Sort of. I wanted to talk to you. To both of you, actually."

"About what happened?"

Nut up, buttercup. "No."

Rob frowned, but didn't interrupt him.

"Look, there's a reason, beyond the obvious, that I didn't hassle you and Laura about your…relationship."

"Go on."

"This is coming purely from a personal place. Feel free to tell me to go to hell if you want, but it's nine years since my wife died, and maybe it's time I do something different."

"You want us to introduce you around." Rob phrased it as a statement, not a question.

"Yeah." Bill took another swallow of his beer. "Unless that would be weird, or uncomfortable. In that case, feel free to say no, because I—"

"Sure." Rob used the spatula to lift the edge of one of the burgers to take a look at it. "We'd be happy to introduce you to our friends."

Bill realized he'd expected that to not go as smoothly as it had. "Oh. Thank you. I appreciate that."

Rob glanced at him. "Just to clarify, purely personally, not professionally."

"Yeah."

"Are you busy tomorrow evening?"

"Tomorrow?"

"Saturday night. Any plans? We have a sitter arranged. We go out to dinner with our friends, most of them you've already met. Then we go to the club."

"Dinner?"

"Yeah, food. You eat out, right?"

"Yeah." A snort escaped him. "Pretty much every night."

"We meet at Sigalo's up in Sarasota. You know where that is?"

"I think so."

"Unless you want to ride with us, but we'll be at the club late."

"Thanks, but I'll drive myself."

"Understandable. Meet us there at seven o'clock. We have dinner, shoot the breeze, and then go to the club."

"Aren't most of your friends I met already…taken?" He didn't want to say married because he knew that wasn't the case with some of them. Not to mention, some of them were poly and he wasn't interested in that kind of arrangement.

Rob handed him his beer to hold while he started flipping the burgers over. "Yes, but between them they know a lot of people. Can introduce you to people. And they're all good people I trust who will steer you clear of any whackjobs."

Rob nearly lost one burger but got it flipped over. "Any experience in the lifestyle, if you mind me asking?"

Bill ignored the all too familiar pang that pierced his soul. "My wife and I…not like you and Laura, apparently. But we weren't strictly vanilla."

Rob nodded without taking his attention from the burgers he was trying to not drop onto Doogie's head—or into the dog's mouth. "Okay. You don't need to tell me all the details if you don't want to. I just wasn't sure if you were a total newb or more experienced." He finished flipping the last burger and took his beer back. "You know, next Saturday, Seth and Leah are teaching a beginner shibari class. Rope bondage. They already have a big class list. It'd be a good place to get to meet new people. I can get you in even if it's full."

Bill thought about it. "Beginners, huh?"

"Yep. It's a four-week class. It's fun, and a lot of people who aren't into heavier play enjoy the artistic aspect of shibari."

He considered it. "Okay."

"Great. We'll talk to Seth and Leah about it tomorrow at dinner." Rob looked down at the dog, who lifted his head and stared hopefully up at him. "You aren't getting a hamburger."

The Lab's tail thumped once against the deck before he settled his head down again.

* * * *

Bill gave Laura credit for pausing only the briefest of moments after Rob told her the plan.

"Oh. That's great. We'd be happy to have you join us at dinner."

"Let me guess," Bill said as they all settled into chairs at the table. "You wouldn't have expected it of me."

She'd started fixing her burger. "No, actually, we know a few people in law enforcement who are into the lifestyle."

He froze. "Locally?"

"Tampa and Orlando, mostly. They come down to Sarasota. Less risk of running into coworkers that way."

He relaxed. "Oh. Okay."

A beaming grin broke out across Laura's face. "Sir," she said to Rob, "does this mean I can call Leah and sic her on Bill?"

Rob burst out laughing. "Yes, I guess her matchmaking skills would be appreciated in this instance."

"Oh, goodie."

"Should I be afraid?" Bill asked.

"No, she just likes to see her friends happy."

"That's good, I suppose."

By the time Bill headed home a little after nine that evening, he didn't feel quite so lonely. He'd had a nice time chatting with the couple.

Whatever happened the next evening, he'd do his best to keep an open mind about it.

Chapter Five

Friday morning, Gabe awoke feeling a little disoriented until she spotted Lil Lobo sitting on the bedside table next to her.

Sarasota. Got it.

Looking at her cell phone, she realized it was also just a little after five in the morning. No matter how she tried, she was an early riser. If she tried to go back to sleep, if she succeeded, she'd end up with a killer headache.

Maria had taken care of any late-rising tendencies she might have had. At least it had made her four years in the military a little easier to deal with.

Hell, four years in the army had been a luxury spa vacation compared to her upbringing.

She got out of bed, used the bathroom, and turned on the TV in the living room on her way to the kitchen to start a pot of coffee. It would be the first of at least two pots she'd finish by herself today.

As the aroma filled the condo, she watched the local ABC affiliate's morning newscast. There was something about the city of Sarasota cracking down on the homeless and triggering outcries from various civil liberties organizations. News about turmoil in the county administration.

No murders.

Hmm. It was rare that a Miami news report didn't lead with a story of a homicide, or serious injury from a shooting or stabbing, or gang violence.

She knew the bucolic Sarasota area was famous for retirees, a film festival, and being a former winter home to a circus. Beyond that, she'd readily admit her knowledge about this part of her adopted home state was woefully lacking.

When she walked over to the sliding glass doors that looked out onto the patio, she realized her assumption the evening before had been correct. The condo overlooked a narrow wooded section that opened into a golf course. In the grey light of early morning, it looked peaceful.

Then she spotted the headlights on a golf cart toodling down a path.

At least it'll be quiet here.

Her condo in Kendall wasn't in the best neighborhood in the world, but she wasn't in the worst, either. She had a mix of neighbors, most around her age and older, including a population heavy on retirees.

I could go for a run.

She waffled on that point. In Miami, she didn't jog. Not outside, at least. Not unless she was chasing down a suspect on foot.

Which, fortunately, she didn't have to do very often. She had a gym membership and forced herself to go three times a week despite hating every minute of it. She'd put on a little weight over the years, developing a pear shape from too much time sitting in front of a computer at her desk, but her size eighteen, five-seven frame hadn't tipped over the edge into the unhealthy range.

Yet.

She could still pass the yearly physical, still meet minimum job requirements for running and everything else, even though she wasn't in nearly as good of shape as she'd been in her early army days.

It'd be better to scope the area out first. No sense getting herself in trouble hitting a bad neighborhood by accident.

You should fire up your work laptop and check your e-mail. You should be working.

That mental nagging bore too many hints of Maria's tone. Gabe shoved it away.

For now.

She knew it would come back at some point.

It always did.

* * * *

After three cups of coffee, reading her online newspapers, and eating yogurt and a banana for breakfast, she opted to take a walk around the complex. With a loose, unbuttoned short-sleeved shirt over her tank top and shorts, which helped conceal the holster holding the .380 along the back of her waist, she got her bearings and explored. The pool and hot tub area were nice, clean, and well maintained, like the rest of the complex. She found the mailboxes and for the hell of it decided to check the one for her unit.

Nothing.

Still, it was nice to know where it was. She rarely received any mail anyway. All her bills were handled electronically, and the few people who wanted to get in touch with her outside of work either did so via e-mail or called her.

Well, except for one cousin, Jennifer. They'd connected via Facebook while Gabe was in college after the army. She was one of only twenty-seven friends Gabe had on the social networking site. They had an understanding that Jennifer never mentioned her grandmother's sister—Gabe's grandmother Maria—or revealed to anyone else Gabe's mailing address.

At least I have one person in the world besides my boss who might miss me if I drop off the planet.

Not that she felt sorry for herself over it. She'd learned to eschew self-pity in her childhood.

Maria had done an excellent job of beating that out of her as well.

* * * *

After returning to the condo, Gabe was deciding on her next action when Walker called her on her personal cell. "So? Do you like it?"

"Yes, it's nice. Who's the photographer?"

"Huh?"

"On the walls in the living room. Who took the pictures?"

"Uh, me. Why?"

"You have prints matching the ones in your office. I figured it was probably you or your wife. They're very nice. I like them."

"Excellent, Sherlock. And thank you. It still doesn't get you off the hook."

"Look, I'm here. I'll stay out of the office for twenty-one days. I said I would." Having a little time to reflect upon her actions, she did feel badly that she'd acted unprofessional and put the case, as well as other cases, at risk. "I'm taking time off."

She also couldn't deny she'd felt more than a little satisfaction watching the rivulet of blood drip down Martinez's face.

"I think I actually believe you, Gabe."

"Is there a reason for this call other than wanting to gloat and bust my balls?"

Walker's tone turned serious. "I'm not gloating, and I'm not busting your balls. You have to trust me. You've worked for me long enough to know I don't usually give ultimatums like this."

He was right. "I know," she mumbled.

"So please trust me when I say this was the only recourse. I also want you to understand the level of trust I have in you that I sent you there in the first place. You are probably the only person I would have handed the keys and alarm code to like that."

"I'm honored."

"Damn well should be." He laughed. "And yes, I saw you took files and your laptop. No, I'm not sadistic enough to forbid you to do any work outside of the office. I know that would be stretching the limits of your sanity." His tone turned solicitous again. "I'm simply asking while you're gone that you please strike a healthy balance. All right?"

She felt a little of the weight roll off her shoulders. Yes, she should have known he would have paid attention to that. That he hadn't said anything the day before surprised her and had made her wonder if he was slipping. "Thank you. I will."

"Good. Now go have fun. I'll e-mail you some great local restaurants in a little bit."

"Thanks." She hung up the phone and stared at her work and personal laptops sitting side by side on the eat-in counter. She was itching to get back to work, to run down information on some of her active investigations.

If Walker can make concessions, so can I. She decided she'd like to take a drive through the downtown area. And now that she knew what the condo had in the way of kitchen equipment, she did need to go shopping.

She headed for the bathroom to grab a shower and make her mental lists.

* * * *

She opted for a little cruising first, driving to the downtown area and getting her bearings. She wouldn't call it sightseeing, it was more reconnoitering. She now had an idea of neighborhoods to avoid, where the condo was in relation to those areas, and the relative safety of the area she was in.

Fortunately, she didn't spot any bars on windows of houses in the neighborhoods surrounding the condo complex. In fact, it looked like a gated community of upscale homes surrounded the golf course. Well-manicured lawns and expensive cars were the norm.

It all put her twelve-year-old Honda to shame, but she refused to think about trading in the car despite being able to afford something newer and better. It still ran great, was cosmetically in decent shape, and had been paid off years earlier.

It would be wasteful to buy a new car when hers was perfectly fine.

She didn't fail to recognize the irony that some of her condo neighbors might be a little suspicious of her because of her car, and yet she was law enforcement.

It was well after noon when she returned home with groceries, several bags of the fiber stuffing she used to fill her amigurumis, and a bag full of yarn from a shop she stumbled across during her explorations. And Walker had e-mailed her.

You'll love these places. Definitely give Ballentine's a shot. Excellent prime rib.

She thumbed through the rest of the message. Not only had he sent restaurant recommendations, but places to go see, like Mote Marine and the Marie Selby Botanical Gardens.

This was the most non-work-related contact she'd had with her boss in several years. She wasn't so emotionally dead she couldn't recognize that he felt concerned about her and was trying make amends for sending her away in the only ways he could.

The only ways she'd let him.

Hey, my boss is *telling me to go do "fun" stuff. Maybe it's time I start to listen.*

Maria's voice tried to argue, but very faintly.

Screw it.

She sent back a quick e-mail from her phone. *Thanks, I'll try Ballentine's on Sunday. I don't want to go out on a Friday or Saturday night when it's too busy.*

She hoped that made him happy that she was trying, too.

After putting away the groceries and making a sandwich for lunch, she forced herself to look away from the laptops. She'd left the bag of yarn on the coffee table.

There's something soothing.

Even though the yarn shop had offered to ball the skeins for her with their machine, she preferred to do it by hand. She turned on the TV and, one by one, began unwinding each skein and transformed it into a ball. As she worked her way through them, she ran through the list in her mind. She had the patterns committed to memory that she made all the time. Newborn hats, mittens, and booties. Lap robes. Shawls. Adult hats, which were mostly used by the elderly since south Florida sported very few days cold enough to need a heavy coat, much less a warm hat. Fingerless gloves, also more popular with the elderly.

She'd also packed some amigurumi patterns, little whimsical animals that were always a hit with kids, like dogs, rabbits, alligators, dolphins, and other cute designs.

But not bears.

Never bears.

She had more than enough to keep her busy for a while. At least for the nearly four weeks she'd be there in Sarasota.

If nothing else, I can get caught up on all the donation projects I want to make.

* * * *

As the yarn pulled through Gabe's fingers, she eventually started ignoring the TV, which she'd tuned to the Weather Channel. Her breathing slowed, her pulse calmed, her mind drifted. She knew it was a form of meditation for her, the only kind of spirituality she felt despite Maria's best and most painful attempts to beat her draconian version of Catholicism into Gabe.

I'm a Yarnist. I should start my own cult. "All hail the fuzzy and the slubs, the frogged and the finished."

She mentally giggled at that.

It was, in fact, how she'd gotten Lil Lobo nine years earlier. The day she'd taken charge of a terrified little girl they'd just rescued from a horrifically abusive situation as an accidental byproduct of another investigation they were conducting. One of several children, it turned out, who'd been abused by the perpetrators. Gabe had immediately scooped the girl up in her arms and carried her outside to the vehicle she'd rode to the scene in, where she had her purse.

Inside, a just-finished alligator she'd completed while waiting several hours for the signal to make the approach for the entry. She'd sat with the little girl in the car, air-conditioner running and doors closed against the noise and disruption of the raid, and spied the green amigurumi sticking out of her purse.

Grabbing it, she'd handed it to the child. "You look like you need an attack alligator to keep you company. I was looking for someone to give him to. He really likes to help people by protecting them. Would you like him?"

The little girl, who turned out to be six-year-old Rachel Dunning, victim of parental abduction from a good foster home by her drug-addict parents a few weeks earlier, nodded and clutched the alligator to her.

Gabe never wanted kids of her own, but even she didn't understand the affinity she had with the little victims she had to deal with on a regular basis.

She wouldn't question it, either. It was something that made her good at her job, able to break through to kids when sometimes even trained mental health professionals couldn't get them to open up and speak to investigators about what they'd been through.

After safely shepherding Rachel to the hospital personally and awaiting the arrival of her frantic foster parents, Gabe had finished her official duties for the day and then went home to make another amigurumi.

Another alligator, the only way to get her mind to zone out, to try to not think about the horrific pictures they'd found on a digital camera at the scene, of Rachel and other young children being sexually abused, the pictures being sold online.

The next day Lisa, Rachel's foster mom, called Gabe and said Rachel wanted to see her. When Gabe arrived at the hospital room, the little girl held a crudely wrapped blob in her hand.

As Gabe approached the bed, Lisa whispered in Gabe's ear, "She picked it out from the gift shop downstairs and wanted to wrap it herself. The nurses got us some tape. She insisted on doing it. I've never seen her so adamant about anything."

Rachel sat up and waved it at Gabe. "This is for you!" In her other hand, she clutched the crocheted alligator. Gabe had to force the smile to stay on her face as she tried to ignore the bruises on the girl's cheeks and arms. She knew from the reports and evidence that the child had plenty of other injuries in places no child should ever have to endure.

Gabe sat on the bed and took the present from the child. "Thank you, sweetheart." She unwrapped it to find a small grey and black stuffed wolf. "I love him! What's his name?"

Rachel hugged Gabe. "One of my nurses said *lobo* is Spanish for wolf. How about Lil Lobo? Just like your name."

"That sounds perfect."

Rachel made her alligator kiss the wolf on the nose. "Now I have Alex to protect me, and you have Lil Lobo to protect you." She nodded firmly, finalizing it.

Gabe pulled herself out of her thoughts as she finished the current skein she was balling. Rachel was now a freshman in high school, an honor student. Her foster parents had adopted her, and she was one of the handful of friends Gabe had on Facebook. Rachel still had Alex the Alligator and frequently took pictures of him with her in various places she went with her family, such as on vacation to the Grand Canyon.

Likewise, Gabe took pictures of Lil Lobo and sent them so the two animals could continue their long-distance "friendship" over time. Unfortunately, the girl hadn't emerged emotionally unscathed from her trauma. She dealt with issues such as cutting, and bouts of depression.

But as they'd talked throughout the years, Gabe giving Rachel insights to her own trials during childhood, Gabe knew the girl would eventually be okay.

She put the ball of yarn aside and started on another skein.

Maybe I'll make some more alligators tonight.

Chapter Six

Bill gave thought all the next morning to his discussion with Rob and Laura the night before.

Why not *go to the class?*

As far as he could tell, the private club was operating completely within the law. He suspected the members he'd already met through the course of the investigation would be more than willing to keep his identity a secret.

And it was a fairly innocuous class. Basic rope bondage.

Cart before the horse. First, he had to make it through dinner with everyone that evening. Depending on how that went, he might decide he didn't even want to go to the club that night, much less attend next weekend's class.

He finished his morning workout and headed outside to mow the grass. By the time he was done with the yard work, it was nearly noon and he debated whether or not to cancel going to dinner.

In the bedroom, he stopped in front of a picture on the wall of him and Ella at their wedding and took a deep breath.

He knew she wouldn't want him to be alone. They'd had this conversation early in their relationship. Just as he'd told her if he didn't come home one night that he wanted her to move on and be happy, she'd wanted the same for him.

Although, in all truth, he'd never expected to lose her so young, or during what was, by all accounts, supposed to be a routine operation. The agonizing four weeks she'd lain in a coma after her stroke on the operating table were something he hated to think about.

He knew she wouldn't have wanted to stay hooked up to machines when there was no chance of her ever coming back. It had broken his heart to do it, but he wouldn't let her body suffer when the essence of her had ceased to exist in the middle of a gallbladder surgery.

Reaching out, he stroked the glass over the picture. "Miss you, babe. Every damn day. I hope I'm doing the right thing. I know I can't ever replace you, and I don't want to try. But I know you'd want me to keep moving forward."

Okay. I need to do it. I need to go. Resolved, he headed to the bathroom to get his shower.

* * * *

Bill was standing in the restaurant's lobby twenty minutes before the agreed upon time when Rob and Laura pulled into the parking lot.

They both greeted him with smiles and hugs. "Glad to see you didn't back out," Rob lightly teased.

"Well, I almost did. I talked myself into coming."

Laura touched his arm. "Look, I don't mean to be forward, but even if nothing else comes out of this, you'll make a good bunch of friends. You saw how supportive they were for us during…last year." She nodded. "They're really good people. You'll like them."

"To be honest, that's sort of what I used to get myself here." And he had. All through his shower he'd rationalized that he needed more than Dori and Papa Tom, Al and Sue, Craig, and the handful of people who took pity on him. He used to have friends, he and Ella. She had been more the social, and he hadn't done his part after her death to keep them close once the shock and initial grief wore off. And in his job, there were plenty of days the last thing he wanted to do after work was socialize.

He had more than enough self-awareness to recognize that was all on him.

The hostess led them back to a far corner where several tables had been arranged together. "We're regulars," Laura said. "We call them every week to give them a head count and they prepare for us."

"Ah. Where do you want me?"

She patted the chair next to her and grinned. "We won't throw you into the deep end of the pool without floaties, I swear."

"Good to know. I appreciate that."

Everyone else arrived fairly soon after. Another round of introductions, or reintroductions, as the case was. He'd met pretty much everyone there through the investigation the prior year.

He was also relieved to see no one acted overly wary of him or his motives for being there.

As the meal continued, he was struck by how absolutely freaking normal everyone appeared and acted. He was well aware of the significance of things some of the people wore, like collars, bracelets, and the like.

But if it wasn't for that, and his prior knowledge of their lifestyle, he never would have assumed anything out of the ordinary about any of them.

It was a welcomed relief to know that his introduction into a more public aspect of this area of his life would be chaperoned by a group of people he suspected he would quickly come to trust.

Hell, he already liked them.

Toward the end of the meal, the conversation turned to the invisible topic at hand. From across the table, Seth Erikkson got Bill's attention. "By the way, we do have room in our class next Saturday."

"We'd love to have you," Leah added.

"I don't have any…equipment," he said, glancing around to nearby tables to make sure they weren't being overheard.

"It's all right," Seth assured him. "No special 'equipment' needed. We have plenty of extra."

"I'll warn you, I've never done anything like this before."

Tony Daniels hooked a thumb toward Seth and Leah. "Then it's the perfect class to introduce you to it. If nothing else, even if you decide it's not for you, they're excellent teachers and you'll kill a few hours."

"I'm looking forward to it."

And if he didn't lie to himself, he really was. It was nice to have something to look forward to other than yard work.

Hell, it was just nice to have a group of people he could spend social time with who weren't in law enforcement or the restaurant business.

They were waiting to settle their checks when Rob said, "Oh, you know what? I totally brainfarted on the munch tomorrow." He turned to Bill. "Did you want to go to that? We'd be happy to go with you."

"Munch?"

"Our once a month group dinner," Tony said. "Vanilla, don't worry. It's a larger group. This month we're having it over at Ballentine's off Bee Ridge. In their meeting room in the back. Starts at six."

"They don't mind you doing that?"

"They love it," Laura assured him. "We rotate between a couple of restaurants. We average thirty or more people per munch. That's a guaranteed busy night for them, and we tend to tip well. They know what we're about, but they don't mind because it's more than worth it to them, and we're careful not to disturb any other diners."

"Who else is going?"

Other than Sully, Clarisse, and Mac, who lived up in Tarpon Springs, it appeared nearly everyone else was going.

He didn't give himself time to think about it. *Take the damn risk.* "Sure. That sounds like fun."

* * * *

There were already over a dozen cars sitting in the parking lot when they all arrived at Venture. The club occupied space in a two-story, nondescript warehouse building in an industrial complex east of I-75.

Bill was a little surprised to realize he didn't feel nervous at all. In fact, a pleasant tingle of anticipation ran through him.

That was something he hadn't felt in too damn long.

He met up with Laura and Rob in the club's lobby. Other than some items hanging on the walls and some books for sale, it really didn't seem very shocking. Hell, a lot tamer than the scattering of adult video and toy stores down in his home turf of Charlotte county.

Stop thinking like a cop. You're here for fun.

Although it was hard to turn off his cop brain, he was determined to stay several hours, at least, and force himself to do something fun besides sitting in front of the TV and watching History Channel reruns for a change.

Okay, so maybe not for fun, but at least for a distraction. Something to get him out amongst a better selection of the human race than he usually had to deal with as part of his job.

After getting his club membership handled and finding out he had a comped entry that night courtesy of Seth and Leah, Rob and Laura led him to the door.

"Ready?" Laura asked.

"No, but let's do it anyway."

"That's the spirit," Rob said with a grin.

Rob opened the door and they walked inside. The main lights had been dimmed, but there were several colored lights scattered around the space and highlighting various pieces of equipment. It looked clean, which was a start. A long buffet table was set out on the far right side, where there was a grouping of round tables and chairs for people to sit and socialize.

Also on the right side of the space sat several groupings of couches. On the far left and merging into the middle of the space were various pieces of play equipment. He wasn't sure what all of them were for, but from the looks of one woman, who was strapped to an X-shaped wooden frame in one corner while her male companion went after her with what he guessed was a flogger, it wasn't difficult to imagine.

Bill noticed while several of the couples and triads he'd just eaten dinner with had brought various rolling suitcases or duffel bags into the club with them, Rob and Laura hadn't. Laura only carried a large bag he thought was her purse.

"You look like you're traveling sort of light compared to the others," he noted.

Rob grinned. "You'd be surprised what little we can use to play with when we get creative."

"We're not as implement-intense as others," Laura said. "Besides, my ass is still bruised from the beating I got last week." She hooked her arm through Rob's and looked up at him with something Bill could easily label adoration. "He's going easy on me this week."

"A little rope bondage, a little forced orgasm torture." He playfully swatted her ass. "Go get changed, baby girl."

"Yes, Sir." She eagerly hurried off toward the bathroom, where some of the other women had already gone to get changed.

Rob leaned in. "Don't get me wrong, play is fun. But most of what we do as part of our dynamic doesn't involve play, or even sex, a lot of the time. There's no wrong way to do what you want to do as long as everyone's on board with it."

Bill nodded, trying to remain neutral. He wasn't at a point yet where he felt comfortable discussing with Rob what he'd had with Ella, but knew if their friendship grew that might very well happen.

Landry and Cris walked over after they'd set their gear down on the far side of the room. "Feel free to ask any questions," Landry said. "Or if you want to try anything out with someone, we can arrange it." He slapped Cris on the back. "He's always a good demo dolly."

Cris smirked. "Thanks, Sir."

"I appreciate that. I suspect tonight I'll mostly be watching and asking questions." Not to mention while he didn't have a problem with it, he personally wasn't into guys.

"Not a problem," Cris assured him. "No pressure. It was a big first step just coming out in the first place."

"You got that right," Bill said.

He couldn't really say anything he saw over the course of the evening shocked him. As a cop, he'd seen a lot. He didn't feel anxious over any of it, because he knew it was all between consenting adults, and no one seemed to be doing anything to violate the club's rules.

If nothing else, the evening allowed him to rule out sadism as a turn-on. He could understand why some people enjoyed it, but he also realized if he met someone who had that kind of need, he likely wouldn't be able to meet it for them. The control and domination of someone in bed—and even out of it, in some ways—absolutely, that would stiffen his cock every time.

On the other hand, after watching Seth truss Leah up in what appeared to be a very intricate and artistic rope harness before doing some forced orgasm play with her, Bill knew he'd hit upon something that interested him.

After their scene, once Seth was able to talk again after giving Leah aftercare, Bill walked over to him. "Is that the kind of thing I'll learn in class next week? It looks awfully complicated."

"We'll be teaching the basics that can eventually lead to that, yes." He smiled. "Why? See something you liked?"

"Yeah. I think that's something I could really get into."

"Good. You going to come to the munch tomorrow night?"

Bill nodded. "Yeah. Yeah, I really think I'm going to. You think you can teach someone like me with no experience?"

"All you have to have is a willingness to learn and practice, and a lot of patience."

"And someone to practice on."

Seth smiled. "I'm sure we can arrange that."

* * * *

When Bill got home, after taking a shower and grabbing a cup of hot herbal tea to relax him, he fired up his laptop. From last year's investigation, he already knew Rob and Laura were members of a site called FetLife. During dinner, everyone had encouraged him to sign up and friend them there.

It would, they said, allow him to connect with more people from their area.

After a few minutes he finally decided on a username and used a throwaway e-mail account to sign up for the site. He sent everyone from dinner a friend request before taking a few minutes to peruse the site. Most of the people from dinner had marked they were going to an event, the munch.

What the hell, why not?

He clicked the option on the event's page that he was going, too.

Then he sat back and stared at the screen for a moment, looking at some of the other usernames marked as *going* or *maybe*. Some of the usernames were…

Interesting.

As were the personal avatars some of the people used. Everything from Hello Kitty to cock shots.

Well, I suppose it is a kind of pussy.

He felt the corners of his mouth curl in a smile, surprising him.

It felt good to be amused again.

Felt good to have a little anticipation for something in his personal life for a change.

Chapter Seven

Gabe spent all day Saturday curled up on the couch, in baggy shorts and a T-shirt, TV on, coffeepot working overtime, and crocheting her way through nearly a dozen amigurumis.

She also spent it forcing herself to keep her focus on her task and not on any other thoughts that struggled to make their way through to the front of her mind.

Like cracking open her work laptop and…oh, working.

Slacker.

She shoved that thought away, which had arrived with way more than a tinge of Maria's shrill voice, and got up to pour herself another cup of coffee.

I'm doing what my boss ordered me to do. That's following orders and being a good employee.

By Saturday night, she sat back and stared at the lineup of crocheted animals arranged on the coffee table. Four alligators, three dolphins, three rabbits, and a dog.

That was the most she'd been able to complete in one sitting in…years.

See? I was productive.

She wasn't sure who she meant that comment for, but no internal monologues dared contradict her.

After popping a microwave dinner in to cook, she glanced at the laptops again. Five minutes later, when the bell dinged that her food was ready, she already had her work laptop booted and running.

She set it on the coffee table next to the animals and went to fetch her dinner. *Hey, I'll just Google that restaurant so I'll know where it's at.*

Yeah, even she didn't believe that.

She checked her work e-mail, replied to a couple of messages, skimmed through a few files while eating, and, finally, brought up a browser screen to run a Google search on the restaurant.

It was fairly close, as a matter of fact. She could drive there in a few minutes. Even better, they listed "casual dining" on their website, meaning she could get away with jeans.

Perfect.

It would make Walker happy if she could report she'd actually taken his advice and gone there to eat.

She clicked on the Events link and scanned their website. Tomorrow night a meeting of something called the Suncoast Society was gathering in their meeting room.

Crud. Did that mean the restaurant would be busier than usual? Now that she'd decided she did want to go, the thought that maybe she'd have to wait another day pecked at her impatient side.

She clicked on the group's link out of curiosity, then froze. The link took her to an event page on a blog for a local group called the Suncoast Society. Skimming through it, it appeared to be a Sarasota-based BDSM group who held a monthly dinner munch that rotated between several restaurants.

Two mental voices waged silent war within her mind. *Stay home, you have groceries. Why waste the money?*

The other voice played sneaky. *Maybe this is something you should look into. For work. Walker did recommend you eat there. Maybe he did it on purpose.*

Logic tried to insert itself. *There are groups like this in South Florida. They aren't the kind of people you have to worry about. They don't involve children or anything heinous like that. It's just adults doing adult things to each other. There are* real *criminals out there to spend time trying to catch.*

She also hadn't treated herself to good prime rib in way too long.

I could always pretend to be a newbie and sit in on their meeting. I'd likely get faster service as well as satisfy my curiosity that they're harmless.

She also knew she'd be lying to herself if she denied any personal interest in the matter. She wasn't a virgin by any stretch of the imagination. Over the past several years, her solo sessions had veered off into the world of less vanilla fantasies. She'd even started reading a few erotic authors on her Kindle, one of the few indulgences she allowed herself with the rationalization that e-books saved her money and space.

In South Florida, there was no way she'd ever visit a BDSM club or munch or coffee group, even though she knew there was an active scene in the area. Not unless she was doing it as part of an undercover investigation. She couldn't risk the possibility of running into someone she worked with.

Or worse, someone she'd arrested.

Normally when faced with personal conundrums such as this, she chose the easiest or most logical option. Retreat, forget about it, ignore it, don't do it. Stay home.

Deny yourself.

She stared at the line of amigurumis on the coffee table.

Is this what my life boils down to? A notation on the donation sheets of several charities, and my name listed as investigator on too many cases to count?

She thought about Rachel. During their last talk just weeks ago, she'd counseled the girl to take personal risks despite the possibility of failure. That failure was always an acceptable option as long as you tried your best.

Maybe for once I should heed my own advice.

No one knew her here. She was all the way across the state, for chrissake. If nothing else, maybe she could, for once, not spend an evening totally alone.

After finishing her meal, she washed out the plastic bowl and put it in the recycling bin to take downstairs when she emptied the trash. Returning to her computer, she shut it down, closed the lid, and returned it to the counter.

I don't need to decide tonight.

She sat on the couch, picked up her hook and yarn, and descended once more into her safe crochet haze.

* * * *

By the time Gabe reached the restaurant the next evening, she'd talked herself into not joining the munch group. Why do something like that when she wouldn't be here that long anyway? It was stupid and pointless, and she was kidding herself if she thought she should try it.

Then she realized how full the parking lot was.

When she walked in, the main dining room appeared full, with several couples and groups waiting in the lobby.

She walked up to the hostess, who looked up with a cheerful smile. "Hi, welcome to Ballentine's."

"Um, how long for a table?"

"For one?"

She nodded.

"It'll be at least thirty minutes, I'm sorry. Would you like to wait?"

A couple walked in and waved to the hostess, who nodded and waved them through.

Before she could think about it, Gabe asked, "No offense, but why did they go in?"

"They're with a group who's reserved our meeting room tonight."

"The Suncoast Society?"

The hostess brightened. "Yes. Are you with them?"

"Um, yeah. Sorry, guess I should have said that. It's my first time."

The hostess' smile broadened. "No worries. Believe me, they get a lot of nervous newcomers we're pleased to see return again and again." She motioned Gabe over and pointed toward a door that was just swinging closed behind the couple. "Right through there. Sit anywhere you'd like. They have the whole room reserved."

"Thanks."

Before her nerve could escape her, or Maria's voice could chime in, Gabe hurried through the busy dining room to the door. Inside the meeting room there were at least fifteen people gathered. Large, round tables seating eight people each were arranged throughout the room.

A woman, who was hugging the couple who'd entered before her, spotted her and swooped over. "Welcome! First time?"

Gabe forced a smile and nodded.

The woman extended her hand. "I'm Laura Carlton." She pointed to where two other men were standing and talking with another couple. "That's my husband, Rob, on the left. The other is our friend, Bill. It's his first time, too. Come join us."

Gabe's original plan had been to sit by herself off in a corner where she could keep her back to a wall and observe, but the woman was already calling over to the two men to get their attention.

Terrific.

Gabe switched her purse to her right shoulder, suddenly very self-conscious of the feel of the Bersa pressing against the back of her right hip. The short-sleeved blouse she wore unbuttoned over her tank top and jeans kept the weapon from printing, but she didn't want to risk someone brushing against her while she was standing and possibly feel it.

Laura turned back to her. "I'm sorry, I didn't catch your name."

She thought fast. "Ella. Ella Wolf." Wasn't the first time she used the last part of her first name as a pseudonym, or anglicized part of her last name during an investigation. Made it easier to remember the ruse.

You're not here for work.

Focus!

"Ella, this is my husband, Rob Carlton."

"Nice to meet you," he said.

She shook with him. "Likewise." The husband was dressed in what Gabe guessed to be a county paramedic uniform. Dark blue cargo pants and a dark blue, short-sleeved shirt. Light brown hair that looked like he saw a lot of sun, and soft brown eyes, Gabe wondered which end of their dynamic he was on until she realized his wife wore a necklace with a heart-shaped locket on it.

She must belong to him.

The other man…

Her instincts screamed cop. Around four inches taller than her five seven, maybe a little older than her, definitely not as in shape as the paramedic, but it looked like he was successfully managing to combat middle-aged drift in his midsection. Brown hair and hazel eyes, she realized his gaze had intently settled on her.

He held out his hand. "Ella, did you say?"

She shook with him. "Ella Wolf."

He slowly nodded, then seemed to catch himself. "I'm sorry," he said, his expression softening. "My wife's name was Ella."

Something in his tone pulled at her. He sounded genuine. "I'm…sorry?"

Then he smiled, warming his face and tugging on her heart just a little bit more. "It's okay." He released her hand. "I lost her suddenly nine years ago. It's just I don't run into a lot of women with her name."

Now Gabe mentally kicked herself. "We're, ah, kind of scattered around all over." *Oh, my god, you're an idiot. Shut your pie hole.*

She supposed that was what happened when she went too damn long without any kind of a social life.

Or friends.

Laura took over. "Since it's her first time, I'm going to sit Ella between me and Bill," she told her husband. "If that's all right?"

Rob nodded. "Great. Glad you came out."

Now she couldn't back out without really sounding like an idiot. "Thank you. Sort of a last-minute decision."

"You're not the first, don't worry. We're an easygoing group."

Laura led her over to a chair next to two that had been tipped forward. "Right here," she said, smiling. "Bill's sitting next to you, on your left. Glad you came out tonight. You won't regret it."

"Thank you." *I hope she's right.*

* * * *

Bill wasn't an idiot. He knew exactly what Laura was up to.

Not that he minded, but he felt a little sorry that Ella looked like she'd been caught unprepared for the sudden seating assignment.

Which was fair, because he'd been caught unprepared for her name. Yes, he'd run into a few Ellas here and there in the years since her death, but it always tweaked his guts in a painful way. Less painful as the years wore on, but it never failed to elicit the reaction.

As he settled into his chair next to her, he offered a smile he hoped put her at ease. She looked as nervous as he felt. "So, what do you do for a living, Ella?" he asked.

She'd been reaching for the glass of water at her place setting. "I, uh, no offense, I'd rather not say. Let's just say I've been gainfully and continuously employed by the state of Florida for ten years, and would like to keep it that way."

"Ah. I'm tracking. I have the same kind of job. Looks like we already have something in common." He'd decided not to reveal to anyone he was a cop, and the people who already knew what he did for a living had agreed to keep that secret for him.

He'd feel a little more relaxed if they were in Tampa, or, say, Miami, but considering Charlotte County was only a few miles to the south, he figured it was better to hold back that little nugget of info for the sake of his privacy.

The longer they made small talk, he realized two things. One, she had something to hide, most likely attributed to her job.

The second, he was struck by how easy she was to talk to. Like they had something more deeply in common than just being at the munch.

Maybe she's a cop. If so, he wouldn't blame her for not wanting to divulge much about herself. But while he wouldn't claim to be an expert on every member of law enforcement in the area, she wasn't someone he'd run across before, that much he could remember. Her name definitely didn't ring a bell.

And he would have remembered her, without a doubt. She would have made an impression on him.

She sat at a little bit of an odd angle in her chair. At one point, when she leaned way forward to reach for the bread basket in the middle of the table, he spotted the telltale print of a gun in her waistband.

That immediately put him on alert. If nothing else, she had a concealed carry permit. He hoped. That wasn't anything special, because with over a million permits issued and counting, their state was notorious for concealed carry. Hell, even Laura had one as a result of her attack.

Then again, she had said state. Some probation officers carried. Or she might be with state corrections.

But maybe that was another source of her tension. With some people, it was easy to tell when they carried because they were almost self-conscious about it. If she really was a cop, likely she wouldn't be self-conscious about carrying. Tonight, he carried a subcompact .22

strapped to his ankle. Ballentine's was in a good neighborhood and he didn't feel the need to carry something larger when all he was doing was going right home after eating.

That made him lean even more strongly toward the non-cop theory. Lots of people were employed by the state in non-law-enforcement positions.

Stop it. You're not here as a cop.

Easy to tell himself, but harder to pull off in practice.

Focus on other things, like how pretty she is.

And she was attractive. Not in a supermodel, fake kind of way, but in a natural, doesn't-know-how-pretty-she-is kind of way. She didn't even appear to be wearing makeup. Her long, dark brown hair hung straight down her back.

One of his personal weaknesses in a woman, and one of the first things he'd noticed about her. Didn't look like she colored it, either, a few strands of grey here and there not detracting from her beauty, in his eyes. He liked that she had a very sweet, comfortable natural look about her despite her nerves. She also wasn't a waif. She had beautiful curves and a gorgeous, curvy ass that…

Okay, maybe I could get into a little bit of light spanking. Rounded, and perfectly accentuated by her jeans. In that way, she did resemble his Ella. It was hard not to think about what her flesh would feel like under his hands…

Dammit, I barely know her and I'm already having dirty thoughts about her. Maybe my libido isn't dead after all.

By the time the room filled and Tony Daniels called for everyone's attention to welcome the group, Bill was trying to figure out a way to ask Ella if she was going to the class on Saturday.

He was more than a little surprised to find himself hoping she was.

* * * *

Gabe wasn't proud of the fact that she lied and told Bill she was from the Sarasota area. Technically, she was staying in Sarasota, so had come from there. She did say she was new to the area, which wasn't a lie either, so she hoped the two evened each other out on the grand karmic scale. She didn't like to lie in the course of her personal life. Being undercover to catch bad guys was one thing.

She far preferred not answering questions over outright lying about the answers. Especially to someone who seemed as nice as Bill. Apparently while he was new to the munch, several of the people sitting at their table seemed somewhat familiar with him.

"So how did you end up here tonight?" she asked him.

"Well, I met several of the attendees here last year through the course of my work. When they invited me, I said sure. Why not? Not like I had any other plans tonight."

"Me, either. Other plans, I mean."

A man from their table stood and called for everyone's attention. "Thanks for coming tonight, everyone. We have several new people tonight. I'd like to welcome everyone to our monthly Suncoast Society munch. Our normal procedure is we go around the tables and everyone can introduce themselves, if they want to, and feel free to say a little about themselves. Or, feel free to pass."

He pointed to the farthest table. "How about we start over there with Tilly and her guys?"

A small titter of laughter rolled through the room. Gabe got the impression it was an inside joke. A woman with long red hair smiled and stood.

"I'm Tilly, and this is Landry and Cris."

"Who's on top tonight?" a woman playfully called out from the other side of the room.

Another round of laughter circled the room, louder this time.

Tilly smiled. "Who do you think?"

The two seated men flanking her both pointed up at her, inciting a third round of laughter.

By the time the introductions reached their table, there were several other first-timers who'd stood and introduced themselves, some with just their name, some with more information. Gabe didn't want to stand out by not saying anything. Fortunately, the rotation meant Bill had to stand first.

"I'm Bill," he said. "First time here, but I know a few people. Thanks for having me. I'm still…learning." He sat down and looked at Gabe.

She swallowed back her nerves and stood. "Hi, I'm…Ella." She'd almost said the wrong name. "I'm also new and still learning."

She sat, glad to be through that without interruption.

The wait staff came in to take their orders. While that happened, Laura turned to her. "You know, there's a beginning rope bondage class this coming Saturday. It's a great class."

"To get to know the ropes?"

Laura grinned. "Exactly. Bill's going."

Gabe glanced over at him. "You are?"

He shrugged. "It looks interesting. I don't know anything about it. I have to start somewhere and it seemed like a good idea."

"I don't have any rope. Just a lot of yarn," she added.

"Oh, that's all right," Laura assured her. "Seth and Leah teach it, and they bring lots of extras. You know, if you go, you and Bill could team up."

Gabe felt a tinge of nerves rush through her. She could already see where this was leading and knew she needed to put the brakes on and fast. "I'll see. I'm not sure if I'll be able to. How soon do I have to let them know?"

"By Thursday. The information's on the website. The Suncoast Society blog? Just hit the e-mail link to let them know."

Gabe nodded. She had seen something about classes on there. "Okay, thanks."

She wasn't sure she even wanted to do that. Tonight was likely a huge mistake. Except when her meal arrived, it was a delicious, perfectly cooked slab of prime rib, admittedly the best she'd had in years.

By the end of her meal, she felt stuffed. Between enjoying her time talking with Bill, as well as Laura, she'd made up her mind.

"You know, I think I will go to that class," she told Bill. "I'll clear my schedule and make sure I can go."

"Good," he said. "I won't feel like a fish out of water if there's another newbie there." He smiled.

She thought she could get used to his smile. "Why's that?"

"It'll be nice knowing I'm not the only clueless one there."

She didn't get the feeling he was trying to pressure her. In fact, he hadn't even asked for her phone number or e-mail address. "You don't strike me as the clueless type."

"Eh, when it comes to this stuff, believe me, I am."

"Then why are you here?"

He shrugged. "Tired of fishing in the wrong ponds, and tired of being alone. After nine years, maybe it's time to change the way I'm doing things."

"Been eight years for me."

"Don't know about you," he said, "but work gets in my way a lot."

"Something else we have in common, then."

Before leaving, she made sure to speak to Seth and Leah and introduce herself to them.

As Ella.

"We'll be glad to have you there," Leah said.

When a couple of voices tried to speak up in the back of Gabe's mind, she stomped them down without bothering to identify them first. That in and of itself was a miracle.

She'd been ordered to enjoy herself. To relax. To have some "me" time.

"Thank you. I appreciate that."

She thought about waiting for Bill once she'd paid her check, to talk to him some more, then indecision hit again.

No, she definitely wanted to go to the class. If nothing else, to prove to herself that she could take me time.

Well, when ordered.

She walked over to Bill, where he stood talking with Tony and Shayla, Tony's wife. "I need to go." She shook with them, finishing with Bill. "I guess I'll see you next Saturday, then."

His smile reached his eyes. It struck her he looked like a man not necessarily used to smiling a whole lot, like maybe he carried more on his shoulders than just lingering grief and loneliness. "Looking forward to it, Ella."

As she walked to her car, she briefly wished her name really was Ella.

She liked the way it sounded falling from his lips.

Chapter Eight

When Bill showed up at Marelli's on Monday night for dinner, Dori playfully gave him a hard time. "We were beginning to think something was wrong, or maybe you didn't like us anymore. You missed three days in a row. That's not like you."

He laughed, privately pleased that they'd noticed his absence. "Sorry. Busy weekend for a change. No more plans until this Saturday."

"I told Papa Tom if you'd suddenly met a woman, that you'd bring her in here for us to approve of."

"Of course I would. Love me, love Marelli's. It's a deal breaker."

Bill tried not to think too much about Ella over the next few days. He mentally kicked himself in the butt for not walking her out to her car.

I could have gotten her license plate number.

That thought made him kick himself again, because it wasn't exactly the best way to potentially start a new relationship on the firmest of footings, by running someone's plate.

Besides, it was highly unprofessional. And, in this case, illegal.

Although he had run a Google search on her and didn't come up with anything that looked like it pertained to her.

Not to mention he hadn't exactly been completely open with her, either, regarding his profession. He'd already decided, based on what happened during the class on Saturday, that he would open up a little more to her if he wanted to go out on a date with her. At least reveal that he was a cop so she could immediately reject him if she had a problem with that.

And if she didn't have a problem with what he did, maybe it would entice her to open up a little more, too. He'd gotten the impression it wasn't just because of the munch that she hadn't been very talkative about personal topics. Like maybe she was used to keeping details about her life close to the vest.

That would fit in with several of his theories, the front-runners currently being probation officer, social worker, or DCF investigator. Maybe even corrections in some other form, like an office worker. Those could all be state jobs. He doubted she was a trooper or wildlife officer. But she'd specifically mentioned working for the state, and the state was a big place with a lot of agencies.

Unless she lied.

He hoped she hadn't outright lied to him.

Well, doesn't matter yet. She'll have to come to the class first. And he wasn't even sure she'd do that. He had prepared himself for that possibility. She might get cold feet somewhere in the middle of the week, and he'd never see her again.

He was definitely a realist. Especially after what he'd been through with his Ella. He'd had every expectation of her coming home the next day following her surgery, and everything being fine. Not spending four weeks praying she'd miraculously wake up before finally agreeing to life support being discontinued.

Yes, he'd quit believing in miracles that afternoon, in lightning strikes of the good kind. As he'd watched the monitors chart her decline, so left his faith in happy endings. He'd lost more than just the love of his life that day. He'd lost all the hopes and dreams and plans they'd had. He'd never been much of a "greater power" kind of guy, but that afternoon cemented in his mind that there couldn't be a god or anything else.

And if there was a god cruel enough to take his Ella from him like that, he didn't want to believe in it anyway.

* * * *

Thursday afternoon, his former brother-in-law Craig called him. "Any plans for this Saturday night? Melody's thinking about throwing a cookout."

Bill silently groaned. Normally he enjoyed going over to their home. They'd been an important part of his life, his support during the four weeks following Ella's stroke, and in the weeks and months after her death.

"I can't this Saturday. For once, I actually have plans."

Craig laughed. "Please tell me it's a woman? Mel's bugging the crap out of me to try to set you up again."

Bill leaned back in his office chair. "Sort of. I did meet someone last weekend. Going to go out to dinner with friends." It wasn't technically a lie. He did hope Ella would join all of them for dinner at Sigalo's after the class. He just hadn't confirmed that, and couldn't until he saw her again.

If she even came to class.

"That's great! Any intel I can pass along to you-know-who? She'll bug the crap out of me, you know."

"I met her through friends last weekend. I don't even know if anything will come of it." That was also the truth.

Technically.

It didn't escape him that "met through mutual friends" was also a phrase the Suncoast Society group had told him they used a lot when introducing their kinky friends to vanilla friends and family. "Met through mutual friends" could cover a lot of ground without forcing anyone to outright lie or triggering most people to dig deeper for details.

"Well, I'm sure she'll give you a pass on dinner then. Just don't be surprised if she calls you and bugs you to bring your friend over to meet us."

Melody meant well. She and Ella had gotten along like a house on fire, close friends from when Craig, who'd been three years older than Ella, had brought her home while in college to meet their family.

Bill still felt convinced the death of their daughter at such a young age had contributed to the deaths of Ella's parents. Her father died of a heart attack two years later, her mother nine months after that. Bill suspected her mother had died more of a broken heart than the nebulous "heart failure" listed on her death certificate.

It had hit him as hard as it had Craig, considering he'd lost his own parents years earlier and they'd been like parents to him.

"Please tell her I appreciate the invite, and if anything develops, I'll be sure to let you guys know."

"Yeah, well, I guess she'll have to be happy with that." Craig laughed. "A couple moved in next door last week. There's a few eligible women in their family in your age range, apparently."

Bill couldn't help but smile. "How long did it take Mel to suss that out?"

"About five minutes, I think. Maybe less. You know her."

"Yes, I do. And again, tell her thank you for thinking of me."

Craig's tone softened. "Eh, you really doing okay, man?"

"Yeah." They actually lived over an hour south, down in Naples. He'd fibbed to them a few times and gently refused holiday invites over the past couple of years. It always caused a painfully deep ache in his soul afterward, the holiday gatherings did, that other get-togethers didn't create.

Besides, he always had the Marellis.

By Friday afternoon, Bill was wondering if maybe going to the class was such a great idea. When he found himself back in west county late that afternoon, he stopped by the dive shop. Rob and Laura were both there, the baby asleep in her portable crib set up in the office. Closed in there with the couple, he decided to admit his reservations.

"Maybe this isn't the best idea," he said. "Me going to class tomorrow."

"Are you worried about someone outing you?" Rob asked. "We've been going there for a couple of years, even ran into people we know a couple of times, and we've never had a problem."

Bill sat back in his chair. "Sort of. I don't know."

Laura smiled. "Not sure you're ready to jump back into the dating pool?"

"I don't know. Maybe."

She leaned over and hugged him. "Listen, you said it yourself, you're tired of being alone. Love isn't easy." She glanced at Rob. "Believe me, if anyone knows that, we do. We had to go through it not once, but twice, if you think about it. The second time around, we still chose each other, even though I didn't know who the hell I really was for a lot of the second time. Take a chance and go to the class. If you want, I can ask our sitter if they can take Molly sooner, and I'll go to the class with you."

He didn't want to inconvenience them. "No, that's okay. I guess I should just nut up and go through with it." He looked at Rob. "Does it get any easier?"

The paramedic shrugged. "I'll be honest, the first couple of times I went to events, I felt scared shitless." He rested a hand on Laura's shoulder. "Was it worth it? Absolutely."

She snuggled against Rob's side.

A sad pang squeezed Bill's heart. His mind flashed back to his Ella, to nights snuggled on the couch with her while watching TV. To sweet times spent in bed together.

Standing vigil at her bedside, mentally begging her to open her eyes and look at him.

"Scared shitless." He thought about the Ella he'd met at the munch, how something about her wouldn't leave his mind. "That's pretty accurate."

He drove back to east county and was fortunate enough to snag his usual table at Marelli's. With the place relatively busy, he knew the staff didn't have time to socialize with him. After Dori quickly grabbed his order, setting down glasses of tea and water without even asking him what he wanted to drink, he settled in with his work phone to go through e-mails.

He never did this when with Ella. His Ella. They'd always sat and talked during meals. He missed that nearly as much as he missed the intimate contact. Not even sexual, just…being with someone.

With someone.

He missed not feeling like a fifth wheel when out with others.

He missed the life he'd had, the plans and dreams they'd made. They'd wanted children, but then the world imploded.

Now, he knew he didn't want children at his age, even if the right woman miraculously came along. Ella had wanted children. He'd wanted them more because he wanted what she wanted, wanted to do anything and everything to make her happy. He knew he would have loved them every bit as much as she would have. She'd wanted to put off having them, and had actually started talking about trying to get pregnant before her gallbladder problem cropped up. And then…

All those talks fell by the wayside. Kids, with her, would have been great.

But without her…

No, he'd be better off with a cat. Life had soured him since losing her. Turned him bitter in some ways. Inflexible. He'd grown so comfortable with being alone that if someone was meant to be in his life, like Ella 2.0, they'd have to be able to love him and accept him the way he was, right now. Just like he would accept them.

He was too mature to play games. Too set in his ways to chase someone down. He wouldn't tolerate passive-aggressive antics to try to elicit a reaction from him. They either took him as he was…or they didn't.

He'd seen too many of his friends and coworkers divorce in the time since he'd lost his Ella. He wouldn't set himself up for that, if he could avoid it. That meant not settling. That also meant not trying to be things he knew he wasn't.

And it also meant the stars aligning, and whoever walked into his life not being a doormat who would do anything just to have a relationship. Tony and Rob had both given him that warning, about new sub "frenzy," the buzz of new relationship energy switching off the main breaker in peoples' brains and turning them utterly stupid.

He was a cop, used to keeping his cool. Ella 2.0 appealed to that in him. She didn't seem overly eager to throw herself at him.

Caution like that was something he appreciated.

Now let's see if she gives me a chance to see more of her.

Chapter Nine

Monday morning, Gabe went for an early-morning run and then stood under the shower, water as hot as she could stand it, letting it drum against her scalp and sting her flesh. Her dreams had been filled with all sorts of wild, crazy, and sexually explicit scenes starring Bill.

Of letting him tie her up and do things to her.

I really need to get laid.

Unfortunately, the vibrator in her suitcase couldn't hold her as she drifted off to sleep at night, or have conversations with her. She could lie to herself all she wanted, say she didn't need it, but something deep inside her soul craved and cried out for intimate human contact. Someone to snuggle with on the couch while watching TV. Someone to curl up with in bed while falling asleep.

Someone to touch her without recoiling from her physical and emotional scars.

Someone she could trust enough to let go to, to give her a break from her high-pressured life every once in a while without worrying her burdens were too much for them to bear.

Fat chance of that happening.

After she got dressed she sat on the bed and picked up Lil Lobo. He went with her when she had to leave home for more than a day. He'd become her security blanket, and she wasn't too stupid to see that. He was the reminder that no one could take him away from her.

Unlike Bear...

She forced that thought from her mind. Maria's voice had remained strangely silent that morning. Gabe didn't want to do anything, *think* anything, that might awaken it.

Yes, she knew her life was of her own making from the first step she set outside Maria's door after graduation. She was well aware of that. Aware that she'd spent her initial time away from Maria cocooning herself in armor-clad layers of emotional protection, not letting anyone close enough to hurt her again. The army had been a great help in that respect, rewarding tough personas, encouraging her to push herself as hard as she could. She even had plenty of acquaintances and got along fine with people she worked with. She simply chose not to give anyone a chance to disappoint her, hurt her, let her down. She didn't expect anything from anyone.

Although she expected the world from herself.

She set the stuffed wolf on the bedside table after giving it a final pat on the head. Also a tangible reminder to her that her job was important. Saving lives was important. Saving children, especially. She didn't want kids of her own, not when she saw what could happen to them.

Not when her own childhood had been so hellish.

The little amigurumis were important, too. Even if Gabe only made a positive impact in Rachel's life with the little animals, that alone was worth it. Validation of her efforts.

A reason to continue.

She went out to the kitchen to pour herself a cup of coffee, fighting the urge to log onto her work laptop. Instead, she focused on the growing army of amigurumis on the coffee table. If she kept it up at this rate, she could return to Miami with several dozens of them, meaning that many potential kids could have their days brightened, at least a little.

That's important, too.

It helped her make up her mind. She turned the TV on and tuned it to the Weather Channel before settling in on the sofa and picking up her yarn and a crochet hook.

She'd finished twelve more of the animals by the time she called it a day at eleven o'clock that night. Smiling, she arranged them all on the coffee table, which was rapidly running out of room.

A little army of crocheted critters just waiting for their new homes.

With a pleased nod, she turned off the TV and headed for bed.

* * * *

Tuesday morning started much like Monday had. Dreams kept her tossing and turning all night long, so that when she finally gave in and climbed out of bed a few minutes before five that morning, she felt like she'd barely gotten any sleep.

Again she thought briefly about using the vibrator, then decided against it. She wasn't a fan of masturbating in the morning. The problem with that being she frequently wasn't feeling like doing it by the time she got to bed that night. Especially if the day had been filled with emotionally difficult work.

Like the Martinez case.

She threw on running clothes and headed out the door. Mentally, she chafed at being temporarily off the case. Tracking down the money man topped her list of priorities upon getting back to work. One way or another, she would figure it out, find the son of a bitch, and haul him in for justice. She suspected he'd been involved in another case she worked on two years before, with similar MOs, but no proof tying the two together. Martinez had apparently never met David Muniz, the defendant in that case who was now serving a life sentence without possibility of parole.

Nothing obvious tied the men together except for the way everything had been handled.

Muniz had refused to hand over the money man in that case, too. But she found it hard to believe a petty crook, who hadn't even graduated high school and whose worst crime before that had been dealing in stolen property, could suddenly be kidnapping girls from various countries in the region, smuggling them into the US, and setting up an elaborate network to find johns and arrange deals.

It didn't compute.

Whoever it was, they had a lot of money to buy the guy's silence. The only differences in the cases were that Muniz hadn't personally raped any of the girls, and they were all at least sixteen years old.

Not that those facts made the situation any less heinous. Gabe hadn't successfully convinced Walker or anyone else that the cases were linked by the same backer. She also wondered if two other cases within the past ten years were also linked, but she hadn't been involved in those. In both cases, the primary suspect had been killed in prison.

Considering that Muniz had endured three attempts on his life already, had been relegated permanently to isolation for his own protection, and yet he still refused to talk, she suspected he would never reveal his backer.

Martinez, however, was squirrelly enough that she might be able to shake a little information from him.

Unfortunately, that would have to wait until she was officially back on the job.

By the time she returned to the condo almost an hour later, she'd pushed herself nearly to the point of exhaustion. The hot water of the shower soothed her muscles and lulled her mind into a temporarily calm state.

Maybe Walker's right. Maybe I do need the break, to gain a little perspective, if nothing else.

As she stepped out and toweled herself off, Maria's voice tried to shrilly break through with claims of slacking off, dodging her responsibilities.

She shoved the voice into a mental closet and locked the door. Walker had ordered her to relax, so she would. It would only be a matter of time before Maria's voice escaped and started chattering at her again, but Gabe would keep repeating to herself that she was following orders.

She headed into the kitchen to start the first pot of coffee of the day and add to the growing amigurumi army.

* * * *

Wednesday morning, Gabe had to go out to buy more yarn in a few colors she'd run out of. Especially the green she used for the alligators. They were always one of the most popular amigurumis, their cheerful, goofy smiles making kids happy. She also thought about taking a drive over to Siesta Key, to the famous beach there, and decided against it.

I've got plenty to do.

Walker called her that afternoon on her personal cell phone.

"So, how are you doing?"

"You tell me," she said, propping the phone between her cheek and shoulder as she made the beginning loop for a new animal, a dog this time. "Aren't you checking the alarm logs?"

He let out one of *those* sighs. "Gabe, I'm not checking up on you."

"I thought you said you were."

"I was busting your balls, geez. That's why I'm calling you. To see how you're doing."

"You'll be happy to know I did try Ballentine's on Sunday night."

"Oh? Good. How was it?"

"I had…a very good meal."

"That's it?"

"You want a written report on your desk about it?"

"That's not what I meant and you know it."

She mentally swore as she goofed up the starting stitches and had to rip them out and begin again. "Then what do you mean?"

"I'm concerned about you, all right?"

The tone in his voice caught her attention. She set down the hook and yarn and grabbed the phone again. "Why?"

"Because I consider you a friend in addition to a damn good employee, that's why."

He could have dropped his pants and mooned her and she wouldn't have been more surprised. "Really?"

"Uh, yeah. I know you aren't much into having friends, but that doesn't mean people can't consider *you* their friend, you know?"

She hadn't really thought about it like that. "Oh."

"Why do you think I keep inviting you over to our house, even though you turn me down every time? Why do you think I sent you to my personal condo? Get your head out of your ass and look around you for a change. Maybe people like you. Maybe people respect you. Sometimes you have to give a little in return to get more than you currently have."

He hung up on her.

She stared at her phone, his words pounding through her brain. She didn't have friends. Not really. Although, yeah, Walker would be someone, if pressed, she could label a "friend" and not just a coworker or acquaintance.

Am I really that much of a dumbass I can't recognize when I have friends? Or am I just truly that broken?

She tended toward the second.

Setting her phone on the table, she picked up her yarn and hook, consulted the pattern, and started over again.

* * * *

Walker hadn't checked in with her again by Saturday morning. Gabe changed her mind countless times about going to the class until his words rang through her brain again.

Sometimes you have to give a little.

No one knew her here. What would it hurt? It would get her out of the condo for a few hours. She could stop somewhere to have dinner.

She would broaden her horizons, as they said.

If nothing else, it would allow her to picture some things more clearly when she got back to reading her Kindle. Which she'd done precious little of due to the amigurumis.

She pulled up the website again and studied the class description. Something she'd done several times over the space of the last few days.

What if Bill doesn't show up?

He doesn't owe me anything. We just met.

I would deserve it if he ditched the class.

Shut. Up.

She sat back and scrubbed at her face with her hands. She'd eschewed her morning run since she'd hit it hard every other morning. Her body was starting to feel the effects of the flat-out runs in a bad way.

And I am *going to be forty in a couple of months.*

Not that it bothered her. No midlife crisis for her. It was a pointless waste of time and energy. She would get older every year regardless of her feelings on the matter, and to wring her hands about it was useless.

After making a sandwich for lunch, she finally set her mind and went to get a shower.

What does *one wear to a rope class?*

Chapter Ten

There were already a couple of cars parked outside the club when Gabe pulled in thirty minutes before the class was scheduled to start.

Finally, after debating the issue back and forth for a while, she decided to lock her weapon in the small gun safe bolted to the floor of her trunk. Depending on how the class went, it might be difficult to conceal it. From the description provided on the website, it looked like students would be encouraged to try the techniques they would be taught.

If she was partnered with Bill, she didn't want to have to make dumb excuses as to why he couldn't tie her up.

Besides that, the club's rules on their website specifically prohibited firearms.

Although as active law enforcement, technically she could circumvent that. Except for the fact that she was there for personal reasons, not undercover, not officially in the slightest. Meaning she was supposed to adhere to the club's rules.

She locked the .380 in the trunk and headed inside. When she had to provide an ID and fill out paperwork, she had to stop herself from presenting her official credentials and offered up her driver's license instead.

I need to be careful.

Maria's voice tried to sound off in the back of her brain and Gabe shoved it away. She wanted to do something for herself for a change. Maybe it was an unusual choice over, say, something like sightseeing, or taking up a hobby, but the pictures she'd seen of intricate and artistic ropework fascinated her.

Not to mention, if she ended up gaining any official knowledge she could use in future investigations to help weed out predators from innocent people, that would be a bonus.

She certainly wasn't looking for a man out of it. The last relationship she'd tried nearly eight years ago had lasted all of three months. When he couldn't handle her independence, combined with what she did for a living and the sometimes unpredictable nature of her hours if she was involved in an investigation, it had almost been a relief to end things when he told her he didn't think it was working out.

It meant she no longer had to pretend or make excuses for what or who she was. Or try to change herself to fit into the relationship.

It also meant no more trying to dodge him in the bathroom, or insisting the lights be off when they made love so he couldn't see the scars on her back.

By the time she paid her class fee and headed through the inner door into the club proper, she was struggling against her nerves. She thought about turning around and leaving right then, except Leah spotted her and called out a greeting.

"Hi, Ella!" The woman walked over, a friendly smile on her face. "Glad you made it. Let me introduce you around."

Gabe had no choice but to follow her over to one side of the space, where several round tables were located. Glancing over to the other side of the large space, she could see various pieces of equipment were set up, most likely used for bondage pursuits.

A dozen people or so, male and female alike, were sitting at the tables. Leah's husband, Seth, stood talking with one of the men.

She didn't see Bill.

He arrived a few minutes later while Leah was still making the introductions. Gabe tried to ignore the way her pulse sped up, thrumming, when she spotted him and his gaze locked with hers.

And the smile that suddenly enveloped his face.

That was a smile she suspected she could grow quite used to seeing on a regular basis. Her heart raced in an unfamiliar way.

Unfamiliar, since there was no risk of an "in the line of duty" kind of death right now, which was usually the only time she felt a rush like that.

Stop it. You won't be here more than a couple of weeks.

Still, it didn't keep her body from reacting to him.

"Glad to see you made it," he said by way of greeting when he walked over.

"Thanks. You, too." She hoped that sounded more noncommittal than it had come out.

When the class started, Seth and Leah went over the basics of what they'd be covering throughout the full class series. Following that, Seth, using Leah as his model, went over safety issues, including how to evaluate the rope bottom for health or physical concerns that might affect how to tie them. Also, they covered what did and did not constitute a safe hard point for suspension, and what to look out for. Gabe appreciated the fact that they wanted people who thought they might only bottom to also be versed in safety issues to help protect them from unsafe rigging practices.

"Don't be afraid to question your rigger," Seth told them. "I'm not saying you have to be rude, but always speak up if you have concerns. This is your body you're talking about. You have a responsibility to yourself first to keep safe. And never let someone rig you in a suspension tie unless you know they've had experience. If they want to gain experience, they need to be doing it under the supervision of someone who is experienced with suspensions, or at the very least they need to have an assistant who can help catch you in case of a fall."

Gabe enjoyed watching the dynamic between Seth and Leah. It was easy to see how much in love they were. It practically radiated through the air between them.

"We won't even be touching suspensions in this class series," Seth told them. "We'll be covering the basics, the most common ties, how to do basic restraints. The next class series will cover more advanced ties, leading to basic suspensions. If there's enough interest, we'll put together an artistic series where you can start widening your skills into decorative and functional ties."

They took a brief break for everyone to have a chance to hit the bathroom, or for smokers to grab a quick one before they started on the class participation portion.

"Not a smoker?" Gabe asked Bill when he didn't move.

He shook his head. "Nope. Never cared to try it."

One more point in his favor.

She caught herself thinking that and tried to shove it out of her mind. Leah walked over at that moment, giving Gabe a mental respite. The woman carried a small duffel bag, which she set on the table for them.

"Here's your loaner kit," Leah said. "There's more than enough rope in there to cover what we're going to do today."

"Thanks," Bill said, standing to unzip the bag and peer inside. Gabe craned her neck to see, but didn't stand. She'd finally managed to get her pulse under control. She didn't want to have any more close contact with the man than necessary and send her heart racing again.

"I guess this won't be anything like crochet," Gabe muttered.

Bill smiled. "Probably not. You enjoy doing that?"

"Yeah, you could say that." She thought back to the overflowing amigurumi menagerie back at the condo. They covered the coffee table, the entertainment center, both end tables, and had started taking over the kitchen counter. She knew she could bag them up, but didn't have the heart to do that just yet.

She liked seeing them fill the space, their cheery colors and smiling faces lightening her mood a little bit.

It made her feel good to see them there. It made her feel less empty.

When class commenced again, the first thing Seth went over was basic techniques on how to wrap the rope around someone. He had everyone try making a basic rope gauntlet on their own arm, including all the people who were bottoms for their partners. Then it progressed to doing it to their partner.

Bill, in jeans and a short-sleeved collared shirt, held out an arm to her with a smile. "You first."

"Really?"

He shrugged. "If I'm going to learn how to do it, I definitely need to know what it feels like, right?"

Everything he said seemed to make her like him even more. He didn't strike her as an arrogant know-it-all, like one of the men in the class, who seemed bound and determined to comment on every single thing Seth said. Gabe noticed the girl the man had brought to class with him looked increasingly uncomfortable with his behavior.

Asshat.

Bill had sat and apparently soaked up every comment, paying close attention to what Seth demonstrated to the class.

After Gabe wrapped the gauntlet around Bill's lower arm, Seth walked over and checked her work. "Good job, Ella," he told her. "Nice technique." He continued on to the next couple.

Gabe blinked, a sudden wash of emotion threatening to spill over as she quickly unbound Bill's arm.

"Are you all right?" he softly asked her.

She nodded, quickly coiling the rope as Seth had shown them and handing it off to Bill. She held out an arm. "Your turn."

She didn't want to admit that it was the first time since before her parents died that someone other than her boss had given her genuine praise. And that it had taken her by surprise.

And that she wanted to hear it again.

* * * *

Bill paused after taking the coil of rope from Ella, studying her features closely. It almost looked like she'd been close to tears for a moment, but he couldn't figure out why. Seth had praised her work.

Nothing in her demeanor telegraphed domestic abuse survivor. She seemed to be a confident, steady woman. Yet there was no mistaking the way her eyes had suddenly gone too bright, or the way she coughed, quickly brushing her fingers across her face and turning away for just a moment.

He dropped his voice. "Are you sure you're okay? Would you like a break?"

"I'm fine. Your turn."

He would suspect she was anything but fine, although he didn't know why. He also barely knew her and had to take her at face value.

If asked, he'd swear Seth's praise of her work tying the gauntlet had nearly started her crying.

Taking his time, he replicated the rope gauntlet on her arm, making sure to be gentle and not get the ropes too tight. The more time he spent with her, the more time he wanted to spend with her.

The more he wanted to unravel her secrets. He was convinced she hid something beyond her true occupation. Something likely painful. She'd made no talk about family, friends, or hobbies, other than the crochet.

The next step was making a basic chest harness. Bill laughed as he stared at her. "Make sure not to wrap my man boobs too tightly."

The comment caught her off-guard, making her laugh. "You are funny. You are far from man boob territory." He wasn't exactly ripped, but he knew he wasn't fat. Then he stripped off his shirt.

No, he definitely didn't have man boobs. He patted his stomach, which maybe had a couple of extra pounds of padding, but didn't jiggle.

"You're too kind," he said. "Unfortunately, middle age is catching up with me."

"It catches up with all of us. The alternative isn't that great." She realized what she said. "Sorry. That was insensitive. I—"

"No, it's okay." His hoped his smile echoed his words, reassuring her that she hadn't hurt his feelings. "Believe me, it's all right. It's been nine years now. I'm okay. But I do appreciate the consideration, thank you." He pointed at the rope. "Ready to get started?"

"You don't mind me pawing at you?"

He loved the spark in her eyes. "Not at all."

It took nearly a half hour for her to get the rope harness tied. As she worked to duplicate Seth's example as closely as possible, Bill watched how she seemed to intently focus, as if this was more than just an exercise in tying rope.

He suspected she was like this in all areas of her life.

More than ever, he wanted to get to know her better, all sides of her, to see what drove her.

When it was his turn to tie her, he wasn't sure how to proceed at first. Some of the women, there with their partners, didn't hesitate to strip down to bare skin, or at least down to their bra.

While he wouldn't have minded if Ella did the same, he wasn't going to come off sounding like an asshole and ask her outright to do it.

Fortunately, he didn't have to. She slipped off the short-sleeved blouse she wore over her tank top. "I'm not wearing a bra," she said before wryly smiling. "And don't worry about incidental contact. It won't freak me out."

She's a good sport.

He started working on the chest harness, trying to keep an eye on her expression to gauge her reaction. He didn't want to do anything to upset her. Especially when he really liked her and realized how perfect her sweet, rounded curves would fit pressed against him.

When he circled around to her back, he paused. Just under her shoulders and the nape of her neck, exposed by the way the initial turns of rope around her torso had pulled down her tank top a little, he spotted several angry scars leading down and out of sight.

"You forget what you're trying to do?" she asked, cutting through his shock.

"No, just trying to figure out how to do it without groping you and pissing you off," he shot back a little more sharply than he'd meant to.

"I'd like to talk you into going to dinner with several of us tonight," he quickly added. "I'm afraid if I get too fresh, you'll say no."

She tipped her head back to look at him. "Maybe I'll say yes."

* * * *

Gabe wasn't a dummy. Now she swore for even doing this in the first place. He'd seen her scars. The look on his face told her that much. At least he'd tried to pretend he hadn't.

And if seeing a little of them had freaked him out that much, if he saw the full extent of them he'd likely run the other way.

But he'd earned points for trying, she gave him that much credit.

"And maybe I don't mind a little pawing," she added. "Maybe I'd like it."

She hoped he didn't sense how nervous she now was, how anxious to get his attention off her back. Feel up her boobs?

If it meant he wasn't looking at her scars, sure thing. She was plenty good with that trade-off. Besides, fair was fair. She'd gotten to paw at him a little, too, and it had taken every ounce of self-control she'd had to keep from running her fingers over his pecs. She'd never been a fan of gym rats. Bill was a real guy who had been trying to keep himself together.

To be truthful with herself, she knew she was a little rounder in the ass and thicker in the hips and thighs than she wished she was, but she wasn't in the army anymore with daily PT to endure. She spent too many hours a day in a chair behind her desk, or in a car, and eating food that wasn't necessarily the best for her.

"So, is that a yes?" he asked.

"To what?"

He smiled. There was something simultaneously sad and sinful about it. "Dinner. Tonight. Not just the two of us, but several others. They go out every Saturday. You met most of them at the munch."

Baaaad idea.

"Sure," she said, shoving the voice away. "Why not?"

Chapter Eleven

In her mind, Gabe changed her decision to go to dinner at least a dozen times between walking from the club out to her car. She didn't want to be rude and suddenly tell everyone no, she didn't want to go to dinner with them.

Especially when she *did* want to go to dinner with Bill.

Going out to eat like this, twice in the space of a week, with a group of people she didn't work with, was a record for her life.

She liked that when she asked if he minded if she drove her car, he didn't argue or try to get her to change her mind. He didn't appear to be put out in the slightest by the request. He also didn't assume he was invited to ride with her.

She liked that, too.

After getting the address for the restaurant in case she got separated from the rest of them, it took a massive amount of willpower on her part not to turn off on a side street and make a dash for freedom. Beating deep inside her heart, a determination to see the evening through to a natural conclusion and not running like a coward.

Yes, all right, fine. I want to prove Travis wrong. I can *relax and meet people and enjoy myself.*

She also wanted to disprove the annoying voice in her mind. The one that sounded like Maria and comprised all her doubts and self-recriminations.

She wanted to make sure *she* wasn't the one who was wrong. That Travis Walker and the voice were the ones off-base.

Unfortunately, deep inside, she suspected that wasn't what she'd discover.

Bill had pulled into the parking lot ahead of her and met her at her car. When he offered her his arm, she felt a pleasant little thrill as she hooked her arm through his.

Although it meant she didn't have a chance to retrieve her gun from the lockbox in the trunk.

Oh, excuse me while I get my sidearm, k tks bai.

Yeah, like *that* would go over well. It would also entail her trying to come up with an explanation for having a permanently mounted gun safe in her trunk. It wasn't like everyone had one of *those*. Or a bulletproof vest. Or a rain jacket with FDLE emblazoned on the back.

It would mean either flat-out lying to him, or revealing her true identity, and neither option was one she liked at the moment.

The restaurant appeared to be in a nice area, and they would be with a group of people. The chances of her being involved in a civilian situation right now, where she would actually need a firearm, were probably as close to zero as she could statistically get.

I guess it stays.

Gabe walked into the restaurant on Bill's arm. She felt slightly uncomfortable as the momentary center of attention while Bill introduced everyone at the table. Most everyone there she'd met or at least seen at the munch. They appeared welcoming, genuinely happy to have her join them.

It didn't help totally dispel her "fish out of water" feelings, but at least she didn't get a snarky vibe from anyone.

If you weren't wasting time on this nonsense anyway, it wouldn't be an issue to start with.

Aaaand there was Maria, back with a vengeance.

At least Gabe had no problem ditching the vestiges of religious guilt Maria had tried to inspire in her. She'd decided years ago, in her early teens, that she wanted nothing to do with Maria's religion if it could permit the woman to do what she did. As an adult, Gabe had seen too much, worked too many horrific cases, to believe in any kind of a loving deity.

People could be good, and people could be evil.

But the work ethic guilt and financial arguments, those were harder to shake. Those made sense.

In some ways, those had served her well throughout her adult life.

Once the server had taken their orders, Leah turned to Gabe. "So, when did you become interested in the lifestyle?"

She wasn't sure how to answer and decided the best answer was the honest one. "I don't know. I've read some books and been curious, but my work situation never allowed me to really do anything before. It was sort of a coincidence I ended up at the munch in the first place."

"No harm in that, Ella," Shayla said from across the table. She smiled as she looked at her husband. "I sort of fell into it myself."

"One of us…one of us," Tilly chanted with a playful grin.

"Just remember that the books aren't always close to real life," Shayla cautioned. "Believe me, I had my eyes opened to a whole new world when I started. In some ways, reality is even stranger than fiction, in a good way."

"How did you get into it?"

"I was assigned to do a story on it," she said. "For the magazine I work for." She looked up at Tony again. "Loren and Ross introduced me to Tony, and we sort of couldn't figure out where my assignment was supposed to end and we began. So we made it permanent."

"You're a reporter?"

"Don't worry," Leah assured her. "Even when she was writing about us, she took great pains to make sure no one was personally identifiable."

Shayla dug a business card out of her purse and handed it to Gabe. "Here's the magazine's website. Just search my byline, and my maiden name, Shayla Pierce, with the term 'BDSM.' The series will come up for you."

"Thanks." She slipped it into her purse.

Leah looked down the table at Tilly and grinned. "I see you got into it with a 'won twue wayer' on Facebook the other day."

Tilly shook her head. "Ugh. I hate those damn asshats."

Gabe was relieved to see Bill looked as clueless as she felt.

Leah filled them in. "You'll sometimes see it abbreviated as 'WTW' on the Internet. It's someone who insists if you're not doing BDSM their way, then you're doing it 'wrong.'"

"I missed this one," Tony said, looking amused. "What was it about this time?"

Tilly set her glass of tea down while both her men looked like they were settling in for the duration of her rant. "Get this! Some Fucktardo the UberDom insisted it's not possible for a sub to sink into subspace unless they're beaten there."

Everyone at the table except Gabe and Bill burst into laughter.

"Seriously?" Clarisse asked. "How the hell did I miss *that* one? I would have loved to take a whack at that asshole."

Leah helpfully filled Gabe and Bill in on the subject. "You know how runners get that thing called 'runner's high'?"

"Uh, sort of," she admitted. "I hate running, especially when I'm doing it."

"Join the club. Subspace is sort of like that, different for everyone in how they experience it or get there. It's most commonly described as a nice, floaty feeling, like the whole world goes away. And I know most of the women here"—Tilly coughed from her end of the table—"who consider themselves full-time subs or slaves will agree it's completely easy to be talked into subspace if they've got the right partner."

Landry leaned forward and focused on Tilly. "And why did you cough, love?"

Tilly's face went red, but she didn't respond.

Everyone else at the table laughed.

"Oh, go easy on the switchy girl," Leah joked. "We lubs her just the way she is. You guys screw up the BDSM bell curve anyway." She returned her attention to Gabe and Bill. "The bottom line is that some people never hit subspace, some hit it all the time, and everything in between. It's different for everyone. There is no right or wrong way to do any of it, outside of obvious safety precautions."

"We're pretty much a 'live and let live' kind of group," Ross said. "Your kink might not be my kink, but that's okay."

"I don't even know for sure what my kink is," Gabe said.

"Ditto," Bill added.

Loren shrugged. "That's okay, too. Even if all you do is watch others, that's a legitimate kink."

"Sounds kind of creepy," Gabe said.

"It can be if you're trying to masturbate on top of someone you're watching without their permission," Tony said with a smirk. "But a lot of people spend time watching and thinking before they figure out what exactly it is that turns them on. No harm in that."

Gabe looked at Bill. "You don't know what turns you on?"

He smiled. "Oh, I know what turns me on, I'm just not sure where that puzzle piece fits quite yet."

"So what are you?"

With a shrug, he said, "Toppy. I'm not going to deny that, in the bedroom, I enjoy having a certain amount of control. Maybe even outside the bedroom, too, if someone's amenable to that. I don't think I'm a sadist."

Rob nearly choked as he laughed with a mouthful of iced tea. "I thought I wasn't a sadist either, Bill. I quickly grew into the role and found out I liked it a lot."

"Yeah," Tony said, "but you grew into it because Laura liked it. I think if Laura had not been into that, you wouldn't have gone there. Am I right?"

"Absolutely," Laura said, focusing on Gabe. "It was a partnership. We kind of explored together, and stuff I didn't think I'd ever like, I found myself begging for."

"Warned you," Shayla said with a playful grin.

Gabe had found out at the munch that, of all the women at the table, those two were the closest of friends, although all the women were close.

"Yes," Laura said, "you warned me. Look at what happened to you."

"What happened to you?" Gabe asked, unable to help herself.

Shayla smiled. "Let's just say I've given up saying 'no' to Sir. He has a sneaky way of turning all my 'hell nos' into 'yes pleases.'"

Tony arched an eyebrow at Shayla, a sweetly evil smile creasing his face. With Tony's moustache and goatee, even Gabe felt the residual effects of the heat that sexy smile held.

By the time they were ready to call for their checks, Gabe had decided she did want to go back to the club for the evening.

Just to watch.

At least, that's what she told herself.

These people all seemed comfortable not only with each other and their partners, but with themselves as well. They spoke openly with her about their lifestyle, without pressing her for details about herself.

She felt a little guilty about that, but still didn't think it wise to completely reveal her identity to them.

She was also desperately trying to figure out a way to incorporate this lifestyle permanently and knew, long-term, that might not be a practical option.

Especially once she returned to Miami.

But for the evening, she'd indulge herself in tantalizing what-if thoughts. It was a damn sight better than listening to echoes of Maria bounce around in her head.

* * * *

Bill secretly felt pleased over how dinner went. Ella had been warmly welcomed by the others, and they'd all taken time to answer her questions and include her in conversations.

If nothing else, he knew he'd keep going out with this group of people just for the camaraderie. Never in his life had he known a more friendly and accepting bunch of people.

That they all appeared to have their shit together and were successful in mainstream society in spite of their more hidden pursuits was a bonus. It gave him something to aspire to, that even if things didn't work out with Ella, maybe he could possibly find someone else who he could be completely open and honest with, the way his friends were with their own partners.

Someone he didn't have to worry about accepting him, the same way he would openly accept them for all their quirks.

When they returned to the club, he went in with Ella. He was about to offer to pay for her evening when Seth and Leah stepped forward. "I want to use one of our freebies on her entrance tonight," Seth told the girl at the desk.

"Cool beans," the girl said, tapping the info into the computer. "Done." She smiled at Ella. "We have all your stuff from the class, so you're good to go. Enjoy your evening."

Bill mentally kicked himself for not being there earlier for the class and getting a look at Ella's paperwork when she registered, to see if Ella Wolf was her real name.

Oh, well.

He held the door to the main club space open for her. The overhead lights had been dimmed, the music and accent lighting now on and creating a festive atmosphere. It was like a party, in a way. Part rock concert, part performance art, part selective mini mosh pit. For some of the people, at least.

"Have you ever been to a club play session before?" Bill asked her.

She shook her head. "No, but I'm pretty hard to shock because of my li—" It was like she cut herself off. "I've seen a lot, don't worry."

It sounded to him like maybe she'd been about to say *because of my line of work.* "Good," he said. "You might see some intense scenes tonight, especially if Landry and Cris play, or Sully and Mac. I haven't seen them play hard together yet, but Laura and Rob warned me they sometimes get really rough. She didn't want me to be shocked."

"Duly noted."

He realized he didn't want her freaked out, scared away from returning next week.

In fact, he'd thought about asking her for her phone number, or at least her e-mail address. She had volunteered that she'd joined FetLife, and that he could send her a friend request. He'd do it when he got home that night. Tomorrow, at the latest. He was accumulating more friends on the site and being careful not to friend anyone he hadn't already met in real life.

Seth walked over. "By the way, in case you're interested, we brought the loaner bag of rope in with us." He smiled knowingly.

Bill was up for that, interested in practicing more and spending some close-up time with Ella.

He wasn't sure how she'd react.

He breathed a silent sigh of relief when she smiled. "That sounds like fun."

Chapter Twelve

Early Sunday morning, at her usual time, Gabe awoke feeling disoriented in a way totally unlike she had her first morning there in the condo.

What. The. Hell?

It wasn't just from the sleep deprivation, from the night she'd spent in the company of people she didn't work with.

She ran her fingers up and down her upper arms, where the ligature marks had been last night after her and Bill had spent a couple of hours under Leah and Seth's tutelage at the club, as well as a few others who offered their opinions when asked.

She stared at her lower arms, where she'd marveled at the feel and texture of the marks on them.

Nothing now, just smooth, unblemished skin.

She'd had a great time. That alone had shocked the hell out of her. Bill had been fun to spend time with, fun to talk to, and had stirred something inside her she wasn't sure she wanted to contemplate.

Going out to dinner was great. Feeling like she was welcomed amongst them, not a fifth wheel, not a work colleague people had to watch what they said around.

Friends.

Is this what having friends feels like?

Looking back on it, she definitely didn't regret going. If nothing else, at the very least she'd satisfied a curiosity in her that, until last night, she'd never realized was so strong.

Hell, she'd never realized, beyond the realm of her Kindle-induced fantasies, that she'd ever begin to see them made real.

Usually it required having a relationship, which she didn't have.

Fear set in.

She would have to get to know Bill better if she took the second class. As it was, she'd been able to avoid the issue of her scars.

What if he wanted to go out with her more?

What if...

She shook off those thoughts.

There would be *no* getting closer. She was from Miami. She didn't have time for a relationship.

She'd have to reveal she was a cop.

She closed her eyes and groaned. No, there wasn't a future in going to another class. There wasn't any use to get close to someone. To get her hopes up, or his. Last night had been a really stupid mistake, no matter how good a time she'd had.

Why bother? She was surprised to realize Maria's voice wasn't anywhere to be found.

On any other day, she might consider that a miracle and desperately try to figure out how to replicate the result.

She suspected she knew exactly why.

The subspace they'd talked about in class and at dinner. That fuzzy, warm, leftover feeling. The one she wished she could have more often.

The one she'd felt while letting Bill practice tying her up multiple times last night.

Such a great feeling, one she'd never felt before.

One she knew she could never allow herself to feel again. Not without risking her career or her sanity over silly hopes for a relationship that could never work out in the long term.

I need a run.

She got up, threw clothes and sneakers on, and headed out for the jogging path that circled around and wandered through the complex. Outside, despite the early hour, it was already warm, muggy in a familiar way. She tried pushing herself as hard as she could go, trying to use a punishing pace to drive all other thoughts out of her head, but it wasn't enough. When she returned to the condo and crawled into the shower, she slid down the wall, wrapped her arms around her legs, and buried her face against her knees as she cried.

She wanted more, so much more, and knew it wouldn't be possible.

Deep inside her soul, the lonely little girl who'd never known love after losing her parents still curled up in a bed in a practically bare room in a house she didn't know and cried.

The way she'd silently cried so many nights until she finally managed to silence those cries for good.

And she'd learned early on never to let Maria see her cry. Ever.

Not even over sappy Christmas commercials where happy, loving families gathered over coffee or dinners or even new cars.

But inside her the girl cried, lonely, alone, with no one to console her.

She mourned her parents, in a way taken from her twice. First by the drunk that hit their car head-on, then again by a coldhearted grandmother who harbored so much resentment that she wouldn't let Gabe even talk about them.

I can't do this. I can't get so distracted from my work that I let this take over. I have to stop this now, before it goes too far.

Before he can hurt me. That was a weak little voice she rarely heard anymore.

The voice of the little girl.

Gabe closed her eyes and rocked back and forth under the water.

* * * *

Gabe spent the rest of the day making amigurumis and pointedly avoiding her personal laptop. If she logged on to that, she knew she'd end up on FetLife. And she'd seen an e-mail notice come through her phone where Bill had sent her a friend request.

Breaking up with him in an e-mail is a total dick move.

And despite knowing it was the only option, she couldn't bring herself to do it.

So she ignored it and focused on adding more crocheted crusaders to the stash.

* * * *

By the next Saturday morning she'd made another yarn and fiber filling run. At last count, over one hundred of the animals were now sharing the condo with her. They covered every horizontal surface in the living room area, as well as the bed in the second bedroom.

She didn't have the heart to bag them up. She wanted to see the collection grow, swell, fill the place. They would stay out until right before she had to leave, and only then would she gather them to take back to Miami with her.

And she still had two weeks, going by working days, before she left Sarasota.

Which was both a good and bad thing. The last several nights she hadn't slept well. When she did, her dreams were filled with fantasies of Bill tying her down with ropes before doing things to her, like fucking her brains out.

Even though the dreams left her horny, when conscious thought took over upon waking, all desire left her.

She wanted what she knew she couldn't have.

That wasn't anything to inspire sexual desire in her.

Especially not when she'd seen some pretty sexy forced orgasm scenes at the club the previous week.

Scenes that could have easily been pulled from some of the better books she'd read.

I need to delete all that crap from my Kindle. It's given me expectations I should know better than to have.

She couldn't bring herself to do that, either.

As time drew closer for the class, she forced herself to stop looking at the clock and focus on her crochet. Another alligator had started taking shape as her hook flew and twisted through the yarn. In her mind, she chanted the phrases as they came in the pattern.

Yarn over, single crochet. Skip. Join. Turn.

She let the yarn soothe her and shift her active, conscious brain out of gear. Her fingers took over, knowing what to do.

Not even stopping for lunch, she waited until the light outside the condo's back porch had started turning dark and purple, and she knew she'd missed the class.

And dinner.

Bill would probably hate her now. Even better. She could feel guilty for it and live with that, but at least she knew it was a clean break. Better for him, more than he would ever know, and best for her despite it hurting her heart.

At least, for now, Maria stayed silent.

And that was something she wouldn't complain about.

Chapter Thirteen

Rather than staying cooped up in the condo and going crazy Sunday, Gabe decided to take a drive south. There were supposed to be some great beaches in the area, especially in the southern part of the county.

She knew if she didn't get away from her computer, she'd end up working no matter what she'd promised her boss. She couldn't help it. It was something Maria had, literally, beat into her at a young age.

Working meant you were a productive citizen.

Goofing off meant you weren't.

Sigh.

Leaving the laptop at the condo, she got in her car and headed south down US 41 until she found the turnoff for CR 776 that would take her south through Englewood. From there, she located the Manasota Key turnoff and found her way to the beaches.

She rarely went to the beaches in Miami. They were crowded with tourists, backed up against condos, and it meant battling annoying traffic to get over to the barrier islands. Parking was always a bitch, and by the time she got there, she was always in such a foul mood she might as well have been visiting a landfill.

This was…nothing like that. The pristine white sand was strangely lacking crowds, or even high-rises. Sea grass dunes revealed gorgeous turquoise water she didn't have to fight her way through hordes of people to get to.

It was almost…calming.

Okay, so I get why people like it here.

Miami hadn't been her dream destination. It'd simply been where she ended up after her enlistment had ended, she'd gone to school, graduated, and started working in law enforcement.

After an hour or so of wandering up and down the sand, she returned to her car and continued south, leaving the key from the southern entrance and deciding to follow the road all the way into Port Charlotte, where the map told her it would once again intersect with US 41.

One big, long, lazy loop. No one can accuse me of not trying to sightsee.

When she finally reached that intersection, she found a mall there.

Perfect.

To kill time more than anything, she walked into the movie theatre and bought a ticket for the next show starting, which happened to be an R-rated comedy.

Even better.

After the movie ended, she opted to eat dinner at the mall. When Walker quizzed her about how she spent her time, she wouldn't have to lie. She did sightsee, she did relax.

Sort of.

Unfortunately, all this gave her more time to think, more time to feel guilty about ditching the second class at the club without bothering to try to get a message to Bill.

Well, he probably hates me already. Fuck it.

It was after dark when she emerged from the mall and headed toward her car. She blamed her full stomach, and being absorbed in her self-recriminations for ditching the class without contacting Bill, for not paying better attention. When the group of three teen boys stepped out in front of her from behind a minivan, it took her a moment to get into work mode again.

One of the three boys had something in his hand that flashed in the light from the overhead security lights in the parking lot. He was the tallest and oldest-looking of the three. "Give me your purse."

Knife.

Sound faded away as she stepped in close. She grabbed his wrist with her left hand and pushed it down and away as she drew her .380 and pressed it against his temple.

"Law enforcement!" she screamed. "Get on the ground, *now*!"

"Shit!" One of the boys took off running.

She kicked the one with the knife in the kneecap. He dropped the knife as he screamed in pain on his way down to the pavement. She wrenched his arm up and behind him, her knees planted in the middle of his back.

The third boy looked undecided, wide-eyed, and frozen. She pointed her weapon at him. "Hands behind your head and down on the ground, *now*!"

An older couple from the next row over getting out of their car saw the events. "Are you all right, ma'am?" the man asked.

"No. Call 911. Tell them I'm an FDLE agent and I need police backup right now."

"You mean the sheriff?" the man asked. "We don't have police here."

She fought the urge to swear at him. "The 911 dispatcher will know who to send."

The second boy finally decided he might be better off following her orders instead of fleeing. He didn't look like a hardened criminal. He looked more like a kid about ready to piss his pants.

She slowly stood and grabbed the knife from where it had landed and backed away from the two boys. "You stay facedown, hands on your heads. If you move, I will shoot you." Well, she wouldn't shoot them automatically, but better to give them a threat that would keep them in place than to have to deal with possibly shooting one of them.

She heard the sirens less than a minute later. By the time the first deputy rolled up, she felt the adrenaline kick catching up and hitting her, sweat now pouring down her back.

When the deputy emerged from his unit, a hand on his sidearm, she stepped back and holstered her weapon, holding both hands up.

"FDLE Special Agent Gabriella Villalobos, Miami. They tried to mug me, one had at least a knife, and there's one more who ran. I didn't have cuffs on me."

She kept one hand up while slowly reaching into her back pocket to withdraw her badge holder and ID, extending it to the deputy. He looked at it before nodding. "Thank you," he said.

He tossed her a pair of handcuffs. She cuffed one of the boys while he cuffed the other. Another two marked cars rolled up and the deputies began searching the boys and questioning them. She leaned against the far side of the first car to wait until they were ready to take her statement. Breathing deeply, she clenched and unclenched her fists, trying to ride out the surge of adrenaline now pouring through her.

She mentally groaned. *Walker's gonna kill me. So much for my time off. Drawing my sidearm means there's going to be a shit-ton of paperwork.*

* * * *

Someone called Miami to verify her identity. After the initial frenzy settled and a K-9 unit went looking for the third punk, she gave her statement.

She also felt like an idiot for letting the boys, who were fifteen and sixteen, albeit taller and heavier than her, getting the drop on her in the first place.

Basic urban survival 101, always be aware of your surroundings. Had she been paying attention, she never would have walked that close to the row of parked vehicles, especially one blocking her view like the minivan.

That will teach me to focus on my personal life.

Gabe heard the dispatcher radio the deputies that a detective was on the way to the scene. She let out another silent groan. She wanted to get out of there and go back to the condo. Walker would bust her balls for this, even though it wasn't technically her fault.

I can already hear him now. "Attracting trouble, are you? That bored, huh?"

She snorted.

Worse, it was starting to drizzle.

Greeeaaat.

She told the lead deputy she needed to go get her rain jacket. After retrieving it from her trunk, she walked back and spotted another car, unmarked, pulling up to the scene.

She'd pulled the jacket's hood up and over her head just in time for her heart to seize in her chest.

Fuck!

It's dark. It can't be. It's a coincidence. I'm seeing things…

Fuck!

But as she heard him speaking to one of the deputies, she realized it was.

Bill.

* * * *

"Not telling you guys how to do your jobs, but did someone verify she's really FDLE?" Bill asked one of the deputies.

He pulled on his raincoat, mentally swearing at the weather's timing. Just what he wanted to be doing on a Sunday night, dealing with state wonks. At least once a month they caught some mental midget with a fake badge imitating law enforcement. Sometimes for what they thought was a good purpose, and sometimes not.

Hell, he wasn't even supposed to be working tonight, but he'd offered to take a shift. Anything to get his mind off wondering why Ella stood him up at the class yesterday. She hadn't responded to his private message to her on FetLife, either, asking if she was okay. Somehow, he suspected she wouldn't be back on FetLife, although he had no way of telling if she'd read his message or not. Her activity stream had remained silent, not that it meant anything.

The deputy, Edwards, nodded. "Yeah, Collins checked on her. She's legit."

"Okay. Where is she?"

He hooked a thumb toward another cruiser. "Waiting over there."

"Thanks."

He walked over. She stood on the far side of the cruiser, back to him and wearing a dark blue hooded rain slicker with FDLE emblazoned in bright yellow across the back of it.

Well, they don't sell those at Walmart. "Special Agent Villalobos? I'm Detective William Thomas." He held out his hand.

She turned, the upper part of her face deeply hidden in the shadows of the hood, and shook with him.

That's when the bottom dropped out of the sky.

"Sorry," he said, ducking his head against the deluge and raising his voice to be heard over the rain. "This'll just take a second. Did you already give your statement?"

"Yeah," she said, but her voice sounded…weird. Familiar and yet spiked with nervous jitters. "One of the responding officers took my statement and info."

Likely the adrenaline crash hitting her. "No offense, but can I ask why you are in the area if you're stationed in Miami?"

"On vacation. Staying at a condo in Sarasota. Was sightseeing and stopped here for a movie and dinner."

"Ah." *Just pure dumb luck, then.*

They both jumped as a bolt of lightning split the air almost directly overhead, followed by a thundering *crack* that made everyone duck and let out shouts of surprise.

He handed her a business card. "We'll be in touch if we need anything else. Otherwise, the state attorney's office will contact you if it goes to trial. You'd better get out of here. I'm heading back to my car."

"Thanks." She scurried off. He didn't bother waiting to see what she drove. He turned and ran for his own car. They'd have to sit and wait for the rain to die down a little before continuing.

The K-9 won't find shit in this slop.

As he cranked his car and started the defroster, he stared out the windshield. To the best of his knowledge, he'd never met an FDLE agent by that name, but he'd swear there was something familiar about her.

* * * *

Fuck fuck fuckfuckFUCK!

The initial adrenaline surge had started to fade, but seeing Bill had amped it up again. Her pulse raced so hard and fast in her throat she wasn't sure might not pass out. Her hands shook so badly she almost couldn't get the key fitted into the ignition. She pulled out and around to the far side of the mall, into the busy parking lot of a standalone restaurant on the outskirts. There, she put the car into park and rested her forehead against the steering wheel while forcing herself to take deep breaths.

She'd dropped his card on the passenger seat. After a couple of minutes, once her fingers weren't trembling quite so badly, she reached over and picked it up again.

Bill was actually one Charlotte County Sheriff's Office Detective William Thomas.

Son of a bitch!

What were the odds that the two of them were both in law enforcement? And what the *hell* had he been doing there at the club anyways? Did she miss being part of a bust?

Rational thought tried to get a crowbar into the frazzled adrenaline frenzy clouding her brain. No, he'd been friends with some of the people there. Rob and Laura. And there'd been no recent reports of anything happening regarding the club as far as she knew. From the way he acted, he seemed to be genuinely trying to learn from the class, not gather information to be used later in an investigation or as evidence.

Hell, the club seemed to be doing everything legally and aboveboard. Even had their state sales tax certificate and county business permit posted in the office by the cash register. They forbade alcohol, drugs, and penetrative sex. It was a private, members-only club, with the correct zoning and location for an adult business.

She closed her eyes and replayed the evening. Rob had mentioned something about meeting Bill through work.

It took her nearly twenty minutes to be able to drive again. She found US 41 and headed north, stopping for nothing except traffic lights until she pulled into the parking space at the condo. Running upstairs, she left the wet slicker lying in the tiled foyer by the front door and went straight to her work computer, Bill's business card in her hand.

It took her less than thirty seconds to find the story. Bill had worked the well-publicized attack of one Laura Spaulding over a year earlier. Her fiancé at the time, Rob Carlton, a county paramedic, had been working during the attack and was cleared as a suspect. The attack had left Laura with a severe case of amnesia usually only seen in romance novels and movies, and less often in real life, unless accompanied by traumatic brain injuries.

She was a lucky woman to come out relatively unscathed physically.

After several months, the case had resolved itself when the suspect abducted Laura on one of her shop's boats, but she managed to kill him before the boat sank. She was rescued and recovered her memories as a result of the second attack.

Apparently Laura and Rob had gone from engaged to married at some point.

Shock and relief battled in her already adrenaline-scrambled brain. Starting as snickers, her laughter ended up growing and rolling through her until she sat doubled over in her chair and struggled to breathe.

A stupid coincidence. That's exactly what it had been. But what would have happened had she gone back for the second class? Gotten to know him better? She was from Miami, anyway. A long-distance relationship, even that close of a distance, wasn't something she had any interest in.

Besides, he'd seen a little of her back. That was enough intimate contact.

She made sure the front door was locked before taking her gun off and getting undressed. The hot shower felt good, melting the last of the stress from her system.

Dumb, stupid luck.

Maybe sometimes things really did happen for a reason. She wasn't religious, or even superstitious by any stretch of the imagination, but it looked like getting cold feet had really saved her from an uncomfortable development. He likely wouldn't want to be involved with another law enforcement officer, either. That just doubled their risk of being outed.

Before she went to bed, she hopped onto the Internet again. She found TV station coverage of press conferences that had been held during the investigation of Laura's attack. She did her best to ignore the pleasant little thump her pulse made when she watched Bill…

Sorry, Det. William Thomas…

…make official updates and statements to the press.

I was stupid to think I could have a relationship, anyway. This was a sign. I took my focus off my work and look what happened. That was just a warning shot from Fate across my bow to get my head on straight and concentrate on my job.

She shut her computer down and went to bed. Unfortunately, sleep wasn't soon in coming. Her mind refused to quit thinking about Bill, about what happened.

About narrow misses…

And missed chances.

Chapter Fourteen

Monday morning, Gabe overslept. When her work cell phone rang on the bedside table a little after seven thirty, she groaned as she rolled over and looked at the screen, the headache forcing her to squint to read the display.

Walker.

Dammit.

Actually, she gave him credit. She was shocked he'd waited this long to call her and bust her balls over the mugging. She'd expected someone in Miami to give him a call about it last night since he was her supervisor. She'd have to fill out paperwork on the incident and submit it to him regardless.

She sat up and thumbed the green button. "Villalobos."

Walker's tone sounded all business. "Change of plans. You're going back to work."

She yawned. "Am I in that much trouble, boss?"

"Huh?"

"Over the mugging. Am I in that much trouble?"

A second of silence greeted her comment. "The what? What the hell are you talking about?"

Now she felt a little more awake despite the headache throbbing through her brain from oversleeping. "What are *you* talking about?"

"What mugging?"

"You're not calling to bust my nuts about nearly getting mugged last night and having to draw my personal sidearm?"

She heard him take a long, slow, deep breath on the other end of the line and let it out again before he spoke. "Want to back up and tell me what you're talking about?"

Crap. Was it possible he hadn't been calling about that? "Um, no biggie."

"You brought it up. Tell me."

She did, keeping it short and sweet and not mentioning anything about knowing the responding detective, much less how she knew him.

"Jeez, Gabe," he said. "You know, it's your lucky day. I don't even have time to bust your balls about that."

"Then what do you want?"

"We're setting up a task force to nab some more of the johns from the Martinez case." He quickly detailed how they were sending out agents to several regional offices to coordinate with local law enforcement agencies in the areas where they'd tracked potential suspects. "I want you to work with the Sarasota and Charlotte County area representatives. We'll probably add Manatee and DeSoto to the list as well, once the computer crimes guys get back to me with a list of locations."

She swung her legs over the edge of the bed. "You're not just yanking my chain?"

"No, I'm serious. You're already in the area. We give a briefing day after tomorrow. I'll come up to sit in on it with you and coordinate with the locals for you. I've already contacted the agencies and got them to assign representatives. I'll come up and do the briefing with you before I go up to Tampa for that one. We already have Orlando, Ft. Myers, and Naples, and the east coast scheduled, and I'll be hitting those on Thursday and Friday."

"Work-work?"

He chuckled. "Work-work. Your happy place, if I'm not mistaken?"

"So I get back some of my vacation time, then?"

"Like you really care about vacation time."

"I just thought I'd ask."

"Check your work e-mail. I've sent you notes. I need you to pull together a briefing presentation for this, one that the other agents can use at their regional briefings. You have the case?"

She thought to the files on her laptop, as well as her notes. "I have everything I need."

"Good. Let me see a rough draft by noon before you start on the pretty version." He hung up.

She smiled as she stood and ran to the kitchen to get the coffee started. Her headache had vanished.

Work! I get to work!

Any thoughts she might have had about Bill, regrets about ditching the class, dropped to last place.

She had work to do.

Finally.

* * * *

She actually had the rough draft to Walker by eleven and was on the phone with him shortly thereafter.

"Damn, girl. You've been busy this morning."

She'd also started her third pot of coffee. "I had work to do."

"Look, I'm sorry I had to interrupt your time off—"

"Jeez, boss. Don't ruin the moment by apologizing, okay?"

"You will still take time off. Just after we get through this. Okay?"

"Sure. Whatever you say." She smiled, glad he couldn't see her expression. She knew the truth. After this case, there'd be another. And another.

And another.

The old maxim was wrong. There were three sureties in this world—death, taxes…and assholes who were willing to do bad things to other people.

She was responsible for taking care of the third.

Before long, Walker would forget about ordering her to relax, and she could go on with her life and what she needed to do.

Working.

At least it kept her mind off the empty little gap blatantly obvious to her now. The oddly Bill-shaped gap.

Okay, so maybe not so little.

Suck it up, buttercup, and deal. If you hadn't been stupid in the first place, you wouldn't be feeling like this now. Your own damn fault.

She never should have gone to the munch. She damn sure shouldn't have gone to the class. It was horrible of her to get Bill's hopes up when she knew she wasn't local to the area. He was a really nice guy who deserved to find someone who could give him what he needed.

There was no way in hell she could be that person.

Even though, deep inside, she really wished she could.

* * * *

By the time she collapsed a little after midnight, she'd already run seven different versions by Walker, the last of which he okayed and began distributing to the other agents after she turned in the final "pretty" version.

Gabe also realized she had one little problem, that she had absolutely no work clothes with her, or her usual working carry rig for her sidearm.

Dammit.

She rolled onto her back and stared at the shadows cast across the bedroom ceiling. They'd started becoming familiar to her. The condo felt familiar.

Sarasota and the surrounding area was beginning to feel familiar.

Go shopping, which will cost me, or drive home and back, which will also cost me in time and gas money.

She closed her eyes and pondered it. In the end, she figured she'd spend less money on gas, and less overall aggravation, if she just bit the bullet and went home.

It didn't escape her she didn't even have anyone she could ask to go over to her place, grab things for her, and take them to her boss to bring up to her.

No one else had a key to her condo.

How sad am I?

Without a chance to get to know Bill better, especially now that she'd be working with local law enforcement, she figured she deserved it.

* * * *

She stuck her head in Travis Walker's office a little before noon. "Hiya."

He sat back, shock on his face. "What the hell are you doing here? Did I not make it clear we were doing things there?"

"Yeeeaahh, about that." She shrugged. "My clothes and stuff are here." She pointed down. "In Miami. I had to come get them, unless you wanted me showing up in shorts and a T-shirt. Don't worry, I promise to go straight home, grab my stuff, and get my butt back to Sarasota. You can even check on me and time me."

He buried his face in his hands and let out a moan. "You are going to be the damn death of me yet, girl." He raised his face and stared at her. "I just saw an official copy of the report from Charlotte County. What the hell happened?"

"Okay, you know, in a way this is all *your* fault."

She'd worked on this part on the way over from Sarasota.

"*My* fault?"

"Yeah. You ordered me to relax, have fun, take time off, and sightsee." She opened her hands, palms up. "*Your* fault. I was just following orders."

"*Really?*"

She solemnly nodded.

He stared at her for a moment before shaking his head and pointing at his office door. "Out. Go. Get your shit and get back to Sarasota. And get me your report on the incident by tomorrow. Did you get the info I sent you about the meeting details up there?"

"Yep." She stood. "Anything else?"

He stared at her. "You're lucky I like you so much."

She grinned. "I'm great at my job and you know it."

"Yes, you are. And yes, I do." He pointed again. "Out."

At the door, she turned back to face him. "Oh, do you think I could claim all this mileage on my taxes as work expense, or should I itemize it and submit it for reimbursement?"

"Out!"

She managed to suppress her grin until she turned away from the door and headed toward the elevator.

When she unlocked her front door a half hour later, a realization hit her. This didn't feel much different than the condo she was staying at in Sarasota. In fact, without the ever-growing amigurumi army to greet her, it felt damned empty.

At least she had Lil Lobo in her purse.

She grabbed a larger suitcase and filled it, including grabbing the other gun from her gun safe, just in case. Another 9mm Glock she sometimes carried. And the concealed carry rig she wore while working, a couple of blazers, slacks, blouses, and pairs of shoes. She also took a few minutes to empty some things from the fridge and bag the garbage to drop in the Dumpster on her way out.

As she stood by the front door and surveyed the small condo, she felt a pang hit her. She'd lived there ten years, and yet never replaced the store-bought art on the walls that had come with the place, or the furniture. Just the mattress and box spring.

It had likely been staged by the real estate agent. When she'd asked about including the furnishings, they'd agreed for a nominal charge. That was worth it to Gabe to avoid the aggravation of doing it herself.

She still had a few pictures of her parents in albums she'd brought from Maria's, but had never taken the time to get any of them enlarged into wall-sized prints despite it crossing her mind a few times.

She went back to the bedroom, grabbed another suitcase from under the bed, and packed the photo albums into it. Now she literally could lock the door on the condo, walk away from it, and never return, if she had to. She'd learned to live light and lean growing up, a habit reinforced by the army and her years in college dorms.

I wonder what Bill's house looks like.

Then again, she'd never find out now.

On that sad thought she left, locking the door behind her.

Chapter Fifteen

At least now Bill had something else to take his mind off Ella standing him up at the class and apparently dropping off the face of the planet. He and Al got assigned to a multi-agency task force that would be led by an FDLE agent. They were tracking down customers of a child sex ring operation they'd busted up in Miami a couple of weeks prior. Other agents were handling task forces in other parts of the state. They'd draw in the johns via the computer and arrest them, but they needed to have everybody on board to keep this from turning into a paperwork nightmare. And it would take up several weeks of his time.

Al stood inside Bill's office doorway. "Ready to go?"

"Yeah." He logged off his computer and grabbed his notepad. He wasn't exactly looking forward to this. Joint tasks forces were nearly always a pain in the ass that at some point devolved into a territorial pissing contest between jurisdictions between the different departments.

All he wanted to do was put bad guys in jail and keep good people safe. Period, full stop. Especially sexual predators.

Unfortunately, it was usually the individual investigators who got along well, while the department heads jockeyed for precedent. Especially if they were elected or appointed officials who needed the cachet of a blockbuster operation for their resumes.

And since Charlotte County was smaller, in terms of force, population, and number of perps, they would get shuffled to the back of the line if they were lucky, and treated like incompetent Barney Fifes if they weren't.

Al offered to drive, which was fine with Bill. Hopefully they could be back in the office by early afternoon. Bill didn't relish the thought of wasting an entire workday on this circle jerk.

"You remember the last FDLE guy we had to work with on a regular basis?" Al asked as he pointed his car north on US 41.

Bill nodded. "I heard he finally retired last year."

"What a dick he was."

Bill smiled. "Yes, he was. Glad he wasn't our problem to deal with very often."

"My friend Paul, who's a detective with Sarasota County? He hated him with a passion. Even filed a complaint with the state about him being unprofessional."

"How'd that pan out?"

Al grinned. "The dick retired, didn't he?"

"That must have been some complaint. So what do we know about"—he glanced at his notes—"Travis Walker?"

"I've heard he's good. Reasonable. Bringing in one of his top investigators to run point for the state in our area."

A supervisor who would hand over an investigation to a—*gasp*—investigator? *How novel.* "I think that bodes well," Bill said.

"That's my opinion, and I'm sticking to it."

They were meeting in the south county admin center in Venice. It wasn't exactly neutral territory, but it was centrally located for most of the attendees. There was even a detective from DeSoto County coming over to take part since one of the leads took them to Arcadia. They'd have FDLE overseeing the case, with both the city and county of Sarasota, city of Venice, city of North Port, Charlotte County, DeSoto County, and even a representative from Manatee County since some of the activity was traced close enough to the county line to give them reason to believe there might be jurisdictional issues there as well.

They pulled into the parking lot twenty minutes before the scheduled meeting start time. "Where are we going?"

"Conference room over near the auditorium."

Fortunately, the board of county commissioners wasn't meeting there that day, or the place would have been packed inside and out. They walked in and found the conference room, where three men were already waiting. Bill recognized one of them from North Port, and as they made introductions and took seats around the conference table, Bill sensed at least these three men were all of the same mindset of him and Al, that they wanted to focus on the investigation and apprehensions and let the managers duke the rest of it out amongst themselves.

More people filtered in. Bill actually wasn't paying attention when Travis Walker entered the room, followed by someone else. He'd been head down over his BlackBerry, responding to an e-mail from a deputy who'd been the initial responding officer on a case he was working.

When he looked up for the introductions, he froze. Well, except for his heart, which began thundering in his chest. Behind Walker, and wearing a deer-in-the-headlights look as she stared at Bill, stood one Ella.

"Thanks for coming here today, ladies and gentlemen," Walker said. "We know this is a hassle, but since this case ties in with one that we're working over in Miami, they decided it would be best to put an investigator already familiar with it in place. I'd like to introduce Special Agent Gabriella Villalobos."

Bill watched her throat work as she swallowed hard before nodding to the room. Today she wore her hair back in a tight braid.

Well, I was wrong about her not being a cop. I must be slipping. It took all he had not to burst out laughing.

As Walker went around the conference table to get personal introductions, she stood there, nodding when appropriate, but her gaze never leaving Bill's. When Walker reached him, Bill decided to play a card.

"Detective William Thomas, Charlotte County. Actually, Special Agent Villalobos and I have already met, albeit briefly."

Her face transformed into a beautiful and—in his opinion—well-deserved shade of scarlet behind Walker.

"You have?" Walker asked.

"Yes. Sunday night, she apprehended a couple of muggers who attacked her. We didn't get to talk long because it started storming."

"Oh, yes, seems I heard about that," Walker said, glancing back at Ella—*Gabriella*, Bill corrected himself—who was now looking at a legal pad clutched in her hands.

Bill's eyes didn't leave her face. Every time she glanced up, she looked away again. Walker took a seat at the head of the table as she unslung a laptop bag from her shoulder and got it ready to hook up to a monitor.

"I'm going to let Special Agent Villalobos take things from here," Walker said. "She's going to fill you in on the history and information we have so far, and she's prepared handouts to e-mail all of you." He passed out a paper to everyone. "Her e-mail and contact info is on there, as is mine. Just shoot her an e-mail so she can send it to you."

She seemed to fumble the cable connection as she tried to get her laptop hooked up to the monitor. It took her a few moments to gather herself and start speaking, but once she did, shifting into what was obviously her work mode, Bill's attitude started to adjust.

By the time she finished with the summation an hour later, he was full of admiration for her.

She still wouldn't meet his gaze head-on.

He couldn't blame her.

They needed to break for lunch and were all going to hit the Bob Evans a few blocks down the road. Bill excused himself from Al and stepped over to her, dropping his voice. "We need to talk."

She started to say something, but he cut her off. "I'll ride to the restaurant with you. Or did you come with your boss?"

"Fine," she muttered.

He told Al to head over without him, that they'd be there in a few minutes. Al actually opted to ride with his friend from Sarasota county and a couple of others. Eventually the room emptied, leaving the two of them standing there.

It was obvious she wasn't going to speak first, so he did. "So what do I call you? Ella? Gabriella? Special Agent Villalobos?"

"Car," she muttered. She fished her keys from her pocket, slung her laptop case over her shoulder, and headed out the door without bothering to see if he was following her.

* * * *

Gabe could barely breathe. She'd been praying the little creeps who'd mugged her would plead out, meaning no reason to ever see Det. William Thomas again.

Boy, was I ever wrong.

Never in her life had she dreamed he'd be plopped onto the task force. Then again, had she stopped to think about it instead of being so excited to be on the job again, she would have realized there was a decent chance of it happening.

She suspected Walker would grill her later, once they could speak alone, about her reaction. Then she'd have to come up with a suitable cover story. As it was she fought the urge to break into a run as soon as she emerged from the building into the daylight of the warm afternoon. She turned right, toward the rear parking lot, well aware of Bill following close behind her.

He didn't speak, waiting by the passenger door until she got her door open and popped the locks to let him in. Once they were inside, engine on and AC running, she sat there with her hands on the steering wheel and her eyes facing forward.

"You didn't answer my question," he finally said.

"What question?"

"What do you want me to call you? Unless you meant you wanted me to call you 'car,' which I highly doubt."

"Gabe's fine," she said. "That's what everyone else usually calls me."

"Okay," he said. "I can request someone else be assigned to the task force in my place."

She looked at him. "Why?"

"It's obviously going to be an issue for you."

That got her dander up. "What the heck does that mean? I never said it was going to be an issue for me."

"You could barely talk in there at first."

"I was a little surprised to see you there. Duh."

"Yeah, well since you're not the replaceable one here, it should be me."

"You saying you don't want to work with me?"

"That's not what I said."

"Sounds like it."

"So let me ask you something. Sunday night, you obviously recognized me. I thought there was something familiar about you, but I couldn't get a look at you because of your raincoat. Then it started pouring. Why didn't you say anything then?"

She knew no excuse she gave would sound good.

That's why she opted for the truth. "I was scared," she quietly admitted. She finally looked at him.

His handsome face wrinkled in a scowl. "You were scared of me?" he quietly asked.

"No. Not of you. Of...everything."

"Is that why you didn't come back Saturday?"

"I—" Her mouth snapped shut. "I don't know."

"You didn't want to see me again?"

"No. I mean, no, that's not why."

"Then tell me."

"Why didn't you tell me you're a cop?"

"Probably for the same reason you didn't tell me you're an FDLE agent." He leaned back in his seat. "I called that one wrong. I saw you carrying at the munch, but I honestly didn't think you were a—"

Dammit. "What?"

"Carrying." He glanced at her. "You leaned forward once and your gun printed."

She closed her eyes and groaned. *Rookie mistake.*

"It wasn't obvious to anyone else," he continued. "The only reason I noticed it was I saw how you were sitting in your chair." A corner of his mouth curled in a smile. "Occupational hazard."

"I suppose you weren't carrying? I find that hard to believe."

He shrugged. "Ankle holster. And we're straying off the topic with little time left to talk."

"I can work with you. All right?"

"Really?"

"Yeah, really."

"I'm guessing you and Walker didn't come together."

"No, I drove down from Sarasota. He drove in from Miami this morning."

He nodded. "Good. Then you can drive me back to Port Charlotte this afternoon. That will give us plenty of time to talk."

"What?"

He turned in his seat again to face her head-on. "If you can't spend forty-five minutes talking to me in a car, I might as well request someone else be assigned in my place to the task force this afternoon, before we get too far along."

The truth was she didn't *want* him to be reassigned.

She wanted to work with him.

"Fine."

"Fine you want me to ask for reassignment?"

"No." She shifted the car into reverse and started backing out. "Fine, I'll drive you back to Port Charlotte this afternoon."

* * * *

Lunch wasn't exactly uncomfortable, but it wasn't a fraction as fun as the munch or class had been. Bill sat next to her while they ate and eased up on the staring once back in the conference room. He also used his work phone to run down some information and history on her.

He had to admit he was damned impressed. She had a remarkable record and apparently zero ego about it. He'd unfortunately met more than his fair share of pompous assholes on the job, investigators who liked to flaunt their records as part of their self-worth.

Apparently, Gabe fell squarely into the "just doing my job" camp.

He respected her even more for it.

At the end of the day, he told Al to go on without him. "We're going to discuss the mugging case on the way back. I have a few things I can have her sign off on."

Al's faint scowl made Bill silently swear. "Oookay," Al said. "Whatever you say."

"And I'm going to take her over to Marelli's for dinner."

"Oh." Al grinned. "You'd think he's their personal PR rep," Al told her. "You'll love their food."

Travis Walker came over, wearing a smile. "Ah, so you're the detective that caught her not following orders, huh?"

"What?"

Walker laughed. "I'd distinctly ordered her to take three weeks' vacation and not work, and she ends up tangled with a mugging."

"Hey," she snapped, more than a little testiness in her tone. "I *was* the victim, you know."

"I'm just teasing you, Gabe," Walker said. He leaned in. "See what I mean?" He hooked a thumb at her. "This agent is a massive workaholic. One of the best ever, but I keep telling her if she doesn't learn to balance her life, she's going to burn herself out."

"Work *is* my life," she shot back.

"You do need balance in this line of work," Bill agreed, as if she hadn't spoken.

She glared at him as she shut down her laptop and got her stuff put away, but she didn't respond.

On their way out to her car, she asked him, "Do you think he bought that?"

"What? Who are we talking about?"

"Your friend, Al. Did he buy your excuse?"

He stopped and turned to her. "What excuse? I am taking you out to dinner." He stared down at her. "You have a problem with that?" he softly asked.

Let's see how she likes the real me.

He thought for a second she was going to say yes, she had a huge, fat-ass problem with that, but then she gave a faint shake of her head that threatened to harden his cock right there.

Technically, they didn't work together. They worked for completely different agencies.

Technically, it wouldn't be a problem.

He held up a finger. "And this is my treat. No arguments. Your gas money and your time driving me back down there, and back up, of course, so I get to buy you dinner. Fair trade. Got it?"

She nodded.

"Good." He took her keys from her and walked to the driver's side, unlocking the door and holding it open for her. Once she was in, he walked around and got in.

She was staring at him from the driver's seat.

"What?" he asked.

She looked like she started to say something, thought about it, stopped, then shook her head. She started the car, pulled out of the parking lot, and headed south on US 41.

"Where to?" she asked.

"That way," he said.

Chapter Sixteen

Gabe didn't understand it. She didn't understand why she didn't just tell Bill to go fuck himself when he'd said he wanted her to drive him back. And then buy her dinner?

You know, normal guys do *buy their dates dinner.*

This is not *a date!*

Yeah, she knew she could lie to herself all she wanted, it'd still be a date. The date they didn't get to have.

The date she'd nuked by skipping the second class and standing him up.

Yes, that was all on her, and she knew it. At the very least, she should have contacted the club to forward her apologies. But then she'd run into him the next night at the mall, and it had totally thrown off her equilibrium.

That wasn't a state she was used to.

At all.

"Tell me about the scars on your back."

She nearly slammed on the brakes. "What?"

"The scars on your back. I saw part of them during class. They look pretty bad. Either tell me about them, or tell me it's none of my business. Either answer is acceptable."

Well, wasn't this kind of what she thought maybe she'd been looking for when she indulged in her stupid little fantasies? An Alpha guy she could trust not to be an asshole?

"Courtesy of my grandmother," she mumbled.

"How old were you?"

She snorted. "Which time? I lived with her from when I was eight until the day I graduated high school. The most recent ones are the top layer. Last time she actually got me hard enough to break skin, I'd just turned seventeen."

"What about your parents?"

"They died when I was eight. Car wreck. She got custody of me because my mother's parents were dead, and both of my parents were only children. No aunts or uncles who could take me."

"And then?"

She stopped for a red light before she looked at him. "You're awfully nosy, aren't you?"

He arched an eyebrow at her.

When he didn't say anything, she let out a frustrated sigh. "Went right into basic training after high school. Four years in, college at UF, police academy, then straight into law enforcement."

"Brothers or sisters?"

"Nope."

"You never pressed charges against her for the abuse?"

"I had no other family I could turn to. She had me in a strict Catholic school. What do *you* think I did?"

"Fair enough." He remained quiet for a moment. "You can ask me questions, too, you know."

"Why didn't you get remarried before now?"

"Like I said, I guess I wasn't fishing in the right pond."

"So you did that stuff with your wife?"

He shrugged. "Not really. In bed we weren't vanilla, but we weren't crazy, either."

"I'm not looking for anyone to order me around."

"Didn't say you were, or that I wanted that in a relationship."

She swerved a little as she glanced at him. "Relationship?"

"What?"

"You think we have a *relationship*?"

"Did I say that?"

"I—" She clamped down on it. No, that was not what he'd said, just what she'd jumped at. "Sorry."

He smiled. He did have a handsome smile.

Damn him.

"I went to the club the week before the first class," he said. "The night before the munch. I saw Seth and Leah playing, using rope bondage. It intrigued me. I'm not interested in heavy impact play, really, because I'm not a sadist. I like the control aspect, though. The rope was artistic."

Answered her next question. "I'm not looking to get my ass beat."

"Never said you were. I believe I just said I wasn't interested in that."

She felt like he was running conversational circles around her, and it was her fault for not keeping up.

This was *not* a problem she was used to having. "So why dinner?"

He shrugged. "I want to spend more time with you. Now that it appears we have even more in common, and that we both have a vested interest in keeping this part of our lives separate from our professional lives, it looks like we can trust each other."

"Why do you want to spend more time with me?" she asked.

"Seriously?"

"Yeah."

"Because I like you, that's why. I'm attracted to you. I'm not looking to play relationship games. If you're not interested in me, it's all right to tell me. No harm, no foul. I won't be an asshole about it."

Ask a stupid question. "I don't know what I'm looking for," she admitted. "I'm not even sure why I went to the class beyond curiosity." Well, that was only a half truth. "Okay, I did want to see you again."

"Why did you go to the munch then?"

"Honestly?"

"Of course."

She sighed. "My boss referred me to the restaurant. Non-professionally," she quickly added. "When I went, the place was packed. I'd seen about the munch on the website, saw another couple sail on through, and decided to go for it so I didn't have to wait forever for a table."

"You weren't at all curious about the lifestyle? You just wanted better restaurant service?"

It took her a few moments to finally mutter, "Okay, maybe I was a little curious."

"Did I do something to offend you at the munch? Or at the class, or dinner?"

"No! I told you, I wanted to see you again. I enjoyed meeting you and talking to you."

"Then why did you bail on the second class?"

That was the million-dollar question. "I told you, I was scared."

"Fair enough."

He didn't elaborate.

She felt she owed him more of an answer than just that. "Look, I suck at this relationship stuff, okay? I'll admit it. One thing I'm not good at. Haven't had to be good at. Take it or leave it."

"I'll take it."

"What?"

He shrugged. "I'm not asking for undying devotion. I'm asking for dinner. If that's beyond you, then okay, whatever."

"Dinner?"

"Yeah, dinner."

Suck it up, buttercup. "Okay, fine. Dinner."

"*My* treat."

She grumbled before nodding.

"So does this mean we have some sort of relationship starting?" he asked.

Hell, she had used that word, hadn't she? "Maybe. Is that an acceptable answer, too?"

He nodded, that smile still curving his lips and doing something to her insides that she hadn't felt in too damn long.

If ever.

* * * *

Bill struggled not to burst out laughing. He could tell how hard this was for her. He also knew that had he slipped into sympathy mode over the shocking revelations about her grandmother and what happened to Gabe during her childhood, she likely would have locked up tighter than Fort Knox.

She was over it, or at least claimed she was, so he wouldn't push her. There would be plenty of time in the future to explore that if she decided to really trust him. Plenty of time to get the full story from her.

If they made it that far. Frankly, he was having fun verbally sparring with her and hoped they had more than just one more date.

Right now, he wanted to make it through dinner without her bolting like a terrified rabbit. No, physically she wasn't afraid of him. Her fear came from the inside. Maybe she didn't even realize it, but he could see it. All his years in law enforcement and dealing with a wide swath of people, he wasn't a stranger to reading reactions.

Maybe she didn't even know what she was really looking for. He was okay with that, too. As long as he could coax her into another date after tonight.

And another.

One tentative step at a time, until he could prove to her he was on the level and wasn't looking for a quick lay or a doormat.

She was neither of those.

He never understood abusive asshats who wanted to break a woman's spirit. He wanted a woman who had fire, a strong, stubborn spirit, someone who would willingly want to be with him and, sometimes, willingly want to submit to him. Not because she had to, but because she wanted to.

There was no honor in breaking someone's will. The only honor was in earning someone's trust enough that she willingly wanted to give him what he sought. The thrill of knowing that he was the only person who got to see that side of her.

The only person she trusted enough to show that side of her.

And the more independent the person, the greater the honor, in his mind.

His Ella had been the same way. Everyone who thought they knew her, and him, would have been shocked had they seen their bedroom dynamic. Sometimes even outside the bedroom, although to a far lesser and more informal way than some of the people from the club. He'd never had to demand it.

In fact, she'd been the one to instigate it early on in their relationship. And he'd been happy to know he was the first and only one who'd ever seen that side of her.

Magic.

He yanked himself out of thoughts of the past before he sank too deeply into them.

Ella was dead, but now, just maybe, he'd met someone he knew he could give his heart to.

If she'd have him.

And, more importantly, if she'd let him.

* * * *

Bill was both glad to see Marelli's parking lot wasn't filled, and a little disappointed they weren't busier.

It meant the family would likely be stopping by their table to chat and interrupting his time with Gabe. Normally that wouldn't be an issue, but maybe tonight he should have picked another restaurant.

Dori greeted them when they walked in. "Bill, there you are. And who is this?"

Uh-oh.

"Uh, Dori, this is Special Agent Gabriella Villalobos. We're working together on a task force."

"Ah." The waitress looked disappointed. "And here I was hoping she was your date."

He didn't miss the look Gabe shot him over her shoulder as she followed Dori to a table. He also couldn't interpret what that look meant.

"I take it you're a regular here," Gabe muttered after they were left alone to look at their menus.

"Nearly every night. How pitiful is that? They invite me to their home for the holidays."

She stared at him over her menu. "Seriously?"

"Seriously."

She let out a snort as her gaze returned to her menu. "I dodge invitations to my boss' house every holiday so I don't have to pretend I know how to be sociable."

"You seemed sociable enough last Saturday night at dinner. Leah and the others were very disappointed you didn't come back for the second class."

* * * *

Gabe felt her face instantly go red. "Yeah, well, tell them I'm sorry about that. Feel free to tell them my reasons, too. That I'm a cop."

"I think you should tell them yourself."

She dropped her menu and stared at him. "What?"

He leaned forward, arms crossed in front of him and resting on the table. "The third class is this Saturday. I'll pick you up on my way there."

This wasn't the easygoing man she'd gone out to dinner with.

This man was definitely an Alpha. Still, he hadn't crossed over the line into asshole territory…yet.

"I haven't agreed to go to the class."

"You owe me."

"What? Owe you what?"

"I was really looking forward to seeing you at the second class." He smirked. "And because I was so bummed about you not being there, I volunteered to take a Sunday shift, nearly got struck by lightning in a parking lot, and had to spend a couple of hours sloshing around in the rain and mud at night after a K9 officer doing tracking, all because someone decided not to pay attention while walking to her car. You know how many hours of paperwork I had to go through?"

She met his gaze. There was a hint of teasing in his tone, the barest curve to his lips betraying his true mood.

Deflating, she nodded. "Sorry. I did screw that up. Guess I do owe you for that."

He reached across the table and took her hand in his. "Seriously, Gabe, please go with me to the third class. And dinner." His gentle tone tugged at her. "We can go back to the club later and just watch. Do you have better plans for a Saturday night? Because I know I don't, and I'd much rather spend the time with you than sitting alone at home."

She forced herself to look into his eyes. He'd slid back from the asshole line squarely into Alpha territory.

"They're going to hate me," she softly said.

"No, they won't." He squeezed her hand. "I promise you they won't. I'll talk to them. It'll be fine. They'll understand."

"I'm not normally a flake like that, I swear."

"I get it." He released her hand after one last squeeze. "It's okay. I understand." He arched an eyebrow at her. "Frankly, my opinion is the only one that should matter to you in this situation. Please let me pick you up Saturday for the class. Do it for me, if nothing else."

He was playing dirty. She took a deep breath and let it out again. It felt like she was about to jump off a cliff.

"Okay," she softly said. "I'll go."

Chapter Seventeen

They texted back and forth on Thursday via their private phones. Gabe wouldn't deny it felt good to finally sense she wasn't alone in the world.

It was also a massive relief to have the truth out. To know Bill forgave her, understood her reasons for bailing on the class as well as hiding the truth about her identity from him at first, and didn't hold it against her.

She also wouldn't deny it was a relief to know she would get more alone time with him and rope. The thought that she might never experience subspace again had truly saddened her. How much so wasn't clear until now.

Bill was a nice guy. He was a cop who could understand what she went through, what she did for a living. The stresses she was under, the things she'd seen and had to deal with. If she let things happen between them, she wouldn't feel guilty about missed dinners or blown plans at the last minute because of a case.

He would understand.

He likely wouldn't guilt trip her over it, either.

Friday, the task force met again in Venice. Bill and Gabe pretended nothing had happened between them, although Gabe had trouble keeping her eyes off him. It seemed every time she looked his way, his gaze skipped away from her like a panicked horse.

At least she wasn't the only one who seemed to have it bad, and thank god her boss wasn't there to see what was going on. She suspected he would have easily picked up on it.

And probably would have been highly amused by it, which would have only served to piss her off.

They had agreed Bill would come up to her condo after they finished working. When he arrived a little after seven, carrying a pizza, she nervously let him in. When he walked in and set the pizza on the counter, he looked out into the living room. "Oh, those are neat."

She hurried to get paper plates ready. "What?"

He walked over to the coffee table and picked up a blue dog. "These. My wife used to knit things like this. Ami…amo… What are they called?"

"Amigurumis."

"That's it." He set it down and appeared to be counting the others there and around the room. "Wow. You've been busy."

"I donate them."

"No bears?"

Damn him. Being with a cop would have an obvious drawback. He had a very observant nature, whether by training or temperament, it didn't matter. "No bears."

He turned. "Mind telling me why?"

She started to say yes, she minded very damn much, but then realized it would make her sound like a bitch.

She stared at the floor. "I… No bears. It's not something I really like to talk about. Maybe another time."

"Fair enough." He walked back to the kitchen. "Is it okay if I kick my shoes off?"

She blinked before looking back at him. Apparently, he wasn't going to grill her about the bears. Some guys might have taken her reluctance as a challenge to pry the answer out of her by guilt or guile. "Um, sure, yeah. That's fine."

"You all right?"

"Yeah. I'm fine." *Just shocked as hell.* She'd expected him to want all the answers.

He tilted his head a little as he looked at her. "You realize that I'm not an idiot, right?" He smirked. "I *was* married. I'm not such a clueless guy that I can't recognize when a woman *really* doesn't want to talk about something. Especially when she flat out says so. I told you, I won't play games. I'm a face-value kind of guy."

"Thank you."

"No problem." He kicked off his shoes before walking into the kitchen again. "I do have an admission of my own, however."

Her heart raced again, only in the bad way this time. "What?"

"I called Seth yesterday and told him what happened. Don't worry, he won't out you, believe me. He loaned me the bag of rope, and I have it in the car."

The fear turned to... Well, she wasn't sure what it turned into, only that she now stewed somewhere between turned on and trepidation. "Why?"

"You missed last week's class. If you're going to get caught up quickly, I need to go through stuff with you tonight. Besides, I wouldn't mind the extra practice on you. And I'll be happy to talk you through tying me up first. Fair's fair."

Now she felt badly again. "You didn't get to practice at class?"

"Not really. Laura and Rob came to the class, and she volunteered to let me practice on her, but it wasn't the same."

"Why?"

He smirked. "If you don't remember, Rob's younger than me, and a county paramedic. He can kick my ass. Also, while I like Laura, I'm not attracted to her the way I'm attracted to you. It was definitely more fun working with you, where I wasn't worried about offending you or accidentally touching an inappropriate area."

She blinked. "You're attracted to me?"

"Yeah. I thought I made that fairly obvious."

Okay, yeah, he had, she just hadn't fully processed it. "But I'm—" She clamped her mouth shut.

He stepped close and gently took her hands, waiting until she looked up into his eyes. "If you say you're anything but beautiful, you'll make me want to spank some sense into you."

It suddenly felt very hard to breathe. "Beautiful?"

He cocked his head. "Okay, seriously? I know you said it's been a while, but surely the last guy you were with told you how beautiful you are."

"But I'm not skinny."

"*Really? That's* what you're going with, the old *I'm fat* garbage? I think you're gorgeous. I'm not attracted to skinny women anyway. My wife was five eight and a size sixteen most of the time we were together, and she was the most beautiful woman in the world, as far as I was concerned."

He reached out and lightly tugged on her braid. "Your hair is gorgeous. You have the most amazing, beautiful eyes. You have a body I imagine I could wrap my arms around and squeeze against mine and not worry that I'm going to hurt you. You are a real woman, not fake, not manufactured in a liposuction clinic or too many hours in the gym. And, news flash, I'm not perfect either. Second news flash, it was your personality that drew my attention, not your looks. Your looks were the delicious frosting on an absolutely fantastic cake. But it doesn't matter how great the frosting looks if the cake is just cardboard underneath."

She felt her face heat. No one had ever talked to her like this before. "I don't feel like delicious cake." In fact, for most of her life, she'd felt like cardboard.

He pulled her into his arms for a hug that felt warm, welcoming, inviting.

Loving.

"Gabe, give me a chance. Take what I say as my personal truth. I will never blow smoke up your ass. If I say I think you're a beautiful person, I mean it. It's not just pretty words. If we never get to a point where you feel comfortable taking this relationship to a sexual level, well, I'll be disappointed, but I won't walk away from you just for that. You've brought something into my life I thought was completely gone. For that reason alone if nothing else, I don't want to lose you, however I can have you in my life."

"What's that?"

He palmed her cheeks and stared into her eyes. "You brought me hope."

* * * *

Saturday morning, Gabe awoke early. Bill had left a little after eleven the evening before, their time together a blur of playful teasing and wonderful hours spent tying rope, as well as being tied.

Definitely something that revved her motor. To the point she almost regretted not asking him if he wanted to spend the night.

Then again, they hadn't had the sex conversation yet and she knew they should. Among other conversations.

Was he someone she wanted to sleep with? Absolutely. The more time she spent with him, the more she realized how much she wanted to sleep with him. Considering how rare that feeling was for her, she wanted to take advantage of it.

Tonight wouldn't be that night either, though. She knew that. She didn't want to make a mistake and rush into something just because her hormones had kicked into overdrive.

And it also depended on how the others received her. They might be totally mad at her, despite what Bill insisted, and she might just want to go home after class and be alone.

Although she desperately hoped she was wrong about that.

She was ready when he arrived to pick her up early that afternoon, even though she'd been fighting a horrible case of nerves.

When she set the condo's alarm and locked the front door, he stopped her before they could walk downstairs.

"Are you all right? Do we need to cancel this?"

The concern in his expression and voice touched her. She hadn't realized how strongly she was telegraphing her fears.

It didn't make any sense lying about it. "I'm worried about what they're going to think. Which is bizarre, because I've never worried about that in my entire life."

"It's okay. That's human. Do you trust me to know this will be all right tonight?"

She wanted to. She *really* wanted to.

She nodded.

"If at some point you feel you absolutely need to leave, just tell me, and we'll go. All I'm asking is that you give it a chance. Fair enough?"

"Fair enough."

Her stomach clenched the closer they got to the club. When they walked in the door, she was ready to turn around and walk out again when she spotted Leah standing at the desk and talking to the woman working there.

Leah was faster. She flashed Gabe a brilliant smile before rushing over to hug her.

"Everything's okay," the woman whispered in her ear. "Bill told us. We understand."

The prickle of tears Gabe felt shocked and surprised her. She quickly blinked them away. "Thanks."

"Hey, we're used to cold feet, believe me. And you had very valid concerns. I'm just glad everything worked out for the good this time."

Gabe was about to get her wallet out to pay for her class, but Bill beat her to it.

"I was going to pay for myself," she told him. It was only fifteen dollars, but still, it was the principle of the matter.

He cocked his head at her, wearing that smirk she was quickly coming to associate with him slipping into a more Alpha mood. "The proper response is usually to say 'thank you.'"

"I pay my own way."

He stepped closer. "I asked you here. I can afford it. I want to pay for your class. If you really have a problem with it, or anything else I do, then say *red* and we'll talk."

"I—" Her mouth snapped shut. Code because he paid for her class?

His smirk broadened to a smile.

Dammit.

She knew that he was fully aware of the barrel he'd placed her over, playing with her to see what she'd do. Rather, she'd placed herself over the barrel. Her pride warred over which was the lesser hit to her psyche, letting him actually pick up the tab, or coding over something so—in her opinion—ridiculous.

No, not every sadist is into beating people, apparently.

She sighed in resignation. "Thank you."

His smile turned into a beaming grin. "You're very welcome, sweetheart."

* * * *

Gabe wondered what kind of battle she'd have to deal with at dinner, but he shocked her. When they pulled into the parking lot, he turned to her before getting out. "May I buy you dinner, or would you feel more comfortable paying for yourself? Either way is all right, your choice."

Relief. Their tiny power struggle earlier wasn't going to morph into some monstrosity. Not tonight, at least.

"I would really prefer paying for myself, thanks."

He nodded. "Not a problem. That's why I asked. How did you feel when I made you choose between coding or letting me pay for your class?"

She stared at him for a moment before answering. "Honestly? It pissed me off a little at the time."

"I could tell."

"Then why did you do that?"

He leaned in, gently winding her ponytail around his hand. Today she hadn't braided her hair, just pulled it back with an elastic band. He tugged just enough to make her lean toward him, that playful smirk curling his lips in an admittedly sexy way.

"Because I *could*, sweetheart. You keep worrying about me accepting you. That's a two-way street. There are things I like to do. There are times I want to be in complete control. That doesn't mean I'm a domineering asshole, but there will be things I will insist on. They might seem like little things to you, but they mean something to me. Coding will always be an option for you, but sometimes I will deliberately goad you into choosing to submit to me rather than coding for something you feel silly about coding for.

"The longer we spend together," he added, "the more I will push that barrier, because I need you to see the real me, too. To the point where, hopefully, coding is always an implied option for you, but that you will choose to submit to me when I ask it of you because you want to, not because you're afraid not to. I don't want someone who will blindly do what I say out of fear or because they don't know how to make up their own mind. I want someone who wants to do what I say, even if it's something they don't want to do and even though they know they always have the choice to refuse without there being any kind of negative consequence. And there will *never* be any kind of negative consequence for coding or refusing. Understand?"

She couldn't yank her gaze from his.

She nodded.

"I'd like to hear you say it."

She didn't understand why her heart thumped like that.

No, wait, she did.

He was being dominant. *A* Dominant. He was showing her his other side.

The one only she got to see like this.

She licked her lips to wet them, although the spit seemed to have dried up in her mouth. "I know coding is always an option."

He arched an eyebrow at her.

"What?"

"I'll sit here with you as long as it takes. You'll think of it."

Gabe shoved away the wave of irritation that tried to flood her brain. That wouldn't help her now.

What does he want?

She replayed his last comments.

She still wasn't sure. She suspected she could outright ask him what it was he wanted, or even code and talk about it.

Bill had seemingly pierced her protective wall, figured out how to use her stubbornness against her to his benefit.

She eventually settled on something to try. "I know coding is always an option, Sir."

It was as if a brilliant light flooded from his smile, his eyes, from the very core of his being. He pulled her closer and pressed a chaste, tender kiss to her forehead. "Such a good girl. Very good, sweetheart."

It felt like the breath had been pulled out of her as his words echoed through her soul.

Good girl.

Her clit throbbed. She knew if she checked she'd be soaking wet, her cunt now desperate for a good, hard fucking.

Holy crap, what just happened?

She realized he was studying her, his smile shifting back to that calculating smirk from earlier. His grip tightened a little on her ponytail as his eyes narrowed. "That just struck a good kind of nerve, didn't it?"

She nodded.

Another tightening of his grip. "I need an answer out loud, sweetheart."

"Yes."

He didn't respond.

"Yes, Sir."

He touched the tip of his finger to her lips. "Never forget that phrase," he said, his voice sounding hoarse, strained. "Because it does to me what 'good girl' does to you."

Chapter Eighteen

Sunday morning, Gabe stared at the ceiling after waking up. The light and shadows looked…wrong.

Feeling around blindly, she found her work cell phone and held it up so she could see the screen.

Holy crap! The time read 10:17.

She rubbed at her eyes. This was the latest she'd slept in in years. And she didn't even have a headache. In fact, she felt pretty damn spiffy.

The night came back to her. Class, dinner. Going back to the club.

How she'd longed to be some of the women, and a few of the men, bottoming to their partners.

Not the heavy impact play. She'd had enough of that crap to last her a lifetime.

But the trust, the sensation of turning herself over completely to someone.

To him.

She wanted that.

Badly.

How it had felt being tucked under his arm, against his side as they watched various scenes going on throughout the night.

How everyone had seemed to welcome her at dinner despite her standing Bill up at class the week before.

Leah hadn't lied to her to spare her feelings.

It had surprised her to find out over dinner that Sully was a former cop, although in retrospect it shouldn't have. He had that watchful way about him, like she imagined she had, the way Bill had.

Most importantly, how it felt when he said "good girl" to her. And how he reacted when she called him Sir.

Tonight, he would drive up and cook for her. She knew from talks they'd had the night before that sex wouldn't be on the table, although they needed to talk about it. She appreciated that he didn't seem to be in a hurry to hop into bed with her, that he could control himself and not try to manipulate or pressure her into doing anything.

She also realized that, for once in her life, it was a good thing, because if he'd wanted to fuck her after the first time he said "good girl" to her, she would have gladly let him.

It's my kryptonite.

She rolled over to find a text from Bill on her personal cell phone.

Good morning, sweetheart. How are you feeling?

Normally, she might bristle at the term of endearment.

From him, it sounded…

Just right.

Good morning. I'm good. Just woke up.

Before she could set the phone back on the table, it buzzed in her hand, a response from him.

:)

She liked the way her pulse sped up.

In fact, for the first time that she could remember in her life, she was eagerly anticipating something. Some*one*.

I could get used to this.

* * * *

Bill arrived a little after five and had brought with him the ingredients to make a delicious chicken quiche. Her nervous tension this time stemmed from her anticipation, not dread.

He wouldn't be rushed. She knew that while she had the option to press for deeper conversations, he wanted to be in charge of how and when it happened.

He waited until halfway through their dinner. "So let's make a deal," he joked, his tone light.

She looked up from her food. "What kind of deal?" She hoped he didn't spot the wariness in her eyes, hear the hesitation in her tone. She didn't want to ruin their good evening by putting a halt to things.

"Next weekend, I'll come up here, and we spend from Friday afternoon until Sunday together. Go to the class, dinner with everyone, the club."

She straightened in her chair. "Sex?" Frankly, she hoped sex was part of the picture. If it wasn't going to happen soon, she'd be pretty damned disappointed.

She'd figure out some way to hide the worst of her scars from him in bed.

He shrugged. "Not a deal breaker. Although if you wanted to, that'd be nice. I'm hoping things lead to that eventually, even if not next weekend. That's an instance where I'm not going to press too fast."

She mentally swore when she felt her face redden. "It's been a long time for me."

"Me, too. I'll go to the doctor and get a current set of test results if you want, but I haven't been with anyone since Ella, and I'm clean. Or we can stock up on condoms. Your call."

She glanced down at her plate again. "I'm clean," she said. "On the pill, although I'm not sure why I bother."

He reached across the table and took her hand in his. "We're both adults here, no strings attached. We don't know if this can go anywhere unless we try, right?"

She had to vocalize her remaining fears. "And what if it goes south quickly and in a really ugly way? How do we work together?"

"I'm willing to risk it. I know I'm not going to be sleeping around or doing anything to jeopardize this. I suspect you won't be, either. I trust you."

"How can you say you trust me when you barely know me?"

"You've trusted me this far. I've trusted you. Trust has to grow from somewhere. It's sort of what the word means. Not many people I'd give the benefit of the doubt to like I do with you, but it's worth it to me to get to see where this might go. I think last night and today have been a very good start, don't you?"

"Again I ask, what if it goes really wrong?"

He shrugged. "We back up, figure it out, and try again." He squeezed her hands. "I can't imagine anything so bad either of us could unintentionally do to blow this up so badly we can't fix it. Can you? You're a logical person. You tell me. Are you planning on deliberately screwing around or lying to me?"

She shook her head.

"Okay then. Neither am I. I say we're both adults. I won't play the bad kind of mind games with you. If you decide hey, you absolutely cannot do this, all you have to do is say so, and hopefully we can still be friends. And I'll give you the same courtesy. Deal?"

She nodded. "Deal."

He smiled. The way it tugged at her, hopeful, sexy, sweet, and sinful, all at the same time, it melted her insides.

Maria's voice tried to pop up and she envisioned herself whacking it with a gigantic carnival game hammer before nailing a board over the hole from which it had crept into her brain.

Not tonight.

"Thank you for giving this a chance," he said. "If nothing else, we get a chance to spend some time with another person instead of alone. That's not so bad, is it?"

"No, that's not bad at all." She squeezed his hands back. "In fact, it sounds pretty darn good."

Now all she had to do was make it to next Friday without climbing the walls.

Chapter Nineteen

A blob of tropical weather in the Atlantic ended up organizing enough to be classified Wednesday morning as a tropical depression that would hit directly across the state from them before giving them a couple of days of nasty weather as it slowly crept west.

The fourth shibari class ended up postponed until the next week because of the storm. Apparently the club's parking lot had a bad tendency to flood during heavy rains, making it tricky to get into and out of the complex where it was located. Gabe felt disappointed by that, but at the same time relieved that she would get to have Bill all to herself.

This would be a make-or-break couple of days for them. To see if she could even tolerate someone's close presence that long.

Or if he could tolerate hers.

"You realize we're going to be stuck inside all weekend, right?" he told her with a playful smile. "Might as well get used to it."

"How come they didn't call you in to work?"

He shrugged. "No official tropical storm or hurricane warnings for our area. It's coming in from across the state and won't be more than a blob of weather by the time it reaches us. I'm surprised they didn't recall you to Miami."

"They don't pull us in unless it's a major storm," she said.

He draped his arms around her waist, his expression turning somber. "I want to do a lot of talking this weekend."

"Why?"

"Because I think we need to," he said. "There's a lot about me you don't know. A lot about you I don't know. I want to remedy that, even if I have to tie you up to accomplish it." He arched an eyebrow at her. "Or is that a problem?"

"Talk?"

"If you haven't figured it out yet, I want more than just great sex or a fun time in bed. I do want a relationship with you."

"Isn't that moving kind of fast?"

"Did I say marriage?" He released her and cocked his head as he studied her. "Technically, we already have a relationship. Nothing formal or even permanent, but it's a start."

"I don't even know if I know what I want. I hope you're serious about wanting to take things slow. Marriage is definitely off the table for me for the future, as far as I'm concerned. If that's going to be a problem, say so."

"It's not a problem, and I really mean it. I know life wasn't easy for you as a kid. I want to hear about it. I want to know all about you."

"Maybe you won't like what you hear."

"Stop it."

She flinched at his harsh tone.

He must have seen it, because he grabbed her hands again and held on, gentling his tone. "I am the *only* one who gets to determine what I do or don't like about you. Understand? You don't get to talk yourself down to me. I know I'm not perfect, and I won't lie about my flaws or try to gloss them over, but I'm not going to try to influence your decision about what you think of me. I want you to extend me the same courtesy. You insulting yourself is like you're insulting me and my tastes and preferences, because I like you. Got it?"

No one had ever spoken to her like that before. She stared into his hazel eyes, trying to read what was there. She eventually nodded.

That made him smile. "Good girl."

She simultaneously loved and hated the way her heart sped up when he said it, the way he said it.

How could two words do that to her?

Then again, words had done a lot of bad things to her throughout a large chunk of her early life. Why wouldn't two little words also be able to do good things?

It's just that had never happened before.

His gaze narrowed thoughtfully. "What happens when I say that?"

She swallowed. "Say what?"

The smile again. "That. When I say, 'good girl.' What happens?"

I get wet. But she couldn't bring herself to admit it. "I don't know," she softly said.

"Do you really like it when I say it, or do you think it's condescending?"

Why deny it? "I like it."

His smile widened. "Good."

She felt her heart thrum again, anticipating the second half of that phrase.

He leaned in close. "Good girl."

Her breath caught in her throat. Then he closed the distance, brushing his lips across hers, lightly, briefly, a sweet reward. He didn't press for more and immediately leaned back again. "Why no bears?"

Her blood ran cold. "What?"

He hooked a thumb over his shoulder at the amigurumi army invading the condo one stitch at a time. "I asked you about bears the other day, and you had a pretty hard reaction. I want to know why."

She froze. No one had ever asked her about bears before.

No one had ever noticed.

Hell, no one had been close enough to her to ever notice.

There was a better than odds-on chance the man would be seeing her naked at some point over the weekend, if not in the next couple of hours.

Or sooner.

If she couldn't open up enough to tell him this, then their relationship would be doomed before it even had a chance to put down any kind of roots and grow.

"Tell me, or code. Your choice."

Turning, she leaned against the counter and crossed her arms over her chest. With her gaze focused on the tile floor she said, "I had a stuffed bear my dad and mom gave me when I was little. Bear was my favorite toy. Went everywhere with me except school. When my parents died, Maria basically sold off everything except some of my clothes."

"She sold your bear?"

She shrugged. "She didn't say that, but I figured that's what she did with him along with all my other toys. She told me I was too big for baby toys, and that she had to sell off everything she could to get the money because my parents didn't have life insurance and the guy who hit and killed them didn't have any insurance."

When she risked a look, she read the anger on his face.

"She sold all your stuff? Toys? Everything?"

"Yeah."

"That bitch."

"That's the nicest of names I've called her over the years."

"So she just robbed you of everything?"

She shook her head. "No." A harsh laugh escaped her. "No, ironically, she didn't. She kept excellent records. When I turned eighteen before I graduated high school, she took me to the bank to have the account turned over to me. She'd spent the money only on me, and there was still quite a bit left over, nearly thirty-five thousand. It helped me not have to work full-time during college when I got out of the army."

"Still, I don't understand how she could be so heartless." He put his hands on her shoulders. "Did she ever explain herself?"

She shrugged. "No. She felt she was completely justified. She raised me, never starved me. Took me to the doctor whenever I was sick. Always made sure I was in school and doing my homework. Made sure I had clothes."

"She just beat you."

"Not all the time."

"You're not making excuses for her, are you?"

"Hell, no." She met his gaze. "Just because I can see her logic doesn't mean I understand or agree with it. I'm well aware of her many faults. I'm also well aware that I could have been through a lot worse. I was never sexually abused. I was, in most other ways, taken care of."

"Do you remember much about your parents?"

"Some. I wasn't really allowed to talk about them. Especially my mom."

"I take it she didn't like your mother?"

"Noooo. Despised her. Maria blamed her for my grandfather's heart attack, the one that killed him not long after my parents got married. My grandfather apparently hated Mom because she wasn't Catholic and she refused to convert. Because he hated her, my grandmother hated her."

"Wow."

She nodded and, before she realized what she was doing, she rested her head against his chest.

It felt right.

He slipped his arms around her and turned them so he was the one leaning against the counter, supporting her weight as she leaned against him.

He felt comfortable, their bodies fitting together perfectly like this.

I wonder how it'd feel together in bed.

Maybe, if she was really lucky, she'd get to experience it at least once before he came to his senses about her.

* * * *

Rage seethed through Bill. He wanted a crack at Maria himself. If he ever got to meet the bitch, he'd be sure to give her a fucking piece of his mind.

"Is she still alive?" he asked.

"Don't know, don't care," Gabe mumbled against his shirt.

He held her closer, firmly, a silent promise to never let her go.

A promise he longed to say out loud and knew had to remain silent. For now, at least. It was too soon. Way too soon for deep emotional declarations like that to her. If he tried to move faster than she was ready, he knew she wouldn't hesitate to walk out of his life without a look back.

The more he learned about her, the more he realized that her walking away just might break his heart, and he barely knew her yet.

Resting his chin against the top of her head, he said, "Gabriella Villalobos, you are a beautiful, wonderful woman. Thank you for giving me a chance."

"I've been a lone wolf most of my life," she admitted. "I'm not sure I know how to do this stuff."

"Living up to your name?"

She chuckled and finally looked up into his eyes again. "Sort of, in a way. My grandfather was the first of his family born in the US. They were originally from Spain."

"Did Maria speak Spanish to you?"

"Sometimes. She was from an American family. And she spent too much time trying to fit in with everyone at her church, I think. I learned more in high school and college than I did at home. I was fluent by the time I left the army."

"Good training, huh?"

"Rosetta Stone." She smirked. "One thing I learned growing up was how to be self-sufficient in a lot of ways."

"What else did she do to you?"

He felt more than heard her tired sigh. "She was…stingy."

"Cheap?"

"More than just that. My grandfather had good life insurance, but she made that last. She didn't have to go to work after he died. You know, growing up in Illinois in the winter, it sucks having to walk around the house wearing three or four layers of clothes because she refused to turn on the heat until the temperature inside the house dropped below sixty degrees."

"Wow."

"Yeah."

He felt her relax in his arms a little. "It was one of the reasons I started crocheting."

"Why?"

"To make myself afghans and sweaters. She taught me how to do it. It was the only hobby she had other than her church work. She made stuff and donated it. When I started doing it, too, it was a way to avoid her, even though we did it together."

"How so?"

He tried to focus on her words as she snuggled even closer. She felt so right nestled against his body.

"Unless I was in church, or doing housework, homework, or crochet, I risked her ire. She'd criticize me during housework, correct me for not doing something up to her high expectations, but she vicariously took pride in my crochet. I got really good at it. Her church friends always praised my work, which she took personally in a good way, at least."

"Raised her up in their eyes, or so she perceived?"

"Yep. She liked that. Liked the attention she got because her granddaughter was good at it."

"I guess you never got normal toys."

She snorted. "No. Buying books was only allowed if they were nonfiction or religious. I was allowed to check out books from the library. I received clothes and shoes. Practical things. She didn't believe in 'wasting money,' as she called it."

"I'm surprised you still enjoy crochet."

"I enjoy being able to help others. And if I was crocheting, she left me alone unless I asked for help with something. Except for schoolwork, it was the only time I could ask her for help with something and she'd be patient with me. Otherwise, I risked punishment for a variety of things. Apparently she was raised by a very strict Catholic family, and her parents were from the 'spare the rod and spoil the child' line of thinking."

"Bitch."

"Yep."

* * * *

The protective, outraged fury in Bill's tone warmed her heart. No one had ever sounded like that before on her behalf.

Ever.

Then again, even with her last boyfriend, in their months together she'd never revealed a fraction of her childhood to him as she had in the past few minutes.

She hadn't trusted him as much emotionally.

With Bill, she felt…safe.

"I can't imagine what you went through. I'm sorry."

"No reason for you to be sorry. Wasn't your fault. Looking back, in a way, I guess there are a few good lessons I picked up. I'm pretty cheap myself. It helped me out when I was in college and in life. And I've got a good work ethic."

"But you never learned how to play."

"Well, some might not say that's a bad thing."

"You need a balance."

"That's what my boss keeps telling me."

"He's right." He tipped her chin up so she had to look into his eyes again.

Kiss me. Kiss me. Please, kiss me.

His lips deliciously curled in a playful smile. "I won't force you to do anything this weekend that you don't want to do. You want me to stop, just say 'red.' No bullshit. Got it?"

She nodded, her tongue reflexively wetting her lips.

"I like to be in control," he continued, "but that doesn't mean I want to be an asshole, either. Also doesn't mean I want to run your whole life. I don't have time or energy for that. I want you to *want* to let me do things. It's no fun if you're not willing. But you can't pull some bullshit where we do something and then turn around later and accuse me of going too far. You have to speak up. I promise you, I will not get angry with you for coding. Ever. Are you willing to do that?"

She nodded. *Please, fucking kiss me!*

"Then tell me what you want. What's going through your head right now?"

It felt like she could barely breathe. "I want you to kiss me," she managed to whisper.

His fingers gently clamped around her chin, firmly holding her in place. He slowly leaned in, teasing, until he feathered his lips across hers. Unbidden, her lips parted, a soft whine escaping her when all he did was lightly trail the tip of his tongue along her lips.

It took forever, endless, sweet torture as he finally pressed his lips to hers, kissing her in a way no one had ever kissed her before.

She'd already wrapped her arms around him, and now her hands clamped down against his shoulder blades, fingers ineffectively trying to dig in trough his shirt and draw him closer.

He turned them, pressing her against the counter and firmly holding her in place while still refusing to let her rush him. He took his time, gently, tenderly, slowly increasing the pressure, until finally what felt like hours later his lips crushed hers in a bruising, possessive kiss that threatened to take her knees out from under her.

Kissed before? Hell, she'd *never* been kissed before if this was the benchmark.

When he finally lifted his head she went up on tiptoes, trying to maintain the contact.

He let out a soft chuckle. One hand dropped from her back down to her ass. He grabbed a fistful of flesh through her shorts and squeezed. "Here's what I want to do," he said, his tone husky and dripping with lust. "I want to take you into the bedroom, tie you up, and explore every inch of your body with my lips until you're begging me to make you come. Then I want to experiment with a little forced orgasm torture."

"Huh?"

He grinned. "Make you come until you're begging me to stop." He pulled her body tightly against him, his bulge pressing into the front of her shorts through his jeans.

Her clit throbbed in response even though ingrained responses damped her enthusiasm a little.

His brow furrowed. "What's wrong?"

Nut up. "Can we please keep the lights off?" Fear swelled inside her as soon as the words left her lips.

His expression softened, his arms once again enveloping her, instantly transforming from demanding to comforting, cradling her against him and dissolving her worries. "Of course, sweetheart. If that's what you want."

She closed her eyes and listened to his heart thrumming away under her ear. "Thank you." Of anything, that had probably been her greatest worry, that he'd want the lights on, or he'd berate her for her request. Her ex had always managed to make her feel stupid for wanting the room to be dark when they made love. Thought she was a prude for not wanting to share the bathroom or shower together.

He kissed the top of her head. "Sweetheart, this is what communication is about. You have to speak up and tell me things so I don't do something wrong."

"Thank you."

"You said that already. You don't have to keep thanking me."

"Yes, Sir." He froze, which caused worry to spill through her again. "What's wrong?" she asked.

He began nibbling the side of her neck again with his lips. "Nothing's wrong, except that I just nearly came in my jeans."

"Why?"

When he lifted his head, he wore a huge grin. "What you said."

She thought about it, realizing the phrase had naturally fallen from her lips. "Yes, Sir?"

He grabbed her, his hand fisting in her hair as he crushed her lips once again in a bruising kiss that sucked all the air from her lungs and left her whimpering with need.

"That," he said, his voice sounding throaty and deep, "is apparently the only thing you need to say to get your way with me. I won't force you to say it, but dammit, I love the sound of it."

This was new. This was something she never remembered feeling before with a guy.

Powerful in a good way.

"Yes, Sir," she said, deliberately this time, and with a playful smile.

He grabbed her ass with both hands and ground his hips into hers. "You keep that up, you're getting fucked right here and now. Even if I have to turn off the lights and bend you over the damn counter. It's not nice to tease a guy who hasn't been laid since before the last President was in office."

His cock ground against her, and she really wanted to shove her shorts down and let him fuck her right there.

Then again...

She did just that, his obvious shock nearly making her laugh. Backed against the counter, she boosted herself up onto it. She still wore her shirt, and as long as he didn't make her take it off, she'd gladly let him fuck her right there for the first time. She already felt her juices running, her cunt throbbing and screaming to be filled.

In a flurry of movement, he unfastened his belt and shoved his jeans and briefs down to his knees. He stepped forward then hesitated. "Dammit, the condoms are in my bag—"

"I don't care. I trust you." She spread her legs and grabbed him, pulling him forward, wrapping her legs around his hips and drawing him in. Yes, he was a good eight inches, at least, and his cock jutted forward, homing in on the target.

He grabbed her, both of them letting out moans as she reached between her legs and grabbed his cock, guiding him in until his full length was buried inside her. She closed her eyes and rested her head against his chest, sure she wouldn't come this time because she never had before, not like this.

His deep groan echoed through her, to the soles of her feet, through her clit, winding through her brain. Behind him she hooked her feet together, crossed at the ankles, keeping him there and wanting him deep inside her.

Then he did something that startled her. He reached between them, his fingers finding her swollen clit, where they started rubbing. A cry escaped her, her eyes clamping shut as his hand sped up.

In her ear he whispered, "Come for me, sweetheart."

A spasm swept through her pussy, not an orgasm, but she realized that between the delicious feel of his cock buried inside her, and his fingers on her clit, she was very close to the edge.

"That's it," he whispered, his voice sounding increasingly hoarse and strained, as if he struggled to hold back. "Let me feel you come. This weekend I own you like this, and I'm going to show you how good it can be."

Of their own accord her hips began rocking, back and forth, against his cock and fingers, the tingle quickly swelling into a bubble of need she thought might kill her if it didn't pop, and soon. She held on, her arms around him, hands clutching at his shoulders, until she let out a cry. The bubble burst, her cunt clamping down on his cock, his fingers moving faster.

"That's my good girl," he said. "You can't lie to me. I feel you coming. You better get used to it, because you're going to be doing a lot of it this weekend."

Another round hit her, even harder than the first. It didn't begin to compare to the vibrator, feeling much deeper and more intense than anything she ever remembered feeling before.

He shoved his hips forward, pressing even deeper, not relenting, fingers never stopping. "Such a good girl," he said. "Look at how hard you're coming for me."

She never wanted it to stop. She'd always scoffed a little at how the books she read described orgasms, because she'd never felt one that intense before. Nice, sure.

Mind blowing?

Not hardly.

Wrong...

It felt like the whole world had disappeared, and all that existed was the sound of his voice in her ear, the feel of his fingers on her clit, and her pussy deliciously impaled on his cock. After another forever, he pulled his fingers away and grabbed her ass, fingers digging into her flesh as he pounded his cock into her. His mouth crushed hers and with his pelvis hitting her swollen and throbbing clit with every thrust, she felt herself come one more time.

Now *I get it.*

She understood. Had it really taken her this long to find a guy she was compatible with in bed? Apparently so. Had she known it could feel *this* good, she might have tried a little harder years ago.

Then again, I wouldn't have found Bill.

He lifted his head, a playful smile on his face, his pace never slowing. "You just came for me again, didn't you?"

"Yes, Sir."

He let out a groan as he climaxed. Then he took several more hard, deep thrusts before falling still. She closed her eyes again and rested her head against his chest, both of them trying to catch their breaths.

Then she laughed.

He kissed the top of her head again. "What's so funny, sweetheart?"

"I just got nailed on my boss' kitchen counter." She snickered. "I don't think I'll tell him about this."

He made her look at him, his cock softening but still buried inside her. "Sorry. I meant for our first time to be a lot more romantic than this."

She draped her arms around his neck and pulled him in for another kiss. "It's okay, Sir. I think this might have been better."

His cock hardened inside her again as his grin widened. "Dammit, I'm telling you I get hard when you say that."

"Then maybe, Sir, I'll spend a lot of time saying it this weekend."

He shoved his cock deeper inside her well-fucked cunt. "Then prepare to spend the weekend with my cock buried inside you."

"Maybe that's what I want."

"So much for me taking my time." He slowly fucked her this time. Every stroke built her desire more. "I don't think I've felt this horny since I was a teenager."

She nibbled the side of his throat, working her way to his ear. "Maybe you'll have to tie me up, Sir, to keep me from wearing you out."

"Goddamn!" His hips jackhammered into her. "I can't hold on, baby."

She nipped his earlobe, making him groan again. As he fell still once more, he let out a laugh. "Sorry I couldn't hold on that time."

She squirmed against him, realizing she'd made a tactical error. "Sorry, Sir."

"No, don't be sorry." He reached between them and found her clit once more. "I'll just make you pay for that." He played with her clit, teasing and tormenting her. He kissed her, rolling her clit between his fingers until she finally let out a cry that he swallowed with their kiss.

Only when he was convinced he'd gotten her over did he lift his mouth from hers. "Better, sweetheart?"

She nodded, trying to catch her breath. She felt like she'd just run a marathon. "Yes, Sir."

Stepping back, he kicked off his shoes and socks and shoved his jeans and briefs down and off. Then he scooped her into his arms and headed for the bedroom. "Now it's time for round two."

Chapter Twenty

Bill wanted to get her to bed, tie her up, and take his time with her. He felt a little bad that he hadn't been able to control himself, but apparently she didn't have a problem with it. Not if how hard he made her come was any indication.

After gently laying her on the bed he pulled the blinds shut, which left the room dimly lit. He strongly suspected her issue was her scars, fear of his reaction to them, maybe even more than a touch of self-loathing involved.

He didn't care. If she wanted the lights off, they'd be off. Hell, he'd make love to her while he wore a blindfold, if that was what she wanted.

One day he would work on that issue with her, if she'd let him.

If they made it that long.

Right now, he was hoping they made it for the rest of their lives.

One step at a time.

Outside, a flash of lightning snuck around the edges of the blinds, followed by a loud crack of thunder.

He smiled down at her as he pulled his shirt off. "I think that's a good omen."

"How?"

"Remember the night at the mall?" He reached for his bag of rope and set it on the bed.

"Maybe that's a bad omen, then."

"Nope." He heard the wind pick up as one of the rain bands started to pass through. "I take it as a good omen." He knelt on the bed, staring down at her. "Arms, sweetheart."

"Do you want me to take my shirt off?"

Her tone of voice told him all he needed to know. "That's up to you. I can tell you're sensitive about it. We're here to have fun this weekend."

He watched her throat work as she swallowed, a nervous tell, he'd noticed. After a moment, she pulled her shirt off and dropped it over the side of the bed. She wasn't wearing a bra, and in the dim light he made out the swell of her breasts, her taut nipples peaked and inviting.

He sat next to her and gently took her wrists in his hands and raised her arms over her head, leaning forward to gather and pin her wrists with one hand. This left her breasts within reach of his mouth. He took the left one into his mouth, gently sucking on her nipple, flicking it with his tongue, enjoying the wordless gasps she made.

When she was squirming on the bed, he released that nipple and leaned over to repeat the treatment with the right one. Her breath quickened, every sound she made sending blood back to his cock and getting him hard again.

Had Ella ever done this to him? Yes, a long time ago, especially in the beginning. They'd always had a good and active sex life, but he'd been single almost as long as he'd been with her.

This felt like more than just the first time with Gabe. It felt like the first time *ever*, all over again.

Back and forth he went between her breasts, enjoying the sweet torment she was obviously going through, the way she sometimes tried to pull her arms free, not fighting him, just forgetting he was going to keep her where and how he wanted her, almost melting under his mouth every time he had to tighten his grip on her wrists.

Eventually he lifted his head from her breasts. "I mean it," he softly said. "This weekend, you belong to me. You can always code, no matter what. But unless you code, I'm in control. Okay?"

In the dim light and full of passion, her brown eyes looked black. She nodded.

"You have to say it."

"Yes, Sir."

His cock ached, screaming to be buried inside her again.

But not yet. He'd gotten two out of his system in record time for him. He would savor the next one now that the initial frenzy had been satiated.

"I want you to say the whole thing."

She blinked.

"I want you to ask me for it," he clarified. "Or code. Either way."

One little step at a time.

She ran the tip of her tongue over her lips. "I want to belong to you this weekend, Sir. I want you to be in control."

His heart swelled. "Such a good girl to ask me to take charge." He leaned in and kissed her, enjoying how she raised her head to meet him, her need washing off her in sweet waves.

He shifted his position, stretching out over her, his body pressing her into the mattress, his hands still pinning her arms over her head. "I'm going to tie you up this weekend and work you into a frenzy. I'm going to make you beg me to fuck you, to let you suck my cock, to make you come. And then I'm going to make you come so hard and so much you're going to beg me to stop. I meant it when I said it. I might not be a sadist into giving pain, but I definitely want to see that glazed look on your face, the one that says you know I belong to you, and you're going to beg me to take everything I want to give you."

He felt her breathing speed up a little as she nodded. "Yes, Sir."

He spread his legs, forcing hers apart, his cock rubbing against her clit but making no move to fuck her. She was wet and ready, from her own juices and the two loads of his cum he'd emptied into her. "Do you enjoy giving head, sweetheart?"

She nodded.

"Answer me. No is always acceptable."

"Yes, Sir," she whispered.

"Good." He sat up. "Stay right there." He let go of her hands and reached into the bag, where he quickly found his handcuffs. He snapped them around her wrists. "Don't move." He gave her a kiss and climbed out of bed.

Stepping into the bathroom, he didn't turn on the light as he used a washcloth to quickly wipe down. Maybe once they'd ironed out a few more boundaries he'd make her suck him clean, but he didn't want to push too hard without having conversations first.

A flash of memory came to mind, of Ella handcuffed, naked and kneeling before him after having just bent her over the bed and fucking her brains out, begging him to let her suck his cock clean.

He closed his eyes and shoved that memory away despite the way his cock throbbed again.

He returned to the bedroom, Gabe's gaze following as he came back and grabbed her legs, pulling her farther down the bed. Then he straddled her, his cock inches from her lips. "Start asking, sweetheart."

"Please let me suck your cock, Sir." Her mouth opened wide.

Daaammnn... He felt his balls draw up tight, nearly shooting his load right then. Pre-cum pearled at the slit, threatening to drip onto her chin. He braced himself against the headboard and lowered the tip of his cock just to where she could reach it if she pursed her lips. The tip of her tongue swiped along the slit, eagerly trying to get more of him into her mouth.

"Such a good girl," he whispered.

* * * *

Gabe felt nearly frantic with need. She'd worried that maybe she would panic if he restrained her, but knowing he'd immediately stop and trusting him, it completely erased all those fears. If anything, knowing he would do what he wanted to her, and knowing she'd enjoy it, had only served to amp up her desire even more.

He wouldn't let her suck his entire cock into her mouth, even when she tried lifting her head to reach. Then he grabbed her ponytail and slid her hair under his knee, pinning her that way and keeping her head immobile, now unable to do anything but lie there and wait on him to make his move.

She looked up in the dim light to find him smiling down at her, now understanding *that* smile he had would be her total undoing every damn time.

"You *do* want to suck my cock, don't you?" he asked.

She nodded, mouth still open, wanting it more than anything at that moment. Maybe even more than breathing.

He chuckled.

Yep, definitely *more than breathing.*

He eased his cock between her lips, his moan echoing hers as she finally was able to close her lips around the head. She wanted to deep-throat him, totally engulf him, and couldn't.

She loved it. Loved him taking control, loved the slow-burning buzz deep in her soul that cleared away all other thoughts, everything else but him, in that moment.

With her tongue she swiped and licked at every little bit of his cock he'd let her reach.

"That's it, sweetheart. Just like that." The husky tone of his voice wound tendrils of need around her heart. She wanted him to keep talking like that, sounding like that.

Being like that.

A little more, a little deeper. She traced the ridge around the head, flicked her tongue over his glans, gently sucked and savored the salty tang of his pre-cum. She longed to suck him dry, coax every last drop out of him, drain him.

Her pussy throbbed, reminded of what it felt like just a few minutes earlier to have this same cock buried deep inside her, and wanting it again.

A little deeper, and just as slowly, she couldn't understand how he could be holding back.

He just came twice. Duh.

But she'd just come…well, more than twice, but *really*?

Had she done that to him?

Another gleeful mental tweak of her clit as that thought sent more waves of cramping need spreading through her cunt.

He began thrusting, making her moan that finally he was going to use her, let her do what she'd been longing to do for what felt like forever. It startled her to realize it'd been less than half an hour since he'd reamed her the first time.

Holy crap!

It was going to be a long weekend at this rate.

She couldn't wait.

Deeper with every thrust, to the back of her tongue, toward her throat, and she realized he was testing her, seeing how deep he could go without gagging her.

She appreciated the courtesy, but with her mouth full of his cock she couldn't easily tell him she was fine with him gagging her just a little. Anything to get more of his cock inside her.

Faster, more confident now, it frustrated her that she couldn't bob her head and help, or use her hands.

Then he fell still, deep, the length of his cock along her tongue and the curly nest of hair at the root of his shaft brushing her chin.

"Such a good girl," he cooed.

Her cunt clenched, desperate for a hard fucking. Whining, she stroked the underside of his cock with her tongue as much as she could, trying to make him move, dammit, anything so she could get some relief from the ache making her hornier than she'd ever been in her entire life.

"Aww, someone's horny," he said.

She whined again.

Laughing, he sat up and pulled out, startling her. But before she could complain, he'd turned around, his leg once again pinning her hair to the bed, and the head of his cock brushing against her lips.

Automatically they parted, her happy sigh muffled as his cock slid deep into her mouth again.

Then his weight pressed on top of her, completely pinning her.

His hands pushed her thighs open. "Legs spread," he said, tone firm.

She didn't hesitate.

"Good girl." She felt the breath from his words on her clit, and she had less than a second to regret she hadn't done more than trim down there that morning when his lips wrapped around her clit.

She moaned around his cock, earning her a moan from him in return. He swiped his tongue up and down her clit, flicking it, and triggering another orgasm. This time she screamed around his cock, relief to finally be coming, forgetting for just a moment about sucking him until he rocked his hips.

"Get busy, sweetheart," he said, the vibration rolling through her clit. "I won't stop until you get me off."

She tried. She really did. But then he played dirty and sucked on her clit and made her come again. And again.

And again.

She closed her eyes and felt herself sailing off into what had to be subspace. Nothing existed except her mouth wrapped around the silky, hot shaft between her lips, and his mouth working her clit into yet another orgasm. It felt like the orgasms started rolling together, one long, tingling, fiery sensation the likes of which she'd never thought she could feel before, much less actually be feeling at that moment.

The fucking books were right!

That was the last coherent thought she had as she lost her mind. At least, that was what it felt like. Insanity had to be something like that.

She settled into a rhythm of sucking and slurping and licking at his cock in between moaning around it when he'd make her come again. Apparently what he was doing to her was helping him hold back. His sac dangled over her nose, sometimes brushing against her face as he would take a few strokes into her mouth. She wished she could just bury her face between his legs and explore every square inch of him there, lick and suck his balls into her mouth, hell, anything he wanted.

Everything he wanted.

He slid two fingers into her wet, well-fucked cunt, and slowly started finger-fucking her. She sucked harder on his cock, now realizing how absolutely serious he was about keeping her pinned to the bed until she made him come.

Frankly, she wasn't sure she could take it. In the space of less than an hour, she'd had more orgasms than she had in several years. She didn't know if she'd survive much more.

His fingers found someplace deep inside her and pressed, persistent.

It felt like her mind unhinged. Her back arched despite his weight on her. The walls of her pussy clamped down on his fingers as the strongest orgasm she'd ever felt in her entire life swept through her.

He lifted his head. "Fuck my hand, sweetheart." He buried his face between her legs again.

She did her best, sucking and rocking her hips, the explosion ricocheting through her body, from her clit to her brain to her toes and back again. It went on and on, and she was just about to consider trying to get his attention to code from how intense it felt when his cock grew harder, hotter, and she knew he was close.

Redoubling her efforts, she let him fuck her mouth, faster, harder, until he let out that familiar moan she was quickly coming to love, and jet after jet of hot cum filled her mouth. Then he kissed the inside of her thighs and rested his head against her leg for a moment, his breath blowing across her flesh as he recovered. In her mouth, his cock began to soften.

When she tried sucking on it again, he laughed and sat up, making her relinquish it. "No, sweetheart. I'm too sensitive right now. I need to recover."

He turned around, not releasing her from the handcuffs, and stretched out next to her on the bed. Pulling her to him, he kissed her, deep and slow. She realized she'd never tasted herself on a lover's lips before, not that she'd had many of those to begin with. But he seemed perfectly comfortable and at ease with it.

Cradling her cheek in his palm, he looked down into her eyes. "Good?"

Her eyes fell closed. Nodding, she nestled her face against his chest.

The tender press of his lips against her forehead nearly drove her to tears. Good tears.

Somehow, she held them back. She still soared, her brain floating, mind…gone. Just *gone*.

She didn't want it to come back anytime soon, and tears might make him want to *talk*.

All she wanted to do in that moment was absorb the sensations.

Absorb him.

He chuckled again, holding her close. "Let's rest for a few minutes before I go after you again. I want to get at least a few more out of you before dinner."

She shivered when she realized he was absolutely serious.

Outside, the wind picked up again, howling. Somewhere not too far away, another rumble of thunder rolled through the atmosphere.

And she realized maybe she had just found something—someone—she couldn't simply walk away from.

Didn't *want* to walk away from.

Maybe ever.

Chapter Twenty-One

Work that following week was a sweet kind of torture for Gabe. Fortunately, she didn't have to directly work with Bill every day, because she wasn't sure she had enough pairs of underwear to handle how frequently she'd have to change them.

Just the thought of what he'd done to her, what he could do to her, made her instantly wet.

No one had ever had that effect on her before.

No, he didn't deliberately try to bait or tease her when they were working. He was as professional and dedicated to his work as she was.

Just the thought of him, what he could and had done to her, what he might do to her, was enough to trigger responses in her body that were apparently far beyond her control.

This was *not* a problem she was used to having.

They were supposed to get together on Friday when he called her that afternoon. "Sorry, sweetheart, but I won't make it up there tonight. Caught a case."

From the sound of his voice, she knew it was serious. "Bad?"

His resigned sigh echoed through the line. "Domestic. Murder-suicide."

Her heart chilled. "Oh, no. Kids?"

"Yeah."

She closed her eyes. "I'm sorry."

"Needless to say, it'll be a few hours before I can even think of getting out of here."

She had an idea. "Let me pick us up dinner from Marelli's. I'll come down, and you can give me the high sign when it's okay to order dinner."

He was quiet for a moment. "I'm not feeling very dominant tonight, sweetheart."

"I know. I didn't mean that."

He gave her two addresses and time to write them down. "The first is home. The second is where I'm at right now. Tell one of the deputies to come in and get me. I'll give you my key and alarm code. If I'm out of here before you get here, I'll call you and let you know."

She hadn't been to his house yet. That he was trusting her with his key this soon she knew meant he really had faith in her.

"Okay."

She quickly gathered her work laptop and supplies to crochet, along with a couple of things in case she spent the night. She knew he could be done in two hours or ten, depending on what had happened.

And she was determined to not let him be alone tonight, even if it was just to let him sit there and be quiet while he processed what he'd seen.

She knew that feeling well.

When she drove down the street toward the crime scene, in what appeared to be an otherwise quiet residential neighborhood, she had to park on the street three houses down. Crowds of people stood outside the yellow crime scene tape, and two different news crew vans had set up outside the perimeter.

She grabbed her badge holder and put on her professional face as she headed toward the line and wove her way through people. A uniformed deputy on the other side was about to stop her when he saw her badge.

"I'm here for Detective Thomas," she said in her cop voice.

He nodded and pointed toward another deputy running scene control at the front door.

She cringed over the ambulance and two medical examiner's vans parked in the driveway and in front of the house.

That was never good a good sign.

She showed her badge to the deputy at the front door. "I don't need inside. Detective Thomas asked me to stop by. Said to ask someone to get him."

He nodded and called inside to someone else. Bill appeared at the front door a moment later. When he stepped outside, he pulled off the protective paper booties covering his shoes and the latex gloves from his hands and tossed them into a temporary garbage can set up in front of the house by the crime scene techs. Motioning her to follow him, he walked over to the driveway where they could stand behind one of the ME's vans and not be seen by either news crew.

He looked somber, drawn, haggard. If it wasn't for everyone around she would pull him into her arms and hug him.

He withdrew a set of keys from his pocket and quickly pulled one off, handing it to her. Then he used his personal phone to text her a four-digit code. "Alarm panel is right inside the front door. After you punch in the code, hit the *off* button. Make yourself at home, whatever you want to do is fine."

"Okay." She waited until he met her gaze. "If I don't hear from you by seven, I'll go get our food and I'll heat yours up for you when you get home."

He nodded.

She knew whatever happened inside that house in that otherwise quiet neighborhood had to be even worse than she imagined. He looked haunted, exhausted.

Reaching out, she touched his arm. "We can be just Bill and Gabe tonight, if that's what you need."

He seemed to ponder it for a moment. "I'm not sure what I'm going to need, except I'm not too stubborn to admit I know I'm going to welcome having you with me tonight. I know you'll understand."

She nodded and watched as he turned and headed back toward the house, getting a fresh pair of booties and gloves from the deputy at the door.

Tightly clutching the key in her hand, she returned to her car.

He lived in another quiet neighborhood in eastern Port Charlotte. Not the newest or fanciest, but she didn't count a single house with bars on the windows within a mile of his address.

His yard wasn't elaborately landscaped, but it was well kept, the grass weed-free and recently mowed.

Suppressing her nerves, she unlocked the front door and quickly disarmed the alarm, taking a moment to find the hallway light switch.

The house was neat, tidy. Lived in, but not as stark and bare as her own condo.

On the entry wall hung several pictures, a few of Bill and a woman. From the looks of them, they were several years old.

His wife?

She felt a little uncomfortable studying them without Bill there to provide narration. Turning back to the front door, she brought her things in and locked the door, finding the living room where she set her stuff on the couch.

Three bedrooms, two baths. One of the bedrooms was a home office and workout room, with a treadmill and desk. The other a guest bedroom. The master bedroom was obviously where he spent a lot of time, not messy, but not feeling unused like the guest room.

On the wall hung a wedding picture. Yes, the woman in the other pictures had to be Ella. In this one, they both looked younger still, Bill smiling down at her, her beaming face glowing back at him.

Can I make him that happy?

She hoped she could.

She wanted to.

It was after nine when he returned home. He headed straight for the shower. She first debated leaving him alone, then decided not to. Stripping, she stepped in with him.

He said nothing. But he turned to her, pulled her into his arms, and let out a ragged sigh.

She rested her head against his chest as he held her, more tightly still, as if clutching onto her like a life preserver in a stormy sea.

In a way, she guessed maybe he was.

It took him several minutes to speak. When he did, his voice sounded soft, full of pain. "This is why I know I don't want kids now. I'm too old for them anyway. And bad things can happen to them."

"How many?"

"Three. And his ex-wife, and her mother and father."

She didn't have a response, so she just held him even more tightly.

It took another few minutes for him to speak again. "I don't know how you do what you do. You see horrible stuff all the time. I know this is my job, but it never makes it easier. You are a tougher woman than I am." He let out a ragged laugh. "You know what I mean."

She looked up at him, found him staring down at her. "We're all tough in the ways we need to be."

He cupped her cheek in his hand and leaned in, kissing her. It took on a sudden, frantic feel, his breath coming faster, harder as his lips bruised hers.

She sensed what he needed. Something she herself knew had been missing from her life too many damn nights.

A distraction.

When he lifted his head to take a breath, she whispered, "Would you like to fuck me, Sir?"

He froze only a moment before kissing her again, hard and deep, a groan escaping him as his cock suddenly hardened between them.

Then he turned her around, a hand between her shoulders pushing her against the wall where she braced herself.

Then his cock was inside her, hard and fast and fierce. She reveled in the feel of it, knowing in this way, at least, she could give him comfort, take his mind away from what he'd seen. Not anything close to the subspace she was quickly growing to need, but maybe helping him a little.

Meeting every thrust, she threw her head back. "That's it, Sir. Fuck me hard."

He let out a hoarse cry as he plunged his cock deep into her pussy one last time, falling still and resting his head against her shoulders while trying to catch his breath.

Leaving her still horny and wanting, but happy.

Then he surprised her, kissing her and hooking his left arm around her, his hand cupping her right breast, while his right arm wrapped around her hip and his fingers found her clit.

"Your turn, sweetheart," he muttered, his voice still deep rumbling. "You come for me now."

He pinched her nipple with his fingers as his other hand sped up between her legs, her clit swollen and aching for release.

She was just about there when she realized he could see her back. Her scars.

Emotional vapor lock set in, tensing her whole body.

Apparently, he sensed it. "What's wrong? Am I hurting you?"

"I...no, not that. I'm fine. Don't stop."

He did stop. In fact, he turned her around. "What happened? What's wrong?"

In the face of what he'd just been through, she didn't want to admit it. "My brain tried to break through, sorry. Nothing you did."

He studied her as if trying to decide if she was telling him the full truth. Nodding, he gently pushed her against the wall. "Okay." He sank to his knees, his hands spreading her legs as far apart as she could get them in the tub. Then he used his thumbs to part her labia and covered her clit with his mouth.

"Ahh..." She couldn't think, could barely breathe. He knew how to use his tongue and lips, that was for sure. And now with her back safely against the wall, she could focus on nothing but those sweetly agonizing sensations washing through her and robbing her of the ability to form words. She braced her hands against his shoulders and held on.

Two fingers, then three slid into her wet cunt as he licked and sucked her clit. The first explosion felt that much sweeter when the walls of her pussy clamped down around his fingers. She thought it would overwhelm her, too much, too intense. When she tried to push his head away, he caught her wrist with his free hand and pinned it against the wall.

That triggered the second explosion.

"Mmm-hmm," he mumbled, the vibrations strumming through her clit and into her core. Apparently he liked getting that reaction out of her, because she lost track of how long he knelt there making her come, how many orgasms he forced out of her before the water started going cold.

Only then did he sit back on his heels with a pleased smile on his face. She noticed his cock had hardened again, too. "Okay, so maybe something can make me feel a little toppy tonight." He stood and kissed her, hard, a fist in her wet hair holding her head in place. "Did you eat?"

She nodded, her voice still shaky, "Yes, Sir."

"Good girl. When we get out of here, get dried off, and go heat my dinner, please." He forced her head to the side, where he nipped up her neck to her earlobe. He'd quickly learned the effect that had on her. "When I finish eating, I'm going to take you to bed and fuck your brains again out before we go to sleep. How does that sound?"

"Good, Sir."

He bit her again, harder this time, making her clit throb and pulling a needy cry from her. "That's my good girl." He let her go so suddenly she nearly fell over and had to grab hold of him for balance. "You all right?" he asked.

The playfully evil smile on his face told her he was damn well aware of what he'd just done to her.

And that it was giving him a needed distraction made her determined to keep that smile on his face. "Yes, Sir."

"Good girl." He patted her on the ass. "I'll be right out."

* * * *

Bill tried to focus on the sweetly out-of-focus look Gabe wore. Yes, it'd been one of the worst days of his career. One of the kind he hoped he never had to go through again.

On the rare nights like this when he was with Ella, she'd done the same thing, instinctively knowing what he needed and when. Immediately after, he needed a distraction, just like this, powerful enough to turn his thoughts far away from what he'd seen.

Later, when he could process it better, he would come to grips with the day's events.

But for now, the best medicine was Gabe and losing himself in her. He also wasn't an idiot. She'd forgotten about her scars in her initial worry about him and his mindset.

For that, he knew he had fallen irretrievably in love with her. She'd frozen up when his focus returned to her and she realized he could clearly see her scars.

That was something he hoped he'd be able to help her overcome with time.

Not tonight. He wasn't in a good mindset to do that tonight. Tonight he was content to let her take charge, despite her not realizing that was exactly what she'd done by offering herself to him.

Tonight he was eager to assuage his own scarred soul by letting hers tend to him.

And he couldn't love her more for it if he tried.

Chapter Twenty-Two

The task force was nearly ready to start arresting their suspects that next weekend, meaning Bill and Gabe would miss their Saturday dinner with their friends. They opted to take Wednesday off, giving them time alone together, but not screwing up their prep work for the operations.

In a way, Gabe dreaded the upcoming arrests because it meant a shift to a long-distance relationship. Even though it was only a couple of hours away, knowing she couldn't just hop in a car and quickly be at his house, or see him sitting across a conference table from her at work, twisted her heart in an unpleasant way.

Bill had gone up to Sarasota and spent Tuesday night with Gabe. Over breakfast Wednesday morning, they were trying to decide what to do for the day when Gabe came up with a comment out of left field that left her mouth before she was able to stop it.

"How do you know we'll be compatible outside of the bedroom?" she asked.

"Instead of looking for excuses why this relationship won't work, how about looking for the things that will and do work?"

"I'm serious," she said. "I want to know there's going to be more to this than just in bed." She realized how that sounded. "I mean, bed's great. But I need more than that."

"Okay, fine." He leaned against the counter. "What do you want to do, then?"

"I want to go to a gun range."

He arched an eyebrow at her. "Really?"

"Yeah. Why? What's wrong with that?"

The lopsided smirk he wore made her alternately want to kiss him and slap it off his face. "Nothing's wrong with it," he said. "I just don't meet too many women whose idea of a romantic date is a trip to the gun range."

She smiled. "Well, aren't you a lucky boy, then? I won't even make you buy my targets or ammunition."

He stepped forward, so close she had to look up into his face. "Maybe I want to buy your targets and ammo." He dropped his voice. "Maybe you need to make some concessions every once in a while and let me do things I want to do for you without fighting me about it. Or are you too scared to do that? You can always code if you don't like it, but there's no logical reason for you to fight me on this one. Your choice."

She knew what he was doing. He was challenging her in more ways than one. There was still that sharp edge of their dynamic working its way through, and he knew she knew the last thing she wanted to do was code for something that didn't involve sex or impact play.

More surprisingly, she realized she didn't mind. "Okay," she agreed. "Fine. You can buy my targets and ammo. Sir," she added.

He grinned as he pulled her in for a hug. "Now was that so hard?"

"You might change your mind when you see the price of 9mm ammo."

He kissed the side of her neck. "I'm going to wear you down eventually. You realize that, right? I'm going to show you this is right for both of us."

"That's what I'm afraid of," she mumbled against his chest.

He made her look at him again. "You don't have to let Maria live rent-free in your head any longer. Hell, you don't have to let her live there even if she was paying her own way. You have to make a choice to get rid of all that crap and be happy because it's the right thing to do. You're a strong, intelligent woman with a good head on your shoulders. You don't need that old bat's voice in your head. It's only holding you back at this point."

"There you go using logic again," she tried to joke.

"Yes, me and that damned devil logic. Evil stuff. Might actually make you happy."

"I don't know if I *know* how to be happy," she admitted before she even realized the words were out of her mouth.

He took her hands in his and held them pressed against his chest. "I know it's hard for you," he said. "But can you trust me at least this much? I know what happy feels like. I had happy, and then I had it ripped right out of me. So when I say *this* feels good, feels *happy*, believe me. I know both ends of the spectrum. This is what it's supposed to feel like."

"Terror? Uncertainty? Like the world's spinning out of control?"

He smiled. "Yep. That's happy."

"You sure?"

"I'm sure."

"Huh." She let him pull her close again, her cheek resting against his chest. "I didn't know fear and happy could go hand in hand like that."

He rubbed his chin against the top of her head. "A lot of people don't."

"I don't know if I'll ever want to get married," she admitted.

Where the hell did that *come from?*

"That's all right," he assured her. "I'm happy with what we have. I also know long distance might take us a little getting used to, but we'll handle that as it happens. I'm willing to take you as you are, right now, without any pressures about what should or shouldn't happen in the future. I'm good with that. If you decide you want more, I'm not going to lie and say I wouldn't like that, too. But I'm not going to get greedy. I *never* thought I'd ever be this happy again. So I'm more than willing to take you the way I have you right now, and just be grateful for every minute I get to spend with you."

"Snarky and terrified and confused?"

He chuckled again, a sweet, low sound that rumbled through her body. "Beautiful and perfect," he insisted. "Let *me* decide how I see you, not defined by how you see yourself."

* * * *

By the middle of the next week, they were knee-deep in the paperwork end of things, having arrested over fifty suspects in four counties. Gabe had forgotten it was her birthday, but Bill hadn't.

"We are taking tomorrow off," he told her that evening when she arrived at his house. "I already cleared it with my boss and yours."

She felt her face heat. "You did?"

"Yep, I called him."

"What did you tell him?"

He grinned. "That I thought you were working yourself to death, and considering you and I had become friends, I wanted to go over your head and get you time off that I knew you wouldn't take for yourself."

"What did he say?"

"That he was glad I told him, and that if you try to do any work tomorrow he'll have your head."

"So what are we doing tomorrow?"

He grabbed her braid, removing the elastic band from the end and finger-combing her tresses before releasing her hair from the other elastic band at the base of the pony tail. He wrapped her hair around his hand and used it to gently tip her head back.

She felt her body melting, instantly responding. "We are going shopping tomorrow, sweetheart," he told her. "And I am buying you a couple of things."

"What things?"

"Presents. Same rules, you have the right to code, but I want to do this for you as a birthday gift. In other words, please don't spoil my fun. Got it?"

She nodded as much as his grip on her hair would allow. "Yes, Sir."

Leaning in, he kissed her. "That's my good girl."

That was all it took to finish her off. When he called her that, no matter what, she knew she'd do anything, everything he asked of her.

Between that and that damn smile of his, he had a sneaky way of getting her not only go along with him, but to enjoy it.

He'd ordered them pizza. After eating, he took her by the hand and led her into his bedroom, where it was dark except for a shaft of dim illumination from the nightlight in the bathroom slanting through the door. She loved that he made every attempt to keep the lights down for her in bed, knowing her hesitation.

He began undressing her. "Time to turn your brain off, sweetheart," he said with a smile. "You completely belong to me for the next twenty-four hours."

When he had her naked, he kissed her, his clothes pressing against her bare flesh and sending tendrils of need coursing through her body. Her clit throbbed, a quick study in knowing what this man could do to her body.

He grabbed her ass with both hands, fingers digging in as he ground his hips against hers. Through his slacks she felt the rigid, swollen outline of his cock. "See what you do to me, sweetheart?"

"Yes, Sir."

He reached into the bedside table and grabbed a pair of handcuffs. In one fluid movement, he had spun her around, cuffed her wrists behind her head, and pushed her facedown over the bed.

He stepped between her legs, folding his body over hers, his mouth barely inches from her ear. "Tonight, sweetheart, I plan on fucking you long and slow and using one of your own toys against you." She heard the familiar *click* of the vibrator she'd brought with her, at his insistence.

Now she understood why.

It hummed to life and she jumped when he reached between her legs with it, pressing it against her clit.

"You belong to me tonight, sweetheart. And I want to hear you moan and scream my name." The comforter rubbed against her nipples, which suddenly ached to feel him sucking or nipping or pinching them. "How's that sound?"

"Good, Sir."

He removed the vibrator and flipped her onto her back, lifting her ankles to his shoulders. It left her cunt open and exposed to him.

He slipped two fingers between her labia, into her pussy, and a grin filled his face. "You are a very wet girl, aren't you?"

"Yes, Sir."

"Did I do that to you?"

"Yes, Sir."

He replaced his fingers with the vibrator, easing it in as deeply as it would go and leaving it there. Then he knelt down and buried his face in her pussy, her thighs shoved apart by his shoulders.

She let out a cry as the first orgasm hit her, between his tongue flicking at her clit and the vibrator hitting her G-spot, she was helpless to stop it. He reached up with both hands and found her nipples, adding deliciously sharp pinches to the sensations.

A second orgasm slammed into her. "Sir!"

He lifted his face from her pussy and sternly ordered, "Take it or code, sweetheart. You're going to keep coming until I'm ready to let you stop."

His tone triggered number three inside her even before he lowered his face back to her clit and began sucking on it.

She didn't know how long she lay there taking it, pleasure so intense she burst into tears at one point even as she was moaning her way through yet another orgasm.

Wanting it to end, she never wanted it to end, and the paradox slammed into her just as hard as another orgasm.

Only when she was shattered and helpless and weak, trembling, did he relent. He withdrew the vibrator and turned it off, tossing it onto the bed. He sat up and unfastened his slacks, shoving them and his briefs down. Climbing onto the bed, he lifted her legs over his shoulders again and pressed her thighs back until they touched her chest as his cock slid deep inside her.

He reached up and clasped her hands. She lay cocooned in his embrace, the world no longer existing.

She stared up into his eyes in the dim light, wondering how she could ever love anyone as much as she loved him, terrified it might end one day, scared he might come to his senses.

He smiled as he took a long, slow thrust. "Oh, sweetheart, I plan on making this last. I want at least one more out of you like this, if I have to stay here and fuck you all night long."

His fingers tightened around her hands. She couldn't have wiggled free, with the handcuffs securing her arms behind her head, if she wanted to.

"You have no idea what this does to me," he said, "hearing you come like that, your eyes glazed over when you realize you have to lie there and take what I give you because you don't *want* me to stop and you're afraid I might."

He knew. He'd seen it. How had he appeared in the middle of her heart like this?

"This is me," he whispered. "You want me? You've got me. And I've got a brain full of dark desires, things I'd like to do to you." As he talked he fucked her, his cock gliding along her clit with each stroke. "Rope ties I've seen that I would love to do to you. Fantasies of installing a hard point in the ceiling in here so I could tie you in a sex swing and fuck you all night long like that. Getting you used to nipple clamps and making you beg to come because I spend hours teasing and tormenting you without letting you get over the edge."

His teeth grazed the side of her neck. "I never want to hurt you, sweetheart. I just want to own you as completely, as thoroughly as you'll let me."

The orgasm startled her, creeping up on her as his pelvis bumped against her clit with each stroke. "Yes," she cried out, trying to rock her hips against him for more traction and unable to do so with his weight pinning her down to the bed.

"Good girl." He slammed into her, hard and fast, fucking her, owning her, trying to catch up with her and come before the last echoes of her climax finished rebounding through her. Once he did, he lowered her legs but didn't move, kissing her, caressing her face.

Then, he yawned, making them both laugh.

"Sorry," he said. "Early morning." He propped himself up on his arms. "Maybe we should go to sleep. I have a lot of plans for you for tomorrow."

"Do you mean it?" she whispered.

His brow furrowed. "Mean what?"

"Did you mean it when you said you want to own me?"

His expression softened. He sat up and reached for the handcuff key, freeing her. Then he pulled her up into his arms. "Sweetheart, I want you in my life however you want to be here. Vanilla, kinky, any way. Do I want to own you? Absolutely. Because you already own me and you don't seem to realize it."

He kissed her, holding her tightly. "So yes, I want to own you, do dirty things to and with you, love you, and have you by my side. As long as it takes for you to be okay with that, I'm good with that, too."

She held on to him tightly, never wanting to let him go. "Thank you, Sir."

"Of course, sweetheart."

* * * *

She fell asleep immediately, soundly, tightly snuggled up against him. The next morning, he started the day by holding her hair while she gave him a blow job.

He grinned as she whined after he told her she wouldn't be allowed to come just yet.

After taking her out to breakfast, they went to the mall. She didn't bother asking him why they were there, because she knew from failed attempts earlier to get it out of him that he wouldn't spoil the surprise.

The first stop was a high-end department store, the lingerie section.

She didn't own any, for starters. She had bras and panties, and that was it.

She'd never purchased dainty, frilly things when she had no one to wear them for.

He leaned in. "We're here for a camisole. Black, thin. Something you can wear under different dresses or blouses."

"Why?"

He made her face him and dropped his voice as he cupped her chin. "Because I want to play with you at the club, and I don't mean just tying you up. I mean I want to tie you to a bench and go after you with a vibrator." He smiled. "And want you to have something on so you will spend your time focused on me and what I'm doing to you, not what you're worried people can see."

He kissed her. "And I don't care how much it costs. Find one you like that fits you, and I will buy you two of them. Either both black, or black and another color, if I like the other color."

She nervously nodded.

He cocked his head.

"Yes, Sir," she whispered.

He grinned and leaned in, kissing her. "Such a good girl."

She balked at the next stop. He carried the shopping bag with not only the two camisoles, but several pairs of satin panties he'd liked and purchased for her after asking her what size she wore.

She didn't even think about coding, despite the expense. The smile on his face, the way he said good girl to her, she would have done anything for that.

But this stop…

"What are we getting here?"

"I think Lil Lobo is lonely and needs a friend."

Terror filled her. "I…I can't."

He turned to her. "Not a bear," he said. "They have something else I have in mind."

He led her inside the Build-A-Bear store and over to the bins of stuffed animals, stopping in front of a German shepherd. "That," he said, whispering in her ear. "So when I'm not with you, you can hold him and remember how much I love you."

There was that prickle of tears again. She brushed them away as she nodded.

"Good girl," he whispered, waving to get the sales clerk's attention.

Fortunately, since it was a weekday, they were the only customers in the store. He even selected a voice box that allowed him to record a custom message. The clerk took him into the back room, where it was quiet, and he emerged a few moments later with a playful smile.

He wouldn't let Gabe play it yet.

Just a few minutes later, Gabe sat in front of a computer terminal, registering her new stuffed animal's name and information.

He leaned in. "Put your name and my address," he said. "And his name is Max."

She looked up. "Max?"

He smiled. "Short for Maximum Overload." He pressed his lips against her ear and whispered, "Because it's what I can do to your brain when I get started, and I want you to get wet every time you look at him. I want you to think of me every time you look at him."

Hell, she was getting wet right now. She had to backspace several times to correct typos as she filled out the form, because she couldn't focus.

Bill had a way of short-circuiting her brain.

And she loved it.

When they finished that part, he started to look at accessories for the dog, but she put her hand out and touched his arm. "I don't need anything for him, Sir," she said. The voice of Maria threatened to make itself known, that it was wasteful to spend money on *toys*.

She didn't know if she could hold it back much longer if she gave in now, on this point.

Today, at least.

He studied her for a moment. "Have I pushed you close to the edge, sweetheart?"

She nodded. "I appreciate it, but…really. I don't need any. Please?"

He pulled her in for a hug, kissing her forehead. "Such a good girl. If you really don't want any, we won't get any."

"Thank you, Sir."

"I guess this means I shouldn't take you by the Sanrio store on our way out of here and get you a Hello Kitty cover for your phone, huh?"

She laughed, realizing he was serious. "I think I need a little more time, Sir."

He kissed her. "You realize I am going to get you to the point where I can buy my sweet girl whatever I think you should have, don't you?"

She nodded. "Yes, Sir."

"We're going to build up to other things. Today, I'm very proud of you for letting me do this for you. Now let's get checked out and go home." He grinned, sending her a playful wink. "Time to get you tied up for a few hours."

Chapter Twenty-Three

They were over four months into their relationship now. This weekend would be their first weekend together in two weeks. The weekend before, she'd gotten involved in an investigation that required working through the weekend, screwing their plans.

Not this weekend.

At least she'd had Max standing watch over her with Lil Lobo. She never would have imagined before how much emotional impact a stuffed animal would have on her, even after what she went through as a kid. Every time she looked at Max, or held him, she was instantly transported back to that day at the store, Bill standing behind her and whispering in her ear as she went through the process of having Max created before their eyes.

It wasn't a substitute for Bill, but it meant more to her than she ever would have realized before.

And when she pressed Max's paw, where the little voice box was located, Bill's voice said, "You're *my* good girl. I love you, sweetheart."

Gabe left Miami later than she'd intended on Friday afternoon and managed to hit traffic on Alligator Alley, where it was backed up several miles for an accident. By the time she finally reached Port Charlotte, it was nearly nine at night and her nerves were shot.

Bill opened the front door and walked out to help bring her things inside. "You all right, sweetheart?"

She let him pull her in for a hug. "Exhausted," she mumbled against his shoulder. "Traffic was terrible."

He kissed the top of her head. "Inside. Give me your keys. I'll get everything."

"Thank you."

She handed them over without complaint and headed into the house. She was too tired and frazzled to argue.

She didn't want to argue. She would admit that, tonight, his help was more than welcomed.

She'd been looking forward to this time together from approximately the second he'd pulled out of the parking lot of her building after their last time together. Especially since he'd been teasing her via text and Skype for the past two weeks.

Once she was unloaded and settled, he pulled her into his arms, a playful grin on his face. "Ready for a good ravishing, I hope?" He gave her a kiss and headed toward the kitchen.

"Absolutely. What's the plan?"

"I want to tie you up in bed."

She stared at him. "That's it?" Considering the way he'd been winding her up, she'd hoped for more than just that. Although, that was always good, and always fun, but it wasn't anything different from what they usually did.

He smiled as he crossed his arms over his chest. "Well, then I'm hoping you'll let me screw your brains out. I kind of thought that was a given at this point in our relationship, but we can clarify it, if you'd prefer."

Her head spun. "What, exactly, are you proposing? You don't need permission to do any of that. We've done it before."

He cocked his head to the side. "Tying you up. Making love to you. Maybe some forced orgasm play mixed in with that. What I want is permission from you to totally do it *my* way. *My* rules. You can code at any time, of course. That never changes. But you don't get toppy from the bottom. You don't try to control the situation. You either code, or you let me do what I want, the way I want. What I'm asking is for you to trust me and not code for anything other than a problem like your arm's going to sleep or something."

She'd never had to code with him while playing. He was always careful when trying new things to constantly check in with her, to watch her reactions, to back off just before she thought she might have to.

She did trust him. Absolutely.

"No spanking or anything?" she asked.

"Not unless you want it and ask me for it."

"Why?"

"Why no spanking?"

"No. I mean why do you want to do this now, asking like this? I kind of thought we were at this point already."

He walked over and sat next to her on the couch, where he took her hands in his. "I don't know what you're feeling or thinking. I'm going to lay this all out on the table for you. All I know is I love being with you. I love making love to you. I enjoy playing around in bed with you. I love it when you let me take charge. I love tying you up. And I would really love mixing all of that together into one, knowing I have the go-ahead from you to do what I want until or unless you code. Knowing I have a conscious decision from you to completely take full and utter control of you for the weekend, however I want."

She wasn't sure what to say.

He kissed her hands, squeezing them. "It's okay to say no."

"Yes." The word was out before she realized it.

He smiled. "Did you want spanking, too, or was that just a question before?"

"I…" She stared into his eyes. "I don't know. Maybe. You get me so horny it gets hard to think. That's a problem I've never had before I met you."

"Getting that horny?"

"Well, yeah, that, too. I meant the not being able to think straight part." She took a deep breath and let it out before softly admitting, "I like that. I like it when you make me feel like that because I know you'll never try to pull anything. I've always been able to trust you. I don't want to screw this up with you."

His expression softened. He gathered her into his arms and kissed her. "Sweetheart, if you were to tell me right now all you wanted to be was friends, I think it might break my heart, but I'd do it just to still get to spend time with you. If you think I'm about to do anything that might screw up your trust in me, think again. I'd rather go way too slow and have you begging for more than to rush things. Slow is fun."

"Slow's sometimes a kind of torture."

He laughed. "Very true."

She looked up into his eyes again. "What are your rules? Doing stuff your way, what does that mean, exactly?"

Stroking her cheek, he looked like he was trying to figure out how to phrase it. "Well, for starters, I want to turn the lights on."

She felt fear already building inside her when he spoke again. "You can have a blindfold, if you want. And I won't turn the light on until after I have you tied up. But your body is beautiful, and it's yours, and I love every square inch of you. I think we're at the point where we need to work past this issue when it's just the two of us. I don't want you to be afraid of me seeing you, all of you, in the light."

That wasn't an unreasonable request. She suspected there was a lot more he was rapidly growing interested in as they played and watched others playing during their trips to the club and during private parties at their friends' houses, all on the more sensual side of the scale. She didn't fear for her physical safety with him. She trusted him, for starters. Knew he wouldn't blow through a safeword.

And she knew with her military and law enforcement training, they were likely close to evenly matched in terms of physicality.

But could she allow herself to completely let go of the control she'd spent her entire life cultivating? She thought maybe, at some point, she might like to explore more with him. Barehanded, over-the-knee spanking—probably. The intimacy more than just discipline. The connection. The give and take.

Books were fiction, and she wasn't an idiot. Some of the books she'd read… She'd never had that connection before, ever, with another human being. She wondered if that was bullshit, too, or if it was possible.

Shayla and Tony looked happy, like they had that kind of connection. Laura and Rob. Leah and Seth. All the others.

And she'd felt happy, too.

Maybe it wasn't just fictional bullshit, that part of it. Maybe there were people in this life who really did have those kinds of fairy-tale relationships.

Maybe it wasn't too much to dream about having one for herself.

With Bill.

Bill was the first person she'd ever allowed inside her defenses. The first person she genuinely believed wasn't after anything other than what he said he was after. To have fun, to not blow her trust.

Sex was definitely way more than just fun with him. He'd glimpsed her scars, the physical and emotional ones, and hadn't run from them or been repulsed by them or overcompensated by making a big deal about what a big deal they were not.

He'd just taken them as part of her, part of the whole. Part of her whole.

She took a deep breath as she stared into his eyes and nodded.

That smile, the one he gave her, the twinkle in his eyes, the way the lines creased the outsides of his eyes in a way she suspected hadn't happened very often before they met, it twisted her insides completely.

He leaned in and kissed her again. "Thank you, sweetheart."

"For what?"

"For trusting me."

* * * *

He led her into the bedroom and pulled her into his arms again. The light from the master bathroom slipped into the room through the half-closed door. Enough he'd be able to see by to tie her.

Kissing her, he slipped his hands under her T-shirt and raised it over her head. She forced herself not to freeze up, not to draw away. She knew he'd stop if she did.

And she most definitely did *not* want him to stop. Now that she'd made the jump into the abyss, she wanted to fall all the way, knowing his love would catch her.

He took his shirt off and dropped it onto the floor, joining hers. Then he pulled her close again.

The feel of his warm flesh pressed against hers, it was something she savored every time.

Something so simple as human contact.

Loving human contact. Tender and gentle contact.

For the first time in her life, it didn't come with her brain screaming things at her, warnings and recriminations.

Maria's voice was nowhere to be heard.

Bill silenced the voices just by his presence, his patient ways, his kind and caring manner, his confident nature that didn't stray into asshole territory. Protective without being overbearing. He'd stepped in and taken control and made her want that, want *him*, before she'd even realized what had happened.

Once they were both naked, he got a duffel bag and set it on the bed. When he unzipped it, she realized it was full of rope. "I've been shopping," he said, removing several coils of rope just like what Seth and Leah had loaned them for class.

And a soft leather blindfold. He held it up. "Ready?"

She nodded. He buckled it around her head before guiding her to sit on the bed.

Then he got started. He took his time, caressing and teasing her with his fingers, slowing as she tensed when his attention was on her back, distracting her with playful tweaks to her nipples and fingers stroking her clit.

She didn't know how long it took him to tie, her but by the time he was finished with the harness that also pinned her arms in place, she knew she was deep in subspace.

He turned the bedside lamp on. She heard it, felt the light even though the blindfold didn't allow any to penetrate. Cringing, she ducked her head.

"Don't do that," he gently said, taking her chin and tipping her head up. "Don't ever draw away from me like that. You're beautiful. And when you're not blindfolded, unless I've ordered you otherwise, you are always to look me in the eyes. Understand?"

She felt the tears threatening to build under her closed eyelids. "Yes, Sir," she whispered.

She felt the mattress dip behind her as he sat. She involuntarily flinched when his fingers touched her back, where she knew one of the scars lay. He slowly caressed it, working around the rope holding her arms securely at her side.

Up and down, back again, moving to another, and another.

"You're trembling," he said. "Are you cold?"

"No, Sir," she whispered.

"Then what's wrong?"

She shrugged.

His hands gently cupped her chin again. He turned her head. "Something must be wrong. Tell me."

She had no answer for him. None that wouldn't drive her to tears, and she was close enough to that already.

He stroked her back. "Did your grandmother do all of this to you?"

She nodded.

He released her chin and returned to caressing her back, her shoulders, her arms. He made no move to reach around the front of her.

It terrified her.

What did he see? What did he think?

Was he fascinated by how ugly she was?

Then she felt the bed move again as he shifted position, followed by the warmth of his lips on her flesh, on one of the scars.

She shivered, choking back the sob.

He froze, waiting.

Despite her best efforts to hold back, the first tear squeezed free, fortunately caught by the edge of the blindfold before it could run down the side of her nose and give her away.

"Why did she do this?" he asked, his breath brushing against her flesh.

She shrugged.

"I asked you a question, sweetheart." Despite his gentle tone, the message was clear. She knew from her own experience as a cop that he wouldn't stop asking until she answered to his satisfaction.

"I don't know," she whispered, not trusting her voice.

"Did she ever say anything?"

Of course she had. Where to start? Countless different imagined slights, failures on her part, sins against God and the Church, perceived and unacceptable willfulness that, Gabe knew from an adult point of view, mostly stemmed from Maria's unreasonable hatred of Gabe's mother and probably more than a little mental illness.

"Yes," she settled on eventually.

His lips feathered across her scars for a few more minutes. Just when Gabe thought maybe she had her emotions under control, he spoke again. "What did she say?"

When she didn't answer, his tone changed a little. Still gentle, but with an edge of firm control. "I asked you a question, sweetheart. Answer me, or code."

Code? Safeword for *talking*?

Hell, by the time she was nine, she'd learned to endure twenty strokes from Maria with a belt without blinking an eye, much less shedding a tear over it. When Maria discovered that no longer induced any kind of fear in Gabe, she'd started using switches, and eventually rods that raised welts, bruised skin, and drew blood.

This emotional flaying was something she didn't know how to process, but she still couldn't bring herself to code.

"She said I was bad, among other things."

Bill was apparently even better than she was at self-control and hiding reactions. She felt a breath across her flesh, but that was the only action betraying his shock. Then his lips started trailing across her back again.

His gentle, whispered words a few minutes later hit her harder and rocked her more than any blow she'd ever taken in her life.

"You are *my* good girl, sweetheart."

She froze, stunned, reeling.

"Say it," he ordered.

She couldn't. Her jaw locked up, throat closed, refusing to cooperate. Her brain rebelled, emotions boiling up from some deep, hidden well she'd sealed so many years ago in her childhood.

Before Bill, when was the last time she'd ever heard someone call her good?

Right before Mom and Dad died.

"Say it," he said again.

She shook her head.

"Say it, or code."

He'd backed her into a corner and he knew it. She *knew* he knew it.

Scrambling for an out, anything to defuse the situation without having to code, she mentally stretched. "It."

Another of those breaths, amused this time, but she knew he wouldn't give up that easily. "I want you to say, 'I am your good girl.' Say it or code, sweetheart."

"Please don't make me say it, Sir," she begged.

He shifted positions again, pulling her to him so her back pressed against his chest, his arms around her, one hand gently cupping her by the throat, his left cheek resting against her right cheek. He whispered, "Say it or code, sweetheart."

She was so focused on not saying it that the tears rolling down her cheeks from under the blindfold shocked her at first.

He kissed the tracks of her tears along her cheeks. In that same quietly firm voice, he repeated, "Say it or code. We aren't moving until you either obey me or code."

It felt like she spoke from the far end of a tunnel, alone, lonely, broken and emotionally bleeding. The little girl curled up in bed, silently weeping into a pillow in a dark, stark room.

She could barely pull air into her lungs to make sound. Somehow, he still heard her. "I am your good girl."

He nuzzled his lips along her ear. "Say, 'I'm your very good girl.'"

The sob escaped her first. "I'm your very good girl," she eventually choked out after several failed tries.

"Again," he quietly commanded. When she didn't immediately respond, he firmly added, "Say it, or code."

The world spun away, pain and anger and grief exploding. "I'm...your very good girl."

"Again."

Over and over he made her say it. Various inflections on different words, until she sobbed, screaming, crying, and at some point he'd changed positions and she hadn't even realized it, now lying on their sides on the bed, her face buried against his chest, his arms around her.

"You *are* my *very* good girl," he firmly insisted, kissing her forehead. Then he slipped the blindfold off her and stared into her eyes, her cheeks cradled in his palms. He leaned in and tenderly kissed her, slowly, sweetly, breaking down whatever barriers she thought she could hold against him.

How pointless and stupid that effort had been. He'd walked right past all her defenses, straight to the heart of what she'd thought had been her well-guarded core.

And proceeded to rip every last beam and timber down, every brick, every stone, every scrap of mortar and nail until nothing but the ravaged, barren landscape of her tattered soul remained.

"Whenever I ask you this," he whispered, "I expect an answer, and I expect it immediately, and you *will* say the entire thing. Who's my very good girl?"

"I'm your very good girl, Sir."

He smiled, his thumbs gently brushing away the tears rolling down her cheeks. "Yes, yes you are. You're my very good, very brave girl." He kissed her again, swallowing her sobs and holding her as the pain ebbed and flowed inside her.

Had she thought she had her life together before she met him? Had she thought she was really just fine?

What a fucking joke.

He lifted his head again to stare into her eyes, a sweet, loving smile on his face. "You are my beautiful girl, my good girl, my sweet little toy."

"I'm a broken toy, Sir."

His smile faded as he shook his head. "*No.* You are *not* broken. You are perfectly you. Are you saying I'm wrong?"

She finally shook her head a little.

His smile returned. "That's *my* good girl."

Now she understood what it seemed like all the women at the club had said at some point or another about their partners. That *smile. That* smile. She'd recognized it before but never understood how deadly it was to any and all will she had. It sank a torpedo straight through the center of her heart, where it exploded.

She'd do *anything* for that smile.

Anything.

Needed it, craved it. Would do anything to make him smile like that. To keep smiling like that.

Everything it took.

No matter how painful.

He untied her, tossing the ropes onto the floor and stretching out on the bed, her body pressed against his and her face buried against his chest. His fingers stroked her back, along the scars.

She didn't flinch.

He'd seen the thing she never thought anyone ever would, stared into the maw of her empty shell and loved everything about her, filling her with what she couldn't supply herself, what no one had since her parents' death.

"Such a good girl," he cooed.

After a while, he rolled her onto her back and reached across her to the bedside table. He grabbed a set of handcuffs and propped himself up on one arm.

"Hands behind your head."

She complied, lacing her fingers together.

The handcuffs clicked around her wrists, ratcheting until he had them snug enough around her arms that she couldn't slide out of them, and loose enough not to dig in.

He smiled down at her. "Spread your legs."

She did.

He reached over her again and grabbed an electric Hitachi vibrator from the bedside table. Apparently he'd plugged it in and set it up while he'd had her blindfolded.

That's new. She'd seen Tony and the others use Hitachis, but didn't know Bill had bought one. It also had a round, six-inch-long attachment on it that curved out from the head at a ninety-degree angle, and looked to be over an inch thick.

"I went shopping," he said with a grin. "Tony made some recommendations. This is going to be stronger than you're used to, but I know you can take it."

The vibrator clicked on. He slid it between her legs, parting her labia, making her gasp when the attachment touched her clit. "Who's my good girl?" he asked.

Now she struggled to answer from the sensations pouring through her taking away her power of speech. "I'm...I'm your good girl."

He grinned.

Oh, holy hell. That was even more lethal than his smile earlier.

"Good girls get rewards." He thumbed the control and it sped up, making her cry out.

"Come for me, sweetheart. Show me what a good girl you are for me."

She gasped for breath, crying out as the first orgasm exploded, washing through her and making her moan.

"Don't close your eyes," he ordered. "Look at me."

She struggled to keep them open as he kept the vibrator pressed against her clit and wave after wave of pleasure rocked through her.

"Who's my good girl?"

"I'm your good girl, Sir."

He crushed his lips against hers, swallowing her moans as he slid the vibrator's attachment inside her wet cunt and started fucking her with it, the head of the Hitachi hitting her clit with each stroke while the end of the attachment perfectly stroked her G-spot with every thrust. Her back arched, her body beyond her control as she started rocking her hips in time with his thrusts.

He lifted his lips just above hers. "That's it, sweetheart," he hoarsely said. "Fuck it for me. Show me how good you are."

Her eyes had started drifting closed. "Open your eyes."

Her eyelids snapped open at his tone.

He stared down at her, that grin still on his face. "You know what I'm going to do, sweetheart? I was talking with Tony and Landry and the others. They said it's easy to rewire the human brain. I'm going to condition you so that every time I call you my good girl, you instantly get wet. Do you like that idea?"

Surprisingly, she did. Not that it would be that difficult since it already pretty much had that effect on her anyway.

Or, maybe it was the feel of his hand slamming the vibrator into her swollen, throbbing clit with each thrust that buried the attachment deep inside her cunt.

"Yes, Sir," she gasped.

"Tell me."

"I…I like that idea."

His grin widened. "Ask me."

"Please train me to get wet when you call me your good girl."

His mouth crushed hers again, her tongue eagerly meeting his. She felt his cock, hard, rubbing against her hip. That only served to fire her need, another orgasm racing through her, the muscles of her pussy clamping down on the vibrator inside her.

Holy…fuck. She'd discovered a lot of things about her body she never knew before being with Bill, but this was different still. She'd never come this hard, or this many times at once.

Ever.

Evvvveeerr.

Somehow, he constantly managed to raise the bar with her, taking her places she never dreamed existed before.

He lifted his head again. "Of course I'll be happy to train you to get wet when I call you my good girl, sweetheart. It'll be my pleasure." He nudged her cheek, making her turn her head to the side so he could nip her earlobe. "I'm going to train you to do a lot of things for me and only me. Things you've never done for anyone else before, things you'll only *ever* do for me. I'm going to own your body and soul, sweetheart. I'm going to prove to you how much I love you and how good it can be. And I'm going to take very good care of you for as long as you'll let me. Do you want that?"

It was hard to think, much less talk with the way he was fucking her with the vibrator. "Yes, Sir."

"You're going to be my good girl, and my beautiful toy. And I promise I will always take good care of you. Do you want that?"

"Yes, Sir."

"They even told me sometimes it's possible to condition someone to come just from a command. I'm going to see if that's possible. Would you like that?"

She'd swear to anything, do anything, be anything to keep him happy and to make sure this never ended.

"Yes, Sir." Hell, even her toes were curling and uncurling, and that had never happened to her before.

"First, we're going to work on the easiest one. I'm going to make sure that every time I call you my good girl, you get wet. Then, I'm going to condition you so that every time I caress your back that it makes you so horny you can't see straight. We're going to work on training you to come on command for me. I want to get so deep into your head and heart that anytime you even think about us in bed, you'll want to beg me to fuck you. I'm going to show you how beautiful and perfect you are. Do you understand me?"

"Yes, Sir."

He suddenly pulled the vibrator out and shut it off, making her gasp. Her hips still flexed involuntarily, looking for that sweet release.

He sat up. She knew she was lost, his smile already twisting her around his heart and soul.

And yes, his cock was hard, rigid, standing straight out. He knelt between her legs, grabbing her behind the knees and pulling them up, spreading her thighs wide open for him. She felt him rub the head of his cock between her wet pussy lips. "Ask me."

"Please, fuck me, Sir."

He slowly shook his head. "No. That's not how you ask."

Her mind raced, struggling to figure out what he wanted. He finally helped her out. "The proper way to ask is, 'Sir, please fuck your good girl.'"

"Sir, please fuck your good girl!"

He slammed home, hard and deep and making her cry out in pleasure when his pubic bone hit her swollen, sensitive clit. He reached up and slid his arms under hers, grabbing her wrists, completely pinning her in place. "Such a good girl," he whispered. "Such a very, *very* good girl."

He slowly fucked her, taking his time, obviously enjoying teasing and torturing her. "From now on, whenever I tell you to ask for a fucking, that is how you ask for it. Understand?"

"Yes, Sir."

"No matter what it takes, no matter how long it takes, I'm going to prove to you how much I love you, and how good it can be between us. I know you need time, and I'm not asking for anything from you right now other than for you to trust me and stay faithful to me. There will be nobody in my life but you, either. Nothing else for now, not marriage, not making you move or quit or anything. But you will be mine, and I will be yours, until you're ready to tell me you want more than that. As long as it takes. Understand?"

"Yes, Sir. I love you, too." A little panic eased, fear she hadn't realized still lay nestled amongst everything else. Faithful to him? Nothing else expected or required? That she could do.

That she *would* do.

"Tell me what you want."

"Please fuck your good girl, Sir."

He picked up the pace, hard and fast and deep as a smile filled his face. "My pleasure, sweetheart," he grunted.

She felt it start, the sweet tingle, not as intense as from the vibrator, but there and growing with every thrust, every time his cock filled her cunt.

"Is my good girl going to come for me?"

"Yes, Sir."

He didn't stop, waiting until he felt her cunt contracting around his cock and she let out a cry of her own to pound into her. Hot, hard, silken steel driving her orgasm and keeping it rolling through her until he finally sank into her one last time and fell still with a moan of his own.

"Did you come?" he gasped.

"Yes, Sir."

He kissed her. "Such a very good girl."

Chapter Twenty-Four

As the new year rolled over, their relationship continued. It sucked spending days apart at a time, but most weekends they managed to get together, taking turns commuting to each other's places.

She had never imagined things could go so well, but they were. They even got to spend extra nights together during the trial phases of the cases, when she had to be present to give her testimony. Then she would stay with Bill, both of them losing their dark thoughts about the crimes they were prosecuting in the comfort of each other's arms.

Or the delicious discomfort of him tying her up before forcing her to come repeatedly, begging him to fuck her brains out between her moans of pleasure.

And Travis hadn't forgotten about her time off, either, much to her surprise. "You still owe me a few days of vacation, you know."

"I know." She'd actually taken a few here and there to spend with Bill, usually a Friday, to give them a three-day weekend.

By February, all the special task force cases were handled either via trial or plea deal, leaving her with the major thorn in her side—Martinez.

Back in Miami, Gabe struggled at work with the Jorge Martinez case. He would go to prison for life, no doubt, despite his attorneys' best attempts to get him off and discredit witnesses, when they weren't stalling the proceedings with what she considered bullshit tactics.

But she wanted more.

She wanted the asshole backing the operation. The whole thing could easily be wrapped up if she could just get her hands on the money guy. Gabe knew the arrests of Martinez and his cohorts would be a temporary distraction to whoever was behind this. It would only be a matter of time before the money man found someone else to take over and the cycle would start up again.

And again.

And again.

She kvetched about it to Bill via a Skype session with him one night. "I've turned over every freaking rock I can find to get a name for this guy. Short of kidnapping one of Martinez's attorneys and chopping his toes off one by one, I don't know what else to do."

"Well, sweetheart, that's illegal for starters." He smirked. "But I like your outside-the-box thinking."

"Then give me an idea. I'm open to any suggestions."

"Time to lean on that guy. The one you clobbered."

She laughed. "Jorge Martinez. Hey, he claims he clobbered himself."

"Sure he did. And I'm Pope Francis."

"You said chopping off toes is frowned upon."

"Yeah, of course it is." He grinned, making her wish she could crawl through the screen and join him right then. "For you."

"Well, technically it's illegal for anyone to do."

"True. You know where he's being held? The facility, I mean."

"Yeah. Isolation. Protective custody."

"So go pay him a visit."

"He won't talk to me. And someone hired him lawyers. Good ones."

"Probably his backer. Listen to me, sweetheart." His tone made her pussy as well as her heart flutter. "You know where he's being held. You know a lot of people in Miami law enforcement, do you not?"

"Yeah?"

"Find out about some of his neighbors inside. Maybe someone in there either serving time or waiting for his court date. Someone who doesn't take lightly to child rapists."

She thought about it. "Yeah, but he's still in isolation."

Bill shrugged. "Ask the state attorney's office if they mind him getting moved. Overcrowding, you know. I'm sure there's got to be at least one guy badder than him who needs to be in isolation, who's been stuck in a hospital ward or something somewhere. All I'm saying is you need to ask around."

"I love you."

He smiled. "Love you, too, sweetheart. Keep me posted."

"Will do."

* * * *

The next morning, she'd already made several phone calls before heading into the office. And she had a name.

That afternoon, she ran a couple of errands, talked to a few more people, and had made arrangements to speak early the next morning with one Da'ron Calder, forty-two and serving a nine-month sentence for battery against a guy accused by a neighbor girl of molesting her.

The extenuating circumstances of the case allowed the public defender to get the case pled down to a misdemeanor. It wasn't Calder's first brush with the law, but nobody disputed his vigilante justice wasn't justified.

When he was brought into the secure interview room, she'd asked a guard to stay with them.

And the video monitor had been disconnected.

The large black man stared at her as he sat at the table, shackle chains rattling. "Who are you?"

She got straight to the point. She unrolled the three pieces of paper, placed them on the table, and slid them across to him. She'd already received permission to give them to him.

His eyes narrowed a little, but that was the only reaction he allowed before looking up at her. "What is this shit?"

"Lawanda drew them for you," Gabe softly said, treading lightly. "And I'd like to show you something." She pulled her personal cell from her pocket, thumbed through to the videos, and hit play before holding it up so he could see it.

On the screen, he watched his little daughter and long-time girlfriend waving at him. They said hi and said a few things to him. By the time the five-minute video finished, a tear was rolling down his cheek.

He gruffly wiped it away as she took her phone back.

"What do you want? I'm no snitch."

"I just want you to listen."

"What?"

"Listen. That's all." She nodded to the guard, who opened the door.

Gabe stood. Calder looked up at her. "What are you talking about?"

She walked around the table to the doorway. "I didn't say anything." The guard stood there, holding the door open for her. Another guard came in and helped Calder to his feet.

"Don't forget your pictures, man," the guard softly told him.

"I can take them?"

"Yeah. She cleared it."

The man tenderly rolled up the papers and held them in his large hands as if they were fragile, Fabergé eggs.

Her background check had shown Calder wasn't a violent man normally, despite his gang involvement.

But he had connections.

Lots of connections.

And he was a devoted father.

They brought Calder to a stop in the corridor as two more guards were leading Jorge Martinez into the interview cell area.

Gabe broadly smiled. "There's the man of the hour," she said a little too loudly.

Martinez glared when he spotted her. "I told you, lady, I ain't talkin'. Talk to my lawyer."

She waved down his objections. "Yeah, yeah, I know. No *hablo* and all that bullshit. Listen, how is my favorite baby rapist doing today?"

His eyes widened. "Fuck you! I didn't rape no babies!"

"No, sorry. That's right, you just raped several little girls."

Now Martinez was paying attention to Calder, who stood just a few feet behind Gabe.

"Fuck you, lady!" Martinez yelled. "Hey, take me back to my cell."

Gabe snapped her fingers. "Oh, that's right, you haven't heard yet. We're moving you out of isolation and into general population. They're moving your shit right now."

"What?"

"Well, you were whining to your attorney about lockdown, so I talked to the state attorney's office. They approved your move into general."

She looked over her shoulder and spotted the hatred on Calder's face, directed at Martinez. Returning her attention to Martinez, she grinned. "You're going to be sharing a cell block with Calder here, as a matter of fact. Just a couple of cells down, from what I understand. Even better, you get a roomie."

Now Martinez struggled against his guards, trying to back away from her and Calder. "No! Fuck you, you're insane! I want my attorney!"

"And people in hell want ice water, asshole. Hell, I want the name of the money guy behind your operation, but I guess none of us are getting what we want today, are we?"

"You…you're fucking crazy! You're trying to get me killed!"

She feigned hurt innocence. "I don't know what you're talking about. You bitched about lockdown, I got you general. There's just no pleasing a guy whose distinct pubic mole was identified by no less than six of the little girls he raped and pimped out, is there?"

She shook her head and turned to Calder again, hooking her thumb back toward Martinez. "You believe this guy? What a fucking ungrateful asshole."

"No, fuck you!" Martinez screamed, now panicking. The guards were struggling to keep him from turning around and bolting back to the gate. "Take me back to my cell right now! I want my fucking attorney!"

"I think they still need a few minutes to finish moving all your crap, buddy. But, hey, I'm sure Calder here will be happy to introduce you around while you're waiting." She looked up at him.

He slowly nodded, the skin at his left temple twitching, his jaw tightly clenched.

She barely tipped her head to him in a nod.

His eyes swiveled toward her and he slowly blinked before his gaze refocused on Martinez.

She was walking toward the exit at the other end of the corridor, which would take her through the secure checkpoint, when one of Calder's guards came hurrying after her. She'd learned the guards liked Calder, because if they gave him respect, he gave it right back and tried to get his fellow inmates to do the same. That, and he had zero tolerance for sexual criminals of any kind.

Especially ones who committed sexual crimes against children.

"Big guy asked me very nicely to tell you thank you," he whispered in her ear. "That he appreciates what you did. And that he was listening very carefully."

She smiled and nodded, turning to look down the hall. She spotted Calder looking at her.

She touched her right ear with her finger.

He nodded.

She walked up to the door and hit the intercom buzzer.

* * * *

Gabe was halfway to the office when her work cell rang.

Walker.

She almost didn't answer it, but then decided it had to happen sooner or later. If not on the phone, when she got to work. "Villalobos," she said, faking a lilt she didn't feel.

"What the *hell* did you do?" he said by way of greeting.

"Hello, Special Agent Walker. And how are you this fine morning?"

"Knock it off. What did you do?"

She hoped Martinez wasn't dead already. That would put a kink in the case, although it wouldn't personally bother her. "Well, can you be more specific, boss?"

"Today. *What*. Did you *do*. *Today*?" He sounded close to blowing a gasket.

"Um, I'm on my way in. I started out with a workout first thing—"

"Were you just at the freaking jail?" he yelled.

"Oh. Well, yeah. Why didn't you ask me that?"

He let out a long groan.

"What?"

"I just got a call from the state attorney's office. Martinez is begging to cut a deal. He's got his freaking arms and legs wrapped around the bars of a door in the interview cell corridor and threatening to make them tase him if he doesn't get a SA there right now to talk to him."

"Huh. Wow, that's convenient, isn't it?"

"Gaaaabe—"

"Ask the guards. I didn't say anything except to tell him the good news that he was being moved to general population."

He groaned again. "And?"

"And what?"

"What else? He was babbling something about another guy."

"Oh. Oh, yeah, there *was* another prisoner right there, come to think of it."

Maybe I shouldn't go to the office right now.

"Gabe, what the hell am I supposed to do with you?"

"Tell me what I did wrong?"

"You set up a defendant to get killed. I never authorized his move."

"I did not. I was trying to accommodate his request to get out of solitary lockdown. And sorry, didn't know you had to approve it first."

Silence.

She checked, and the call hadn't dropped. "Travis?"

"You have got to be the luckiest person on the planet, you know that?"

"Why?"

"He said he'll give us the name of his boss in exchange for protection. He's begging for the witness protection program."

She laughed. "I thought only the feebs offered that."

"He doesn't know that. Yet."

He hung up on her.

She couldn't help the smile. It felt good to smile.

Textbook? No.

Illegal?

Well, that was different. Not technically, she supposed. Ethically, she knew the right attorney could probably get her fired, or reprimanded, at the very least.

She didn't care. If it meant they could take the money man off the street, or at least get the media crawling up his ass, it would mean he couldn't set other little girls up to be raped and abused.

And she'd *never* apologize for that.

* * * *

When she got home that evening, she grabbed a shower before settling in with leftovers from the pot of macaroni and cheese she'd made herself the night before.

I really need to start eating better.

She cruised through her e-mail and newspapers before skimming Facebook. She had a private message there from her cousin Jennifer. But then her Skype alert went off for Bill's call and she never opened Jennifer's message.

Heart thrumming, she clicked on the Skype icon to open the chat window. Bill asked her, "Hey, sweetheart. So, what happened today?"

"Travis asked me to take four days of my vacation time. ASAP."

He winced. "Ouch. Things went that bad, huh? Sorry."

"No, not at all. We've got a name. Martinez is finally cutting a deal."

"Oh, well that's good. Then why the forced time off?"

"Because Travis said he doesn't know whether to slug or hug me, and both of those options can get him in trouble with human resources, one way or another. And that I still owe him time off from before and that for the sake of his sanity and my career, I'd better take it."

Bill laughed. "Hey, remind him that you keep him on his toes. Life never gets boring with you around."

"I did. That's why he added two days onto the original two he ordered me to take."

"How many does that leave you with?"

She ran through it in her mind. "At least another four weeks I haven't used yet total. Including from before."

"So when are you taking the time off?"

"I'm due in court tomorrow for another case, so he can't get rid of me yet. He was not happy to hear that."

"That's the little workaholic I know and love."

A thrill ran through her at his tone and words. Something about that loving, playfully teasing tone always drilled right through her core. They chatted for nearly an hour before she realized how much time had passed.

"I miss you," she said.

"I miss you, too, sweetheart. I'm coming down this weekend."

"Okay."

Her eyes started to prickle. She both hated and loved feeling this vulnerable with him.

Now if she could just kick her hesitation out the window, life would be peachy.

Unfortunately, Maria's voice still came to her from time to time, usually when it'd been too long since Gabe had hit subspace, chattering at her and killing what strides her emotional self-esteem managed to make. Frequently it happened when she was lying alone in bed, curled around the pillow Bill used when staying with her.

"I love you, sweetheart," he said.

Now the prickle threatened to turn into a full-blown, tearful porcupine. "Love you, too, Daddy."

The word had slipped, unbidden, from her mouth.

He reached his fingers out toward the screen and smiled at her. She reached out, too, touching her screen.

"Sweet dreams, my good girl," he said.

"Sweet dreams." She clicked off the connection first. Then she drew her legs up, wrapping her arms around her knees, and cried.

Chapter Twenty-Five

The next Monday, Gabe ended her latest Skype session with Bill and struggled not to burst into tears. Once again she felt lonely. She'd had to go into work that day, her vacation time postponed yet again due to court delays on other cases and work issues that even Travis had to admit she needed to handle.

After having spent the weekend with Bill, she felt lonelier than ever without him.

How much longer can I do this to myself?

Tomorrow, however, began her ordered four days off. And he had depositions and court dates, meaning he couldn't take any time off.

She'd spent a wonderful weekend with Bill, which made her wonder even more why she kept him hanging on when she suspected she would never be able to get past everything to finally allow herself the ability to fully love anyone.

She also knew he wouldn't beg her to come visit him. She wouldn't ask that of him, either, to beg her. She wouldn't play games with him.

She wasn't even sure she was the right person for him. It didn't matter what he said, in many ways she felt too broken to be able to give him what she thought he needed.

Maybe I should just end it once and for all so he can find someone better than me.

The problem was, being with him not only felt right, she knew in her heart it *was* right. She could transfer up to the Sarasota or Tampa area. At the very least, he was only a three-hour car ride away if she stayed in Miami.

Now she was stuck with four days off that she didn't even want, courtesy of her boss. As she stared at the stack of folders she'd brought home with her, which were sitting on the corner of her table, she let out a disgusted snort.

Who am I kidding? I hate taking time off. I feel like I'm slacking.

Another of Maria's lessons still stubbornly slinking around in her brain.

Only losers relaxed. You had to work hard, all the time, to be successful.

She sat back and stared at her computer. Then she reached out and brought up her browser and logged in to Facebook. Now she had messages from Shayla, Leah, Laura—everyone.

Her friends.

She missed them. More than she ever thought she would. And, apparently, they'd all missed her. The munch had been that Sunday.

Being missed.

That was a new experience for her.

Jennifer's message from days earlier still sat there in her inbox.

She clicked on the message and read it.

Dear Gabe,

I don't want you to take this message the wrong way. Please, don't be mad at me. If you never want me to bring the subject up again, I won't, and I completely get it. I know what you said years ago about this, and believe me, I agonized about it for a long time, whether or not to send it. Maybe it's selfish of me, but I wouldn't feel right if I didn't at least pass the whole message along.

My mom told me that, two weeks ago, Aunt Maria was placed in a nursing home just outside of Chicago, because that's where Mom and Grandma are. Maria's got pretty severe Alzheimer's. I guess her place was really run-down and filthy. One of her neighbors called the city, who put her in the hospital until they found family. They've cleaned the place out and are putting everything up for sale to pay for her care. She's got practically no money left, I guess. My grandmother and mother were named her guardians by a judge in an emergency hearing.

When they cleaned her place out, my mom found some stuff, pictures and things, of your parents, and even some of you. She asked me to ask you if you want them. If you do, she said she'd be happy to ship everything to you, or to hold on to it if you wanted to come visit us and pick it up from her then.

Please, please don't be mad at me. I know you hate Maria. I'm no fan of hers, either. I just wanted to pass all the news along to you.

In case you want the information, she's in Willow Acres, room 424, bed B...

Gabe's finger hovered over the touch pad to delete the message, then she paused.

The old bat's in an ALF, huh?

Maybe that wasn't the most charitable thought in the world, but it was the best Gabe could come up with under the circumstances.

She closed her eyes. *It doesn't hurt to think for a moment.*

She thought.

Then she tapped out a reply.

((HUGS)) I'm not mad, I swear. Thank you for writing me. Yes, please tell your mom to send me the stuff. I appreciate it. Let me know the shipping costs and I'll be happy to reimburse her for it.

She sat back in her chair after sending the reply. Then she glanced at the time. It was a little after 9:00 p.m. She brought up another browser tab and typed into it, searching for flights from MIA to O'Hare and Midway.

She could be on one leaving Miami at 7:05 the next morning and arrive in O'Hare before lunchtime.

By the time she went to bed an hour later, she had already packed an overnight bag, laid out a set of clothes appropriate for cold Chicago March weather, and arranged for a rental car.

* * * *

While sitting at the gate the next morning, she texted Bill.
Last-minute trip out of town, just overnight.
He texted back a few minutes later.
Work?
She let out a silent snort. *No, I wish.*
A few moments later, *Stay safe, sweetheart. Let me know when you get there and get home.*

Melancholy washed over her. It'd be so easy to just ask. To open up and admit it. She wanted him.

Hell, she thought maybe she might need him a little.

I need to bury a few demons for good if I ever want my life to truly belong to me, she texted.

They'd just called her flight when he replied. *Hope it goes well, sweetie.*

Her eyes blurred and she had to blink the tears away. *Okay, dammit, he had to be all warm and fuzzy.*

Thanks, I'll keep you posted, she texted back.

Then she shut off her phone. The last thing she wanted to be doing was standing there crying her eyes out.

* * * *

Cold didn't describe the weather. Brutal, biting, insane was more like it.

At least it's not a fricking blizzard.

It brought back her childhood.

And not in a good way. She remembered plenty of cold mornings having to get dressed in the kitchen in front of the stove because Maria wouldn't turn on the heat unless the house was under sixty degrees.

After getting her rental car, she sent Bill a quick text that she was safely in Chicago. Fortunately, there wasn't any ice on the roads despite the bitter cold and overcast skies.

Yep. Florida rocks.

She followed the printed directions she'd prepared the night before from the airport to the nursing home. The young man at the front desk inside the front doors was very helpful with directions and instructions on how to access the locked ward where Maria now lived.

Inside, she stifled a snort.

Maria's on the chain.

She knew that wasn't a very charitable thought either, but it was the nicest one she could muster.

What she didn't expect was the way her stomach tightened, painfully so, her gut clenching as she watched the floor numbers light up on the elevator's control panel.

She'd walked out of Maria's house with several suitcases full of clothes, her books, photo albums, and the checkbook to the account that became hers when she turned eighteen. She had thirty-five thousand in the bank, give or take, and signed papers to report for basic training.

She'd never set eyes on Maria since then. In all honesty, she'd never expected to see the woman again.

Ever.

When the elevator opened into the floor's reception area, she stepped out and walked over to another manned desk. The nurse there was dressed in a scrub shirt adorned with cheerful cartoon cats in rainbow colors.

"I'm here to see Maria Villalobos, room 424."

The nurse tapped into her computer and smiled. "Yes, she should be in there. If not, staff can direct you to the social room."

"Thank you." When Gabe stepped over to the door the nurse pointed to, one of three leading from the reception area, the lock buzzed.

Gabe stifled another totally inappropriate and unpreventable snort of amusement.

Irony is a bitch, right up there with karma, apparently.

She had no trouble following the room numbers down and around the hallway. The facility was clean and smelled of disinfectant and oranges, but it certainly wasn't the newest or best. The linoleum tile floors were scrubbed, but the pattern worn and faded. The halls had been painted a light blue that might have been cheery at one time, but seemed fairly depressing now. The white chair rail running just under the handrail on the wall was dented and scuffed in several areas.

The placard next to room 424's door listed bed A's resident as one Arlene Smith. When Gabe stepped into the room, she didn't see anyone in bed A, which was closest to the door. The bedside table and shelves around bed A were filled with family pictures, cards, and a few knickknacks. Gabe could hear a TV playing on the other side of the room, apparently turned to the Weather Channel.

She walked through the room, past the white curtain with faded green paisley prints on it that separated the two areas. Her stomach rolled, her lungs didn't want to suck in air, and her feet threatened rebellion, to run out without facing the demon for good.

I am stronger than I know.

She took a deep breath and rounded the curtain. Maria lay on her back and looked tiny and dwarfed by the hospital bed. She had her head turned toward the small color TV that hung from a moveable arm attached to the wall.

Jim Cantore talked about how frigid it was in the Chicago area.

No shit, Sherlock.

Maria's rheumy blue eyes bore a glassy sheen.

Thinking maybe Maria hadn't noticed her entrance, Gabe cleared her throat.

Maria didn't blink.

When she started to step around the end of the bed, Gabe's feet finally overrode her brain's commands to keep moving.

In fact, her entire body froze.

The bedside table and shelves around Maria's area were full of stuffed animals. Some of them bore "Get Well Soon" messages, but as Gabe looked more closely, she could see there was nothing personal about the collection, as there was over on bed A's side of the room.

It slammed home exactly what it reminded her of, a child's hospital room, one who either had no family or whose family was poor, or who'd been through a horrifically newsworthy experience and had been inundated with presents, mostly from strangers who felt moved to offer something, anything, to assuage their own need to give, usually after seeing the child's story on TV.

The snort broke free from Gabe's throat.

Maria blinked.

Gabe walked around the bed and sat in the chair next to the TV. "Hello, Maria."

The woman blinked again and slowly swiveled her head on her pillow to stare at Gabe. "Hello."

Even her voice sounded different, faint.

Weak.

Not even remotely like the voice that had haunted and taunted her throughout the years.

Gabe swallowed, but pressed on. "Do you know who I am?"

Maria nodded.

"Who am I?"

Maria blinked and didn't answer at first. "You're that girl from the office. The one who checked me in. My sister said you might be back."

Her voice sounded strained, faded.

The voice of an old woman nearing the end of her life, who'd lost everything, including her mind.

A door lay before Gabe. One she knew she could kick closed and forever remain imprisoned within her own mind, or one she could walk through and nail shut behind her.

She stared at Maria. After a moment, she nodded. "That's right. How are you?"

"Okay."

Nothing else.

"So how is Gabriella doing?" Gabe asked.

"Who?"

"Your granddaughter, Gabriella. Peter's daughter."

Maria looked a little confused. "I think she's at school today. Do you know when she'll be home?"

Her teeth clacked shut, hard, against the scream forming in her throat. After a minute, she asked, "Who brought you all the stuffed animals?"

Maria's eyes, but not her head, looked up, as if trying to see the wall behind her through the top of her skull. "A girl brings them on a cart. She lets me pick one out when she comes."

Gabe nodded. "That's good."

Maria's eyes swiveled again, pausing on the TV before making it to Gabe once more. "Are you the girl from the office?"

She nodded. "That's right. I'm the girl from the office." She stood and shouldered her purse. "Anything you want me to tell anyone?"

The old woman let out a soft sigh. "Can you ask Paul to walk the dog?"

"Sure thing." That would be difficult, since her grandfather, Paul, had been dead for over forty years, and the dog longer than that.

On shaky legs Gabe wasn't sure would support her, she quickly headed out and forced herself not to punch the button by the exit more than once for the nurse to buzz her through.

"Where's the bathroom?" Gabe asked.

"Are you all right?"

She nodded.

The nurse pointed her to another door, this one unlocked, off the reception area. It opened onto a short hallway, leading to three unisex bathrooms.

Gabe locked herself into the last one and held on to the sink as she fought the urge to vomit.

* * * *

Back in her rental car, Gabe didn't feel anywhere close to ready to being able to safely drive quite yet. She needed a few minutes to calm down and let her nerves settle. Instead, she pulled her laptop out of her overnight bag and opened it. Lil Lobo and Max stared at her from inside their compartment on the side of the bag.

As she rooted around for her mobile hotspot, she realized she'd forgotten to pack her laptop charger.

Dammit.

Her original flight plans were to fly home tomorrow afternoon. Now she didn't want to wait. She wanted to get back to Miami tonight. There was no reason to stay here. She'd considered possibly coming back here again, but not now. There was no reason. Maria didn't know her, and Gabe didn't want to see her again. But if she were stuck there in Chicago overnight after all, her laptop didn't have that much of a charge left after having used it on the flight up.

She found the hotspot. First order of business, getting the flight changed. After logging in she found she could change flights, for a premium change fee, of course.

Screw it. It's just money.

She made the change, but she wouldn't be flying out until nearly seven that evening, leaving her several hours to wait with a laptop that was nearly dead.

I need a spare charger anyway.

Before she shut off her computer, she did a quick search. There was an Apple store at a mall not far from the nursing home. On her way back toward O'Hare, as a matter of fact.

Okay, that solves the problem.

She sent the map link to her phone, verified she had the directions, and then shut down the computer. Fortunately, the mall had a parking garage so it wasn't quite so miserable getting from her car inside. She quickly found the Apple store up on the second level and, fortunately, they had her charger in stock. She was standing just outside the doorway, trying to arrange how she was carrying everything, when she looked up.

Directly across the way was a Build-A-Bear store. And, looking down through the break in the walkways ringing the second level, she spotted a Sanrio store on the lower floor.

She'd had every intention of returning to the parking garage. In fact, that was the command she'd given her feet. So it surprised her when she walked around and across to the other side to stand inside the Build-A-Bear doorway.

One of the sales clerks welcomed her and gave her a smile but Gabe didn't answer, just smiled back. She walked around the edges of the store, looking at the doll clothes for sale. Five minutes later, she had three outfits for Max in hand, as well as two outfits designed for one of the mini animals they sold, which she thought would fit Lil Lobo.

Her next stop was the Sanrio store on the lower level, where she bought three different Hello Kitty iPhone cases.

She stopped for a late lunch and wandered the mall before returning to her car and heading for the airport. When she made it through security with over an hour left before her flight, she found herself a seat near an electric outlet and plugged her laptop in to charge. Then she dressed Max and Lil Lobo each in one of their new outfits before carefully tucking them back into her overnight bag.

Just below the surface she felt the constant prickle of tears threatening.

I won't give in. Not here.

Not until she was safely locked behind her own front door and could ignore the world for a while.

She damn sure wouldn't draw TSA's attention by bawling like a fucking baby in the middle of the airport. At least all the other voices, the recriminations, were gone. Silent.

Only one phrase softly drummed through her brain, and it felt more right than anything she'd ever felt in her life.

And there was only one person she wanted to say it to.

* * * *

She'd gassed up her car before leaving it parked in the long-term parking area at the airport. When she got in and locked the doors behind her, she pulled Lil Lobo and Max out and set them on the passenger seat. She'd held them all the way home, in her lap, on the plane.

But instead of heading south, toward Kendall and home, she pointed her car north. It was after one in the morning by the time she hit Alligator Alley. Part of her brain screamed at her to stop and think, to process, to let it out, but her self-control clamped down tightly and kept her calm, focused.

Driving.

A little before three thirty in the morning, she pulled into Bill's driveway and shut her car off. She shouldered her overnight bag and purse, grabbed her phone and the stuffed animals, and took a deep breath before marching up his front walk and ringing the doorbell.

Her pulse pounded in her throat as she stood there, waiting. She was just about to turn and bolt for the car when the front light flicked on. There was a momentary pause she knew was him checking the peephole before he quickly snapped the deadbolt open and threw the door wide.

He wore a T-shirt and shorts and a worried look. She instinctively knew the motion he made was him setting the gun down on the side table as he realized it was her and reached for her. "Gabe? What's wrong, sweetie?"

She had the stuffed animals clutched together in her left hand, the phone in her right. She held the phone up and turned it around, showing him the back. A cheerful, pink Hello Kitty pattern stared back at him.

"I'm *your* good girl," she whispered.

Then there were two, three of him standing in the doorway as her vision blurred from the tears and she broke down sobbing.

A moment later, she was inside, safely in his arms, enfolded in his embrace on the couch. He'd taken her bags and her phone from her and set them down somewhere, but she kept the stuffed animals tightly clutched against her as she finally let it all out.

The rage.

The anger.

The grief.

She screamed and cried until she lay hoarse and broken and empty in his arms and his shirt was sodden from her snot and tears and dawn was starting to cast a glow through the blinds covering the sliding glass doors.

He didn't speak. He kept his arms wrapped tightly around her, his face buried in her hair and his breath warm against her scalp.

When he sensed she'd finally cried herself out, he gently coaxed her to stand and led her to the bedroom. There, he had her sit on the edge of the bed.

"Stay here," he softly said.

She numbly nodded, beyond the ability to think right then.

He left the bedroom. She heard him briefly speak to someone on the phone, then the sound of him popping the magazine and ejecting the chambered round out of his gun before he walked back into the bedroom. He returned the gun to its place in the bedside table. Then he pulled off his shirt and shorts and dropped them to the floor.

Coaxing her to stand up again, he leaned over, patting first her right leg, then her left, so he could remove her shoes and socks. He unfastened her jeans and worked them and her panties off her. Next, her shirt, waiting while she transferred the stuffed animals from one hand to the other when he needed to get her arms out of the shirt. Her bra last.

After getting her situated in the bed, he climbed in next to her. When she rolled to face him, he once again enveloped her in his arms, the stuffed animals pressed between them.

He tenderly kissed her forehead. "Yes, sweetie, you are *my* very, very good girl. Go to sleep. I called in. I'm all yours today, or for as long as you need me. I promise, I'm not going anywhere."

Closing her eyes, she crashed into sleep.

Chapter Twenty-Six

When Gabe awoke, the bedroom TV was on, volume turned down so low she almost couldn't hear it. Her face was still tucked against Bill's shoulder. In sleep she'd draped a leg over his, wrapping herself around him.

He nuzzled the top of her head. "Good morning, sweetie."

"Morning?" She felt horrible, eyes swollen, mouth fuzzy, feeling hungover without even having had the benefit of alcohol.

"Well, afternoon. It's a little after one. Feeling better?"

She took a deep breath and let it out again before considering his question. "I don't know."

"Okay. That's a start. Do you feel like talking about it yet?"

She sniffled, her mind thinking back to where she was almost twenty-four hours earlier. "Yeah," she whispered.

He shifted position a little, propping himself up on one arm so he could face her. He unwedged Max and Lil Lobo from between them and sat them on her tummy. He fingered the stuffed animals' outfits. "Want to start here, or elsewhere?"

She looked into his face, but didn't read anything there except love and concern. He wasn't making fun of her, or light of what happened.

He really wanted to hear it.

She touched the shirt Max wore. "I needed a laptop charger."

Bill didn't comment. He patiently waited for her to continue.

"There was a Build-A-Bear store there in the mall, right across the way. And a Sanrio store. Right there, like it was meant to be."

Still no interruption.

Sniffling, she backed up and filled in the blanks about the message from her cousin, and flying up to visit Maria.

The stuffed animals on her grandmother's shelves and Maria's empty brain.

He reached out and stroked Max's head with one finger, but didn't say anything.

Forcing herself to look into his eyes, she said, "I made a choice."

He met her eyes, his head cocked to the side, but didn't speak.

"The past can't hurt me anymore if I don't let it. I thought I was in control, but it was always controlling me. I don't have to let it control me anymore."

He nodded, his gaze burning into hers. She could tell he wanted to say something, but sensed she wasn't done. He refused to lead the witness. He'd make her get it all out, once and for all.

"I saw they've got openings in the Sarasota office. I could transfer."

Now fear set in, hot, heavy, sending her heart pounding in her chest.

She could barely make herself say it, but she knew she had to. "I am *your* good girl, Daddy," she whispered. "If you still want me."

His expression softened, flowing, melting into a loving smile that started her crying again. He took the stuffed animals from her and set them on the bedside table before pulling her into his arms.

"Yes," he said into her ear, "of *course* I want you. I think I've wanted you from that first night we met at the munch. And yes, you are my good girl. You're my *very* good girl, and I am so, so proud of you."

She held on tightly, clinging to him, her tears this time not a fraction as intense as the night before, relishing the way he held her, firmly, not letting go of her until he was ready to do so. "You belong to me, sweetie, and you're my very, *very* good girl. Always."

Eventually, he rolled her onto his back and palmed her cheeks. "Tell me what you want, sweetheart. You need to say it."

"I want to be with you, Sir."

He brushed at her tears with his thumbs. "I want to be with you, too. We don't have to do it like that if you don't want to, though."

"I want to, Sir."

When he kissed her, she felt the rest of her grief and pain swept away like dead leaves ahead of a stiff breeze. Her soul felt clean, fresh, ready.

She felt ready.

Even better, for the first time she could remember in all of her adult life, she knew what true peace felt like, peace at a cellular level, of being at ease and knowing everything would be all right.

He nodded. "We'll take it slow, okay? Step by step. I don't want to screw this up. I don't need anything from this relationship except you. So whatever form our relationship needs to take to make you happy, I'm good with that. Vanilla, kinky, something in between, I don't care, as long as we're together. Understand?"

She nodded. "Yes, Sir."

The corner of his mouth quirked in a smile, amused. "Then again, maybe I'll have you call me that all the time."

"I hope so, Sir."

* * * *

They were both hungry, but she wanted a shower before anything else happened. With the bathroom steaming up around them, they stepped into the shower in the master bathroom and he took his time washing her, his lips exploring her flesh without even making any overt sexual advances.

It still made her wet. Maybe even more than had he just staked his ownership of her right off the bat with his cock.

He nibbled on her ear. "What's wrong, sweetie?"

She nipped at his throat. "You got me horny, Sir."

"Oh. Did I?"

She didn't even need to look to see his smile because his tone of voice told her everything she needed to know. "Yes, Sir."

He knelt in front of her, making her brace her hands on his shoulders. Then his lips closed on her clit, his tongue flicking as he licked and sucked on her. It took him less than a minute to drive her hard and fast over the edge with an orgasm that felt so good and so sweet it started her tears again.

When he stood up to hold her against him, he slowly rocked her. "Are you really all right?"

"Better than I've ever been."

He reached between her legs, two fingers effortlessly slipping along her clit and into her soaked pussy. She spread them wider, not resisting when he turned her around to face the wall. She braced herself with her hands against the cool tile and moaned when she felt him rub the head of his cock up and down her slit.

When he sank his cock inside her, she moaned again, louder, happy to feel him fucking her.

He took his time, slowly stroking his cock in and out as he played with her clit with one hand. "Give me another one, sweetie. I won't come until you do."

She was so horny she thought she could hump a doorknob and get off. It didn't take him long to make her come a second time, and that was when he started really fucking her, hard and fast until he let out a long, satisfied moan before burying his cock deep inside her.

He pressed himself along her back, kissing her shoulder. "That's how every day should start."

She hooked an arm around him, not wanting to let go. "Absolutely."

He nipped, a little bit of teeth making her pleasantly shiver. "What was that?"

She grinned. "Absolutely, Sir."

"Much better."

* * * *

After breakfast, they returned home and to the bedroom. He stopped by the bathroom to wash up first before joining her on the bed. He tied her in a chest harness that made her breasts jut out and held her wrists behind her back. He laid on the bed, on his back, knees bent.

"Sit on my cock, sweetheart." With his help staying balanced, she managed to swing a leg over him without tumbling off the bed and slowly settled her dripping cunt down over his stiff cock. The position left her open to his view, able to reach her clit and nipples with his fingers, which he tweaked in turn, making her moan.

He grinned and held up the Hitachi. "Get comfy, sweetheart."

Her eyes widened in surprise as he flicked the vibrator on and pressed it against her exposed clit.

She let out a cry, barely able to stay upright as the orgasm drilled through her brain. With his cock buried all the way to the hilt inside her, it only served to intensify the sensation, pressing against her G-spot with every contraction her muscles made.

He pulled the vibrator away after a moment, giving her time to catch her breath. "Holy crap, that was hotter than hell. That is definitely something going into our regular play rotation. Let's do it again!"

Before she could object, he'd pressed the buzzing Hitachi against her clit again. As before, her body responded, out of her control, this time him keeping her coming a little longer, until she was gasping and shaky and afraid she might pass out.

He reached up with his free hand and plucked at her nipples, back and forth, getting them hard and erect and making them ache in a deliciously good way that seemed hard-wired straight to her clit.

"That's what I wanted to see." He turned off the vibrator and reached over to the bedside table, where he pulled out a set of nipple clamps. He held them up. "You want to take these for me, don't you, sweetheart?"

It was hard to nod. She felt the soft blanket of subspace wrapped around her. She'd do any and everything he wanted. "Yes, Daddy."

"Ask me."

"Daddy, please use your nipple clamps on me."

"Oh, such a good girl!"

She let out little yips as he clamped them to her nipples. A chain hung between them. He hooked a finger over it as he picked up the Hitachi again with his other hand. "Let's continue, shall we?" He turned the vibrator on. "My good girl needs to come."

He pressed the vibrator against her clit at the same time he lightly tugged on the chain.

She screamed, unable to keep her eyes open through the waves of pleasure swirling around her, dragging her down like a vortex of electrified nerves.

"Come," he sternly ordered. "Keep coming for me. Don't you dare stop until I tell you to."

The tears came, and she didn't know from where. It felt like her brain's connection to her body had short-circuited somewhere. White-hot pleasure seared every fiber of her being, the delicious tug on her nipples only making the overwhelming buzz from the vibrator that much better.

"Come for me, sweetheart. Keep squeezing my cock like that. Such a good girl."

She threw her head back, long series of wordless moans competing with her lungs for breath. She wasn't sure how she could survive this if he didn't stop soon.

And her greatest fear was that he would stop.

She gasped again when he pulled the vibrator away from her clit, this time trying to catch her breath.

"Look at me."

She forced her eyes open and tried to focus on him.

"Who's my good little sex toy?"

"I am, Sir."

"Who's going to let me fuck her however I want, and whenever I want?"

"Me, Sir."

He tugged on the nipple clamp chain. *How can something painful feel sooo fucking good?*

She didn't know and didn't care, but she was a lot closer now to understanding how some people enjoyed being beaten. If their partners could make them feel like this, she got it.

Totally.

"Who's going to beg me to let her suck my cock every morning when I wake up with a hard-on?"

"Me, Sir!"

As his sexily evil grin spread, she knew she was lost and welcomed it.

"Who wants to worship my cock and balls and ass right now?"

"Me, Sir!"

He let go of the chain, put down the vibrator, and helped her lean to the side enough that she could get a leg up and let him slide free. His stiff cock withdrew from her cunt, still hard and ready.

He scooted farther up the bed, spreading his legs and drawing them up to his chest. It left his cock, balls, and the crack of his ass exposed to her. "Beg me."

"Please, Sir, can I worship your cock and balls and ass?"

"Oh, such a good girl. Of course you can."

It was a little clumsy at first, with her hands behind her back, but she got herself flopped down onto the bed and buried her face between his legs, engulfing his cock first, all the way to the root.

She loved tasting herself on him, worked her way down to his balls, and laved them with her tongue.

His voice sounded hoarse, strained. "Lower, sweetheart." He grabbed his cheeks and spread them. Now she understood why he'd washed up and she had a moment to think about how considerate he was before working her tongue in there.

It was his turn to rock his hips in time with her movements. "Yes, sweetheart. Just like that."

She shoved her tongue against his rim, up to his taint, sucked on his balls and licked his cock before going down again. Up and down, until he was moaning.

"Suck my cock, baby. Drain my balls."

She dove onto it as he grabbed her hair and started fucking her mouth, controlling her, using her. It was hard to say who moaned louder, her or him when he exploded, and she eagerly began swallowing every drop of cum he pumped out.

He lay there for a moment, catching his breath, his fingers still buried in her hair. Then she felt him move and the vibrator clicked on again. He made her release his cock and rolled her onto her back. "Such a good girl," he said. He kissed her, pressing the Hitachi against her, sliding the attachment deep inside her cunt and holding it in place.

She screamed, Bill swallowing every last sound she made, fucking her with the Hitachi. He lifted his head. "Fuck it, sweetheart. Fuck that thing." He sat up and grabbed the chain and tugged, reminding her why her nipples were deliciously hurting and making her cry out again.

He leaned in, voice deep, stern. "Fuck that thing. Show me what a good girl you are for me."

She stared up into his eyes, her hips rocking, unable to stop herself, following his orders as best she could.

His gaze narrowed, lips curling in *that* smile. "Who's going to fuck that vibrator all day long if I order her to?"

"Me, Sir."

He nipped her lower lip. "That's right, sweetheart. You are my beautiful girl and my perfect little toy and I'm going to use you any way, any time, any how I want. And you want me to do that, don't you?"

"Yes, Sir."

"Ask me."

Another wave rolled through her. "I...I'm your little toy and I want you to use me however you want and whenever you want."

He grinned. "Close enough." He lifted the chain, pulling her nipples. "One more and I'll let you stop coming. Come!"

She didn't know how her body could even process the order. Sensory overload hit her, her body beyond her control and his words drilling right to the center of her nervous system. Her cunt contracted around the vibrator and she gave up trying to keep her eyes open as she cried out.

After he was satisfied she'd obeyed, he shut off the vibrator and withdrew it from her. Then he gently removed the nipple clamps. Rolling her onto her side and off her hands, he held her cradled against him. "And that, sweetheart, is me. The real me. Are you sure you still want me?"

Still slick with her tears, she nuzzled her face against his chest. "Yes, Daddy. I love you and want you."

He let out what sounded like a relieved sigh. "That's my good girl. My sweet, beautiful girl."

Chapter Twenty-Seven

Bill went with Gabe when she returned home to Miami a couple of days later to begin the process of moving. She'd asked for, and received, another week's vacation.

She'd figure out how to break the news to Walker that she was requesting a transfer once she got the move mostly completed. Bill assured her even if something fell through, she could likely get a job with Sarasota or Charlotte counties.

Or even not work, if she so chose.

He left it up to her to decide that, and she loved him even more for it.

When she unlocked her door, a note under it on the other side surprised her. It was from her next-door neighbor, who had taken receipt of packages for her in the past.

Hi, Gabe. UPS brought several large boxes for you. I have them for you because I was afraid they might get stolen. If I'm not home, call my cell.
Delores

Bill read the note over her shoulder. "Boxes?"

"Huh." She went next door and knocked, Bill following her.

"Just a minute." A moment later, Delores opened the door. She was a widowed retiree who always made cookies for everyone on their floor during holidays. "Oh, Gabe. There you are."

Gabe put her hands on her hips. "How many times have I told you to look through the peephole? You have to be more careful, even in our building."

Delores opened the door wider and waved her off. "I heard you come home, heard your voice. I suspected it was you." She broadly smiled. "And who is this? Introduce me, young lady."

Gabe felt a little heat wash through her face. "Delores Isaac, this is Bill Thomas." She looked up at him. "He's my boyfriend."

Delores' face beamed. "Boyfriend? You never told me you had a boyfriend," she scolded, reaching for his arm. "Well, come in, come in!"

Bill looked bemused and let the woman lead him inside her apartment. "Nice to meet you, Delores."

"You think you're getting out of here before I have a chance to talk to you, think again. I'm going to hold her boxes hostage until you have at least a few cookies."

She didn't let go of his arm until she'd marched him over to the eat-in counter at her kitchen and made him sit on one of the barstools. Delores had a larger unit than Gabe's, with two bedrooms, two bathrooms, and a larger great room area. Sometimes her children or grandchildren came down from up north to stay with her, but the independent woman steadfastly refused their attempts to get her to move back north now that she was widowed.

Gabe snickered as Bill threw a "rescue me" look at her over his shoulder. She just shrugged and followed them to the counter. She was used to Delores taking charge and keeping her there for friendly chats.

Okay, so maybe she is another friend. She'd never thought about her neighbor in that way before, but realized she was yet another instance of Walker being right. She had way more friends than she realized, she'd just had her head shoved so far up her ass before that she couldn't recognize them as such.

Delores took nearly half an hour to decide she was adequately impressed by Bill's resume and background to declare him a suitable boyfriend for Gabe. Only after they'd both had some cookies and a cup of tea did Delores finally let them take the five large, heavy boxes back to Gabe's unit. Gabe felt a chill run through her when she saw the return label, from Jennifer's mother.

"What's in them?" Bill asked.

"I don't know," she softly said, afraid to open them.

"Who sent them?"

"My...I guess she's my cousin. Maria's sister's daughter. Jennifer's mom."

"Ah." He stared at the boxes for a moment before pulling her into his arms. "You want me to open them for you?"

"No, I guess I should do it." She looked up into his face. "Can you help me, though?"

"Of course I'll help you, sweetheart. I'll do anything you want."

She snuggled safely in his embrace again. "I don't know what they found in Maria's house. I took every picture and photo album I had of my parents when I left." She let out a snort and buried her face against his chest again. "Not like I had any mementoes."

"Then let's do this. Let's go grab some groceries, order a pizza, and then get comfy in the living room before we handle these."

"Okay." She lifted her head again. "I like that plan."

"I hoped you would."

* * * *

It was nearly two hours later when they finally got around to opening the boxes. She was dressed in nothing but one of Bill's T-shirts, had a tummy full of pizza, and was on her first bottle of the evening of hard apple cider.

Bill held the box cutter, and with her sitting close at his side, he carefully slit open the first box. She peered around him as he lifted out photo albums, loose photos, and files full of papers.

She started with the papers. She was shocked to see Maria had saved many of her school papers, all the way back to when she'd first came to live with her.

And even stuff from before, that her parents must have saved.

Report cards, scholastic award certificates, Honor Society papers.

She didn't know how she felt about that, the warmth from Bill at her side barely counteracting the chill in her soul.

Setting those aside, she looked at the first photo album. As she thumbed through it, she realized it must have been one Maria had kept of her dad when he was a kid. She quickly set it aside to go through later when she felt the tears threatening. Another photo album, again documenting her father's childhood. And more folders containing some of his school papers.

By the time they'd finished with that box twenty minutes later, Bill had already gotten Gabe a hand towel from the bathroom for her to use to blow her nose. She was beyond the tissue phase.

He repacked the first box and moved it to the side before pulling the second box close. It, too, was filled with photo albums, papers, and at the bottom something that threatened to crush her.

Her baby book.

She couldn't take it from Bill.

"Do you want me to put it back, sweetheart?" he softly asked.

She shook her head.

"Do you want me to look through it for you?"

She nodded and laid her head against his shoulder after blowing her nose again.

He opened it, smiling as he stared at her baby picture. "You were adorable even as a newborn."

She shrugged, not trusting her voice to respond. There was even a picture of her as a toddler, holding Bear.

As far as she knew, it was the only picture she had of Bear, unless there were more in some of the albums.

He continued paging through it, stopping when he reached age eight and she put her hand on top of his as she leaned forward.

The handwriting had changed. Under age eight, Maria's prim and proper script had taken over. A notation about the date of her parents' deaths, followed by a notation about her new school.

She slowly turned the page.

Maria had faithfully continued to fill out the baby book details, all the way up to her graduation, including annual school pictures.

Gabe took the book from him and pulled it into her lap, going back to age eight and slowly working her way to her teen years again. Nowhere, of course, did it mention the beatings. There was, however, a notation at age nine about her learning how to crochet.

She has beautiful technique.

She didn't realize she was sobbing until Bill took the book from her and pulled her into his lap, cradling her head against him as she cried.

"I don't get it," she eventually whispered. "I don't understand how she could do that to me and then keep my baby book up to date. I didn't even know she had that, or any of this other stuff."

He pressed a kiss to her forehead. "You know how it works, sweetheart. You know how abusers can be. They don't make sense."

"All my life, I'd painted her out to be a monster."

"She *was* a monster. Don't ever forget that. You bear the scars to remind you of that."

"I could never forgive her. All these years."

"You don't have to forgive her. You also don't have to give her any more energy or time."

"I've always heard forgiveness is for the one doing the forgiving."

"Maybe for some, but it's not a law or anything."

She stared at the box. "What else is in there?"

There were a couple of picture albums that had been her mom's. She watched as Bill thumbed through it slowly, giving her time to stare at people who were mostly strangers to her. Fortunately, when she looked, some of the pictures did have notations on their backs.

It was strange seeing pictures of her mom as a young woman. As a child.

Gabe realized she looked exactly like her mom, something she'd never thought about before.

Bill opened the baby book again so they could compare her school pictures to pictures of her mom.

"No wonder Maria hated me," she said. "I reminded her of the woman she blamed for all her problems."

"Stop," he scolded. "Don't excuse what she did."

"I'm not. I'm just trying to…understand it. Make sense of it."

"Why? She harmed you. If she wasn't batshit crazy, I'd go give her a piece of my mind."

"It likely wouldn't have made any difference," Gabe said as she put the baby book aside again. "She thought she was doing the right thing. Whatever her reasons were, she thought they were justified."

"Did she beat your dad?"

"I don't know. I never asked her. I can't believe he would have put it in his will to give her custody of me if she had. I have no memories of my parents ever spanking me, much less doing to me what she did."

Box three contained more of her mother's things, including a new, padded envelope with handwriting on the front.

We found these with the albums, and it looks like your mom is wearing some of them in a few of the pictures, and they were in a plastic baggie, so I thought it best you have them.

She let Bill open it. Inside, they found a man's and woman's wedding band, a small engagement ring, several pairs of earrings, a necklace with a small emerald and diamond pendant on it, and a high school class ring with her mom's name engraved inside it.

She stared at the jewelry lying in his hands. "I never knew she had any of these," she said.

"Did you ever go through her jewelry box?"

"Are you kidding? I *never* went in her room. Not unless I was specifically told to go in there for some reason. That was an instant beating. I think that was the first beating she ever gave me, five with a strap for going where I didn't have permission. I damn sure wouldn't go in her jewelry box."

"Sorry, sweetheart."

Box four devastated her. On the top, sealed in an old, large zip-top plastic baggie and protected from dust over the years, lay Bear.

She reached out with trembling hands and carefully lifted him from the box, her vision doubling, tripling as she easily ripped open the baggie and removed him.

Then, with him clutched against her chest, she buried her head in Bill's lap and cried.

* * * *

Bill knew the only thing he could do was sit there, hold her, and let her do what she needed to do to heal. And she would heal. The progress she'd already made over their past several months together, along with confronting Maria, had brought about massive changes in her.

For the better.

This new development, he guessed, would put her firmly on the road to healing.

He stroked her hair as she cried, waiting her out, knowing it would take as long as it took and refusing to be an asshole about it. She needed to cry, to purge the pain from her system for good. There would likely be many more tears over the next weeks, and maybe even months, as she finished processing everything.

But he could already see the positive changes in her. So different from when they first met that night at the munch, so open and happy and laughing. Willing to take time for herself, guilt-free, and willing to open herself to friendships.

And now she had one missing piece, a large honking piece, of her childhood back.

It took her a while to finally cry herself out. Red-eyed and puffy-nosed, she held the bear sitting up on her chest as her fingers roamed all over him, as if still unsure he was real.

"I don't think Max or Lil Lobo will be jealous," he said.

She let out a tiny laugh. "No," she said, her voice fragile and thin. "They won't. They'll like Bear."

"I don't have any answers for you, sweetheart," he said. "Are you sure you want to keep going tonight?"

"Yes, Sir," she whispered. "I want to finish going through them."

He struggled against the erection threatening to form. He definitely didn't want to be an asshole, but he couldn't deny nothing turned his crank harder and faster than her totally putting herself in his hands like that.

Trusting him.

Letting go and letting him handle things.

He knew how difficult it was for her to get to this point, and he didn't take it for granted. He would *never* take it, or her, for granted.

Bear had apparently been the worst of the revelations. That box, and the last, had held more photos, loose and in albums, and papers, including her parents' high school and college diplomas, their wedding photo album, and several handwritten journals her mom had kept throughout college and the early days of her marriage to Gabe's father.

To his relief, Gabe opted to wait to go through those last things until later, when she felt strong enough to do it. Once he had everything tucked back into the boxes except Bear, which she wouldn't let go of, he helped her to her feet.

"Time for bed, sweetheart."

She looked like a child, with her arms wrapped around the stuffed bear. Gabe nodded.

He kissed her on the forehead. "Let's snuggle in front of the TV, okay?"

She nodded.

He gently turned her around and pointed her at the bedroom before he lightly patted her on the rump. "Go on. I'll be right there."

She went.

He let out a sigh. After picking up their empty cider bottles and making sure the front door was locked, he followed her into the bedroom.

He found her, still in the T-shirt, lying on her right side and facing the center of the bed. He undressed and climbed in with her, waiting until she was snuggled against him, an arm draped over his chest, to grab the remote and turn on the TV.

He kissed the top of her head. "Good night, sweetheart. We'll talk in the morning and see how you're feeling. Okay?"

"Thank you, Daddy."

Whereas "Sir" hardened his cock, "Daddy" always softened his heart to the point of melting. He knew she joked about his smile and what it could do to her.

All she had to do was call him "Daddy" and she could make him do anything she wanted him to.

And he loved it. Especially because she didn't seem to realize that he might be her Dominant, but she wielded absolute and total control of his heart.

"Love you, sweetheart."

"Love you, too, Daddy," she mumbled, already dropping into an exhausted, mentally scalded sleep.

He knew sleep wouldn't be soon in coming for him, however. Too many things ran through his mind, despite what he'd said to her earlier.

He also wanted to know why Maria would take a child's beloved toy from her, and yet save it. Was it because her own child had given it to Gabe? Had Maria really taken things out on Gabe in her anger over Gabe's mom?

No, it didn't matter because it couldn't be changed. But it ate at him. The pain, Gabe's pain, was one thing he couldn't fix for her. And it was the thing he desperately wished he could.

All he knew was he would spend the rest of their lives together trying to make the best life, the happiest life possible for her.

And if anyone they knew didn't think he was "Domly" enough because of it, they could go fuck themselves, as far as he was concerned.

She was his, and he would love and protect her, in his way, the best way for her.

No matter what.

Chapter Twenty-Eight

Today was Saturday, and neither of them had to work. That meant dinner at Sigalo's and a night at the club with their friends.

When Gabe awoke that morning, she realized Bill was already in the kitchen. From the delicious aroma filling the house, she knew he had the coffee going.

She grabbed his robe and pulled it on before hurrying out to the kitchen. There, she slid her arms around his waist from behind and did her best not to slam him into the counter.

He laughed. "Good morning, sweetie."

She kissed his back, between his shoulder blades. "Good morning, Daddy."

She didn't care why, but it felt right calling him that, and he didn't object. It felt less formal than *Sir*, but still a title, in a way.

Daddy's good girl.

Even thinking about the way he said it sent the good kind of shivers up and down her spine, usually ending somewhere in the vicinity of her clit and making her panties damp. He just had that way about him.

"Did you take my robe again?" His tone sounded full of amused mirth.

She kept her arms wrapped around him from behind. "Yes, Daddy."

"Chilly? You want me to bump the AC up a little warmer?"

"Not really. I like wearing it because it smells like you."

That was when he turned and draped his arms around her. He smiled down at her, the lines on the outsides of his hazel eyes crinkling. "Guess I'll need to get another robe and switch them off from time to time, huh?"

Still looking up into his face, she rested her chin against his chest. "Uh-huh."

The past month had been the best of her life, time blurring way too fast for her liking. She was settled into her new office, getting to know her coworkers there.

Making friends with them.

When Walker called her to check on her, he'd asked her if she'd sent a body double in her place.

"Why?"

"Because your new boss says you're the happiest, friendliest agent he's ever had working for him."

"I have a reason to be happy."

Boy, did she ever.

Her attention snapped into focus as Bill's expression turned serious. "I need to ask you something. And *no* is a perfectly acceptable answer and won't change anything between us. I need you to be honest with me, all right?"

Chilling fear slowly started to wash though her. "Okay, Daddy."

He gently pushed her back a step so he could take both her hands in his and bring them up to his lips, kissing them. "Also acceptable is wanting time to consider this before answering me. Or asking me to ask again later. All right?"

She nodded.

"I love you. I'd honestly begun to think, before I met you, that I'd had my one chance at happiness in this life. I never thought I'd ever have it again." He gathered both her hands in one of his and reached behind him, pulling open a drawer. From it, he removed a box and opened it. Inside lay a small, heart-shaped pendant lined with little pieces of blue topaz. "I know we aren't like some of our friends, but I'd like to take a page from their playbook. I'm well aware of your feelings on marriage. And I know we don't do collars or anything like they do, but I'd like to have a small commitment ceremony in front of them some night, if you're okay with that."

The fear immediately transformed into a tearful flood of overwhelming emotions she couldn't process, much less verbalize. She nodded her head, hard, and threw her arms around him.

He softly chuckled as he embraced her. "That's a yes, I take it?"

"Yes, Daddy," she whispered into his shoulder. "Please. I would love that."

He kissed the top of her head and she held her hair out of the way as he draped the delicate gold chain around her neck and fastened it.

Then he wrapped his arms around her from behind and kissed the nape of her neck. "And I'd like to put it on the table that if you ever decide to change your mind about marriage, let me know. I'm happy to have you in my life however you want to be here. I'll never push you for anything more than you're ready and willing to give me. I will follow your lead on that."

She turned in his arms and looked up at him. Knowing the only person with the ability to keep her out of her emotional prison was herself, she took a deep breath. In a tiny voice, she forced herself to say, "Loren's a notary. She married Tilly and Landry. And she performed Shay and Tony's ceremony."

His hazel gaze searched her face, the suspense killing her until he slowly nodded. A sweet smile curved his lips.

The smile. The smile she realized would make her want to do anything if he'd just keep smiling like *that*. "I'll talk to her tonight, then. Everyone is supposed to be at the club next week for Seth and Leah's whip class."

Gabe nodded.

He stepped back and knelt on one knee, taking her hands in his again. "Then next Saturday night, sweetheart, will you please marry me?"

In her mind, the prison walls shattered into dust, carried away on the wind. She could never go back to the way she was, years of loneliness and isolation.

She didn't *want* to go back. She wanted to move forward.

With him.

She nodded, her vision doubling, tripling as she started crying. "Yes, Daddy. Please."

"Aww, sweetheart." He stood and pulled her close again, slowly rocking her as he held her. "Are you sure? I'd rather wait than have you do it just because it's what you think you should do."

"I'm sure, Daddy," she said. "I've never been more sure of anything in my entire life. These are good tears, I swear."

As she closed her eyes, her cheek pressed against his chest and listening to the sound of his heart beating in her ear, she realized that since returning from Chicago she hadn't once heard even the faintest echo of any of Maria's recriminations.

* * * *

The bottom dropped out of the sky on their way to the club. Despite Tilly's beautiful outfit, a long, emerald green gypsy skirt and white peasant blouse, she let out the most unladylike of epithets as she waited for the light to turn green. "Fucking goddamn finicky Florida weather."

Leah let out a giggle and turned to stare into the backseat where Gabe sat with Clarisse. "Hey, I heard rain on a wedding day is good luck."

"Then we must be the luckiest motherfuckers on the face of the goddamned planet every summer," Tilly grumbled as she let off the brake when the light finally changed. "It's only March. Rainy season is still a good two months away yet."

Loren, Shayla, and Laura were already at the club, finishing the preparations there. Tony, Cris, Landry, and Rob were in charge of Bill and making sure he got to the club on time, in one piece, and sober. No one knew what the bachelor party the night before had entailed, except that it had happened out in the Gulf. Mac and Sully had taken Bill and the others out for the evening on their boat, and had promised Gabe there wouldn't be any strippers or loose women.

Of course, that promise had been more for Tilly's benefit, since she'd promised to castrate anyone who considered bringing other women into the equation for the party.

That past Monday, Gabe had put in for a couple of days off, the Monday and Tuesday after the weekend. Walker had called her on her work cell before she'd even made it from her supervisor's office to her desk, asking if she'd sustained a head injury, or been abducted by alien pod people, or something like that. When she told him about her impending nuptials, he'd gone uncharacteristically silent.

"You still there?" she asked.

"Yeah. Congratulations."

"What's wrong?"

"Well, why the hell didn't you invite me? Am I still on your shit list from making you take vacation time? Like I said, I consider you a friend."

She felt a little red in the face. "He just proposed to me on Saturday, and we're doing it next Saturday. I haven't really had a chance to tell anyone."

"Same question, Gabe. What the hell? I thought we were friends."

She closed her door and sat down at her desk. She didn't want to lie and say they were eloping. "We are. It's just... It's going to be held at a private club. I'm not sure you'd approve or be comfortable there."

"What kind of club?"

"This between you and me as friends, or me and a former boss?"

She heard his sigh. "Friends. Off the books."

"It's a...a kind of social club."

"Swinger?"

"No!" She felt immediately ashamed over the way she said it considering she'd met some very nice swingers since joining the club. "No," she said again, "but…it's an alternative lifestyle group."

He let out a long laugh. "*Fifty Shades* sort of stuff?"

She felt fifty shades of red in the face, but she mumbled, "Yeah. Kind of. Not really, but close enough."

More laughter. She heard his voice drop in volume. "Gabe, let me tell you something. You're not the first person, or the last, to be involved in…*that*. I am no stranger to consensual alternative lifestyles, for chrissake. E-mail me the deets. Private e-mail," he clarified, not that he needed to. "My *girl* and I would be honored to attend. If it's in Sarasota, I'm guessing it's at the Venture? We've been members there for years. Why do you think we have a condo in Sarasota of all places?"

She blinked, stammered for an answer, and finally said, "Oh. Um, yes, it is. Okay then. We'd be glad to have you there."

"You know, off the books and friend to friend, I sensed something that day at the initial task force meeting. Something between you and Bill Thomas. I didn't know what it was, but for what it's worth, I'm glad it turned out to be something good for you both. You deserve this. You deserve happiness. You've been unhappy for as long as I've known you, and you're too good a person not to have someone good in your life."

She felt like crying. Did this mean she really did have emotions buried somewhere deep inside that were finally coming out? "Thank you."

"Hey, just out of curiosity, one question. As friends."

"Sure."

He laughed. "Who's on top?"

Laughing felt good. Until now, she didn't realize how little of it she'd done over the years. "I guess you'll find out next Saturday."

Tilly pulled the SUV into the club's parking lot, forcing Gabe's mind back to the present. The week had been a blur of activity of getting a marriage license and making arrangements, all while working. They would tell their vanilla friends and coworkers that they eloped, and invite them all to a reception party at some point.

Of course, some of their kinky friends would be there, too, and keep their secret about the real wedding.

Last night, the women had all stayed at Leah's house to help each other get ready today after a long brunch and hair and nail appointments.

Loren's car sat parked in the club's lot, as was Laura's truck. The women waited inside the vehicle for a few minutes with the engine running until the rain slacked off enough they could dash through the parking lot and make it inside without getting soaked.

Loren, Shayla, and Laura immediately converged on Gabe. "Holy crap, we were worried you'd get soaked," Loren said as she examined Gabe's outfit. Gabe had left her outfit selection up to Bill. He'd chosen a deep purple sundress with black embroidery on it. One with a back that didn't come too low, plus he'd told her to wear her hair loose, meaning it hung down well past her shoulders.

She loved him for the choice, although lately, it'd been very easy to ignore the stubborn pangs of self-consciousness that threatened to dampen her enthusiasm for public play with him at the club.

All she needed to do was focus on his voice, on his eyes, and the feel of his fist in her hair, and she would find herself quickly spinning down into subspace.

When that happened, nothing else mattered but Bill. The world ended just outside the space he occupied when he took control.

"Are the guys here yet?" Gabe asked.

"Don't you worry about that," Tilly assured her. "They will be here or they will face my wrath."

"Holy crap," Laura muttered. "I damn sure wouldn't want to face her wrath."

"Exactly," Tilly said. "So don't worry."

Gabe walked over to the tables set up on the social side of the club. "Wow, that's beautiful!" The cake, three tiers of marbled vanilla and chocolate cake frosted in buttercream, was decorated in beautiful purple-and-green flowers.

She felt tears starting and quickly sniffled them back. They'd assured her the mascara and eye liner was waterproof, but she didn't want to risk it.

"Like it?" Laura asked from just behind her.

"It's gorgeous."

On the top, she noticed, a pair of bride and groom bears.

She fanned her face as she turned away. "Okay, I shouldn't have seen that yet. I'm going to cry."

"What? The cake?"

"The bears," she whispered. Bill had warned her that he'd picked out a special topper for the cake.

She should have known.

And it was absolutely perfect.

"Who made her cry already?" Tilly yelled from where she was helping Loren make a few adjustments to the decorated arbor on the other side of the room. "I will *absolutely* kick some freaking ass if her makeup gets ruined before the wedding."

Laura put her hands on Gabe's shoulders and gently steered her away from the tables. "It's okay. She just saw the cake, that's all."

Tilly put her hands on her hips. "Don't make me blindfold you, kiddo. No tears allowed before the ceremony, happy or otherwise." She considered what she said. "Those *were* happy tears, right?"

Gabe nodded. Tilly had come to be one of her closest friends. "Yes, *very* happy tears."

Tilly nodded back. "Good. Because I don't want to kick a Charlotte County detective's ass. Might not be good for me, you know?"

Chapter Twenty-Nine

Bill and the other men hadn't arrived yet, although there was still nearly an hour before the wedding was to start, when Travis Walker and his wife arrived. She wore a beautiful silver choker necklace around her throat.

Gabe felt a little nervous when they walked over, but his playful smile put her at ease.

"If I'd known all it took to get you to relax was to introduce you to some of my other friends, I would have ordered you to take a vacation years ago." He opened his arms to her. "May I?"

She nodded, gratefully accepting his embrace.

Leah's voice rang out from across the room. "Trav, Jill! What are you doing here?"

She swept in and hugged both of them.

"You know them?" Gabe asked.

Leah nodded. "We've been friends for years..." Her eyes widened. "Oh, my god." She laughed. "You worked with Travis in Miami?"

He grinned. "Yep. Sucked to lose her to you guys, but I'm glad she's happy."

Gabe was about to respond when the door opened again. Bill, followed by the other men, walked through.

She felt her heart thrum in her chest at the sight of him. Black jeans, and a black button-up shirt. Like a piece of iron to a magnet, she wanted to drift over to him and sink into his arms.

"What part of 'call us when you're on the way' did I not make clear?" Tilly scolded them.

Bill shrugged and hooked a thumb over his shoulder at the others. "Blame your guys. No one passed that message to me." But his eyes never left Gabe's. When he stepped up to her side, she automatically pressed against him as his left arm settled around her shoulders.

Travis grinned. "And now I have the answer to my question," he said.

Bill shook with Travis and his wife. "What question?"

Gabe felt her face heat. "Never mind, Sir."

Travis laughed. "*That* question."

Bill kissed the top of Gabe's head. "Who's Daddy's good girl?" he softly asked, but loudly enough Travis and his wife could hear.

"Me, Daddy." The words left her lips without hesitation, without caring who heard her.

She *was* his good girl, and she didn't care who knew it.

"Bill, you're a good man, and I know you'll take good care of her. But one man to another, let me tell you this. I've known Gabe for ten years, and consider her a friend."

Travis stepped in closer and dropped his voice. "You break her heart, I'll make life holy hell for you, trust me." His tone sounded light, but Gabe heard the unmistakably seriousness of the threat. They weren't just idle words.

"No worries," Bill said. "Believe me, I plan on keeping her so happy she won't ever think about walking away."

She looked up into his hazel eyes. "Thank you, Daddy."

* * * *

Gabe would have been fine with a generic ceremony, but Bill wanted a little more than that. She knew he'd bought wedding rings, because the day after he proposed he came home with an engagement ring for her, and when she'd asked him about wedding rings, he'd simply grinned and kissed her.

I wanted a dominant man, that's what I got.

She loved it, loved him.

When it was time for the ceremony to start and their friends were all assembled, Loren called Bill and Gabe to stand in front of the decorated arbor with her. Rob was Bill's best man, while Gabe had asked Laura to do the honors for her. It was hard for her to make a choice between her friends, but considering Laura had been the first one she'd met at the munch, and who had basically introduced her to Bill, and since her husband was Bill's best man, it made sense.

It didn't hurt that her friends assured her none of them would have their feelings hurt regardless who she picked.

Loren held a couple of index cards and told them to join hands. "We're gathered together today as honored witnesses to the joining of our friends, William and Gabriella. Not just in marriage, but more than that. As partners, as a Dominant and his submissive, a Daddy and his girl, an Owner and his cherished love, the yin and yang in a dynamic that only they can define, because they are the only two who matter."

Gabe was a little surprised that he'd asked Loren to use her full name, but realized she shouldn't have when she saw the playful creases at the outer corners of his eyes.

He would have this done his way.

Loren continued. "There are as many ways to hold a wedding, or a handfasting, or a collaring, as there are people involved in the ceremony. And all that matters at the end of the day is that the people involved are happy and satisfied.

"Gabriella, before you stands a man who, in the eyes of his friends and peers, is worthy, respected, and someone we consider a good guy. Someone who wants to take you in hand, by the hand, under his hand but never under anything less than the full love and devotion of his heart, and with the desire to do the very best he can to love, cherish, and care for you. What say ye?"

She smiled. "I say aye."

"You need to say what you want, ask for what you desire."

Okay, Bill had definitely planned this out. She looked him square in the eye despite the tears already threatening to blur her vision. "I want to take this man as my husband, my partner, my Owner, my Dominant." Her voice hitched. "My Daddy. I want him to own me, to love me, to care for me."

There were a few sniffles throughout the room, and Gabe even thought Bill's eyes suddenly looked a little too bright.

"And what do you want to do in return for this?" Loren asked.

"I'll love him—"

"And squeeze him and name him George," someone muttered in the audience, causing a ripple of laughter amongst them and even making Gabe giggle.

Loren cocked her head as she glared at the offender. "*Really*, Gilo? Tilly, I thought you said he was gagged?"

Tilly, a scowl on her face, headed across the room. "Someone get me the fucking duct tape," she darkly muttered.

Loren returned her attention to Gabe. "Sorry, sweetie. Let's try that again. And what do you want to do in return for this?"

Gabe smiled, fighting the urge to repeat poor Gilo's line. "I'll love him, be faithful to him, trust him." She took a deep breath. "I'll obey him because I know he'll only do things in my best interest."

Bill gently squeezed her hands, his smile seared across her soul.

"William," Loren said, "before you stands a woman who, in the eyes of her friends and peers, is deserving of the one man who will make her happy. She asks for that man to own her, love her, care for her. Someone who is worthy of that one man, regardless of the label he takes in her life, be it husband, Dominant, Owner, or Daddy."

Gabe gave Loren credit for remembering what she'd said.

All she herself could do was focus on Bill's eyes, and how warm his hands felt holding hers.

Loren continued. "She's willing to love, trust, be faithful, and obey that one man. Are you that man?"

He nodded, his eyes never leaving Gabe's. "Aye. I am that man."

"Can you give her what she asks?"

"I can."

"Will you give her what she asks?"

"I will."

"Before all those assembled, publicly state your vow, and ask her what you want."

Bill brought her hands up to his lips and kissed them before holding them against his chest. She felt his pulse thundering, matching her own. It reassured her that he was as nervous as she was.

"I promise to love you, trust you, be faithful to you..." He smiled. "And respect you even as I own you. To care for you. To never let you walk this life alone if I can be at your side. I ask you to please be my wife, my partner, my submissive." He kissed her hands again. "My sweet girl. My beautiful toy."

That did it. She did her best to ignore the tears trickling from her eyes.

Loren smiled. "Gabriella, can you give him what he asks?"

"I can."

"Will you give him what he asks?"

"I will."

"Gabriella, your ring."

She hoped Laura had it. Fortunately, she did. Her friend pressed it into her palm with a smile. Gabe turned back to Bill and held it ready.

Loren spoke again. "Rings are usually used to signify the eternity of love. No beginning or end, lasting forever. In our lifestyle, they can mean much more than a pledge of love or fidelity, but also of a trust far deeper than many people ever get to feel in their lives. By accepting this ring, William, you agree to keep this vow you've given in front of all who've assembled."

Loren nodded to Gabe and she slipped it on his left ring finger. She didn't even have time to get a good look at it, although with the tears in her eyes blurring her vision, she could barely see as it was.

"William," Loren said, "your ring."

He turned and Rob handed it to him.

"Gabriella, by accepting this ring, you are freely, of your own will, consenting before all those assembled here today to give yourself to this man." She nodded to Bill, who gently slid the ring on Gabe's left finger, next to the engagement ring. She'd heard that the wedding band was supposed to go on first, but he'd told her he wanted her to keep her engagement ring on throughout the ceremony.

So she had.

"Before you all, these two have taken vows to each other. Is there any reason these two should not be joined?"

No one spoke. Apparently, Tilly had located the duct tape.

Loren grinned. "This is the part I love the best. By the power vested by the State of Florida, I now pronounce you husband and wife, and whatever else you choose to be together. Owner, kiss your toy. She's officially yours."

Everyone began clapping and cheering as Bill grinned and pulled Gabe into his arms before she could blink. Then he crushed her lips with his in a kiss that threatened to have her begging him to fuck her right there in front of everyone.

Good thing the rules prohibit that…

When he finally stood her upright again, she swayed a little on her feet as she tried to get her breath and brains back under control.

Loren hugged her first, whispering in her ear. "Congratulations, sweetie. If he breaks your heart, make sure you have Tilly on speed dial."

Gabe laughed, but knew deep in heart that would not be necessary. Then Loren hugged Bill. After that, it was a blur of hugs and well wishes. Before they could get sidetracked with the reception part of the festivities, Loren called them and Laura and Rob over to sign the marriage certificate.

Now she'd had a chance to dab at her eyes with a tissue and actually look at their bands. Gold, they were a matching set with delicate Celtic knots engraved around the bands.

He leaned in to whisper in her ear. "I thought knots were appropriate."

She nodded. "Yes, Daddy. I love them."

He took her hand and quickly swapped the position of her engagement and wedding rings, kissing her hand after doing it. "I hoped you'd like them."

She motioned him close so she could whisper in his ear. "If you ever wanted to get me a collar, Daddy, I'd wear it for you."

"Funny you should mention that." He smiled. "I was thinking more along the lines for our first anniversary, I want to get you an ankle tattoo. One of those that looks like a bracelet. With my initials worked into it. What would you think about that, sweetheart?"

Her heart raced, pounding.

In a good way. "Only if you go with me to get it done, Daddy."

"Of course. And I was thinking about getting your initials on the inside of my left wrist."

That he was willing to do that for her, it totally melted her. "Thank you, Daddy."

"Want to know why?"

From the evil grin on his face, she knew he wanted her to ask. "Why, Daddy?"

He reached up with his left hand and fisted her hair, gently easing her head back while reaching between her legs with his right hand, easily finding her clit through the fabric of her dress. "Because any time I see it, I want to think exactly about this, the look in your eyes right now, and I'll be able to make a fist with that hand and picture this." His finger stroked her clit through the fabric. "And imagine doing this to you."

She whimpered when he pulled his right hand away and touched his fingers to her lips, which opened automatically for him.

"Such a good girl," he said as she sucked on his fingers, even though the fabric had kept him from getting her juices on them. "Such a very, very good girl. *My* good girl." He smiled.

She whimpered again, knowing she would beg him to spend the rest of her life like this with him if he asked her to, following his commands.

Making him smile *that* smile.

Chapter Thirty

Bill had definitely got her worked up, but a few minutes later, everyone was eating in preparation for getting to the cake. Gabe was glad he had no interest in smashing cake in her face, either, despite Gilo's plaintive begging while dodging Tilly and her riding crop for them to basically frost each other.

After the reception was over, the playspace was officially declared open, in time for the regular club opening to other members. Gabe thought maybe Bill would want to play with her at the club. It had surprised her when he told her no, that he wanted to reserve that for later, at home.

In private.

It also amped up her need to a fevered pitch. She knew he wouldn't strip her fully naked there at the club, even though she realized if he asked it of her, she would do it.

But she'd at least thought to get a couple of orgasms while they were at the club.

Nope, he was content to spend the hours talking with their friends, watching others play, his arm draped possessively across her shoulders and his fingers gently stroking her arm.

Shooting her sexy winks every time he caught her eye.

Winks that, had he not confiscated her panties after the ceremony, would have completely soaked them long before he was ready to leave a little before midnight. As it was, she'd excused herself to the bathroom several times to freshen up and clean up, afraid of a puddle forming on the floor between her feet if she didn't.

He had her totally wet and totally horny.

And from the evil grin on his face, she knew he knew it.

It even shocked her to realize she loved it, the control she willingly gave to him.

The control she knew she *wanted* him to have over her in that way.

Nothing should shock me anymore. Not about him or what we're doing.

In a way, she loved that it did. That there would still be surprises to stumble across.

When they took their leave of everyone and headed home, he opened and held the door of the car for her. As she got in, he smiled. "Make sure to keep your legs spread on the way home."

There went her heart again, racing like crazy. "Yes, Sir."

She took great satisfaction knowing that every time she said that to him, especially when in response to an order, it made him hard. Or harder, as the case might be.

He leaned in. "Lift the hem of your dress and keep it there, sweetheart. I want to see your pussy."

She met his gaze. "Yes, Sir."

He made her strip in the garage after the door was safely rolled down behind them. He confiscated her dress, grabbed a handful of her hair, and led the way inside. In the living room, he led her around the front of one of the matching chairs for the sofa, a soft, upholstered chair with short wooden legs under it, had her kneel facing backward on it, her breasts hanging over the edge of the back.

"Stay," he said. He disappeared into the bedroom and returned with the duffel bag full of rope and the Hitachi.

She suspected what was coming, her juices already running down her legs. Her ass and pussy were exposed like this, and her mouth would be at the perfect height to suck him off.

Subspace started fuzzing the edges of her mind, her body already eagerly anticipating whatever it was he had prepared for her.

Sure enough, he began humming as he uncoiled the first rope and started tying her ankles to the legs of the chair, leaving her legs spread, her pussy exposed.

He next walked around the back of the chair, having her position her arms where it was most comfortable for her to brace herself before he began tying them in a modified gauntlet that led down to the other two chair legs.

A quick rope harness, followed by few turns of rope around her back and under the chair kept her from rising up. She could wiggle her ass, but that was about all she could do. She couldn't pull too far back, and the back of the chair kept her from moving forward.

He stroked her pussy with his hand. "Who owns this?" he softly asked.

"You, Sir."

He lightly slapped her there, making her gasp and jump. "Did that hurt?"

"No, Sir."

He did it again and again, faster, slower, never harder, and hitting her clit with each impact until she realized she was close to coming.

Then he stopped.

She let out a whimper that earned her another laugh. "My poor sweetheart likes having her pussy spanked, doesn't she?"

"Yes, Sir."

He pressed his hand against her lips and she opened, sucking her juices from his fingers.

He grabbed the blindfold and quickly fastened it around her head. "I bought a couple of new toys for tonight, sweetheart. Don't panic. Do you trust me?"

"Yes, Sir."

He kissed her. "Such a good girl."

She felt him move away. When he returned, he tugged at her nipples. "You know what this means, don't you?"

"Yes, Sir." She had a love-hate relationship with the nipple clamps.

He knelt in front of her and took his time teasing her, tweaking one with his fingers while sucking and nipping on the other one, switching back and forth until her clit throbbed, her cunt screaming to be filled, to come, knowing once she started coming she was at his mercy until he was ready to let her stop.

The good kind of fear.

Then, she felt the bite of him attaching the first clamp, followed immediately by the second.

"Such a good girl to take nipple clamps for me." She heard him unzip his jeans, then the head of his cock brushed against her lips. She eagerly swallowed him, working up and down the length of his shaft with her lips and tongue. All the while, he kept one hand on the chain between the nipple clamps, tugging on it, pulling, tormenting her and making her moan in that sweet kind of painful pleasure she wished would never stop.

He buried his other hand in her hair, fisting it, taking over. "I'm in charge, sweetheart. I will fuck your mouth however I want." He withdrew until just the head remained between her lips. "Suck it."

She did, her cheeks hollowing as she pulled at it with her mouth, making him let out a sensual laugh.

"Good girl."

Then he was gone. His cock and his hands. The chain swung free, still giving her delicious sensations as it moved.

A moment later he was back, stroking her ass with his hands. "Do you trust me?"

"Yes, Sir."

"Ask me for your surprise."

"Please give me my surprise, Sir."

"Good girl." She had time to process the sound of something swinging through the air before it smacked her in the ass, and just enough time to process that it was a thoroughly thuddy impact with zero pain before she let out a soft cry.

A flogger. He'd bought a flogger. From the feel of it, a very soft one, although heavy, like a mop flogger. He worked it over her ass and the backs of her thighs, taking his time to make sure some of the falls hit her pussy and adding to the good sensations rolling through her.

The nipple clamp chain swung with every stroke, not giving her any relief there, either.

After a few minutes, he stopped and stroked her ass. "Well?"

"I like it, Sir."

"Good. I hoped you would. I promise, nothing I use on you tonight will be any worse than this. Okay?"

"Yes, Sir."

She felt him step behind her and rub the head of his cock between her pussy lips. "For now, you're absolutely dripping. I think you need a little bit of fucking." He switched the Hitachi on and reached underneath her as he slammed his cock hard and deep inside her. "Come!" He jammed the Hitachi against her clit.

She cried out, straining against the ropes, her explosion taking her by surprise. It was like her body wanted to obey him, too, without any assistance from her.

He held still, his cock buried all the way inside her. "That's it, sweetheart. Work those hips against that vibrator and my cock."

She did, as much as she could, crying her way through the next orgasm and then gasping when he suddenly switched off the vibrator and pulled his cock free.

Then his hand was on the chain again. "Let's make this interesting." The chain grew heavier and she realized he'd clipped some sort of weight to it, tugging on her nipples.

She tried to hold still, but it wasn't possible when he smacked her in the ass with what felt like a foam bat. "Oh, my poor sweetheart. You haven't seen anything yet." It felt like he quickly tied a rope harness around her hips and between her legs, then she felt him insert something.

Her old vibrator.

He switched it on. "Let's change things up a little, shall we?" He snugged the rope, firmly holding the vibrator inside her. It wasn't as strong as the Hitachi, but then he started smacking her in the ass with whatever it was, and every stroke seemed to jostle it inside her as it made the weight on the nipple clamp chain swing.

He sounded like he was about to start giggling. "My poor, poor sweetheart. Feels so good and so bad all at once, doesn't it? Beg me for more."

Her mouth opened. "Please give me more, Sir."

"Why I'd be happy to give you more." More swats across the ass, until she couldn't help it and came again, moaning in pleasure and a sweet kind of pain as her writhing made the nipple clamp chain swing again.

Once she'd worked her way through that one, he untied the hip harness and removed the vibrator. But the nipple clamps stayed on, and he started swinging something else across her ass and thighs. She wasn't sure what it was, because it was light, but firm, and small. Whatever it was, he was going easy with it, she could tell.

He reached between her legs and sank two fingers inside her. "Such a wet pussy. I think you're enjoying this. Are you?"

"Yes, Sir. I'm enjoying it."

"Good girl." He had apparently stripped, because this time when he started fucking her, she didn't feel any clothes, just his warm, bare flesh rubbing against hers.

And the Hitachi again.

She cried out, sobbing as the chain started swinging even harder with every thrust of his hips. He grabbed the rope harness around her chest with one hand and used it for leverage, slamming his hips against her, forcing her clit against the vibrator and tormenting her nipples with every thrust.

"You need to give me at least two more, sweetheart," he grunted. It sounded like his teeth were clenched, as if he struggled to hold back. "Two more good, hard orgasms, and then I'll come and let you take those nipple clamps off."

The first one swept through her, amplified by the pain in her nipples. He pulled the Hitachi away for a moment but still continued fucking her. "Such a good girl. That was one. You only need one more, and then I'm going to fill your sweet pussy with my cum and we'll go to bed and rest."

She moaned, knowing he was deliberately fucking her hard, rocking her, making the nipple clamps swing. She was about to beg him to use the Hitachi again when she heard it click on. She had barely enough time to suck in a breath before he pressed it against her clit.

It felt like the world imploded. Now deep in subspace, she could have been there five minutes or five hours, she didn't know.

His voice broke through, amused. "I said you had to give me one more. I didn't say how long it had to last." He slowed down, chuckling as she moaned, realizing he wouldn't end her torment as soon as she thought he might.

He kept her squirming on it, fucking him, fucking it, her nipples aching and screaming as the weight on the chain kept swinging back and forth with every movement.

"Who owns you, sweetheart?"

"You do, Sir."

"And who's Daddy's good girl?"

"I'm Daddy's good girl."

The vibrator shut off. He grabbed her hips with his, pounding his cock into her and keeping the last vibrations of her orgasm echoing through her until, finally, he let out a groan and finally fell still.

Silence filled the room, the only sounds the two of them catching their breath and her soft, plaintive gasps as the chain rocked.

He patted her on the ass before withdrawing. Then he walked around the front of the chair and carefully removed the nipple clamps.

He stroked her head. "Any regrets, sweetheart?"

She nuzzled her face against his stomach. "No, Daddy. No regrets."

He removed the blindfold and tipped her chin up so he could look her in the eye. "You have no idea how much I'm going to enjoy taking you firmly in hand in the bedroom, sweetheart." He brushed the pad of his thumb across her lips and she opened, immediately sucking it into her mouth and swirling her tongue around it. She'd been a quick study. Anything that he put close to her lips, she opened and sucked it. His fingers, his cock, a vibrator—whatever.

He smiled. "That's my good girl."

Chapter Thirty-One

After getting their showers Tuesday morning, they headed out. She'd asked Bill to pick what he wanted her to wear, enjoying the mental downtime and wanting it to last as long as she could draw it out. He chose one of her sundresses, one that wasn't short, but one she wouldn't have necessarily chosen to wear.

Tomorrow, they'd both have to go back to work. They would take their real honeymoon in a few weeks, a long, leisurely drive up to Boone, North Carolina, where Bill had rented them a house. They'd spend the first week exploring.

Then maybe they'd get out of the house and actually do some sightseeing for the second week.

Maybe.

For now, he'd kept the day's surprise a secret. All she knew was that first they'd eat breakfast out. After they finished that, he drove them to the mall.

As he took her by the hand and led her past stores, she instinctively knew where they'd end up. When he walked her inside Build-A-Bear, she looked up at him.

"More clothes, Daddy?"

He smiled. "Well, yes, that, too." He turned to her and took her hands in his, bringing them up to his lips. "I want you to pick two new bears, sweetheart. We'll make them a boy and a girl. Okay?"

"Bears?"

He nodded, kissing her hands before gently squeezing them. "Bears. I think it's time we send this very last ghost packing for good, don't you?"

Part of her wanted to collapse right there, to break down sobbing in his arms. Not in a bad way, either.

That he knew her so well, better than she knew herself…

There wasn't a single molecule of doubt anywhere in her body that she'd made the right decision. That she could trust him. That she could let him know her, all of her, the pretty and the ugly, the light—and the dark.

He wanted her, wanted *all* of her.

She realized she'd been thinking about it too long when his brow furrowed. "Sweetheart?"

She nodded, smiling. "Yes, Daddy," she whispered.

He pulled her into his arms. In her ear, he softly said, "That's *my* very good girl."

Her clit instantly throbbed, her pussy already growing wet.

Damn him.

She *loved* it.

She loved *him*.

He kissed the side of her neck. "And?"

She closed her eyes and struggled not to burst out laughing. "I'm apparently your very well-trained girl, Daddy."

"Such a *good* girl."

He turned her to face the bins of animals waiting to be chosen and stuffed. Then he gently patted her panty-free ass.

Fortunately they would head home from here. She suspected he'd planned it that way, waiting to trigger her until after they'd reached their last destination so she wouldn't end up with a wet spot on her dress until they returned home.

Although, if he listened too long to Tony, Seth, Rob, and the others, he might develop a little bit of a sadistic streak and start trying more covert things in public that he knew he could get away with.

She loved the possibility of that. Loved that she knew he would never go too far, would never do anything to put either of them at risk.

That didn't mean he might not push her and stretch some boundaries.

With him standing right behind her, so close she could feel the warmth of his body through her sundress, she looked at every bear they had. She tipped her head back to look at him. "The same or different bears, Daddy?"

"Your choice, sweetheart."

She eventually picked out a beige one and a pink one.

"Which is which?"

She held them close and looked up at him, an eyebrow arched at him in disbelief. "*Really*?"

He shrugged. "Hey, I'm not judgmental. You can have a pink boy bear if you want."

Nearly an hour later, both bears had full wardrobes. She'd also purchased several new outfits for Max and Lil Lobo. She carried the boxes holding the bears, while he carried the shopping bags with all the clothes and accessories.

She'd named them Peter and Lydia, after her parents.

After they tucked everything into the backseat and were settled in the car, he turned to her with a grin.

"What, Daddy?" she asked, a tendril of the good kind of fear racing through her.

He arched his eyebrows at her and looked at the hem of her dress.

She was a quick study. She spread her legs and lifted her hem, exposing her shaved pussy to him.

He leaned over and reached between her legs, his fingers gently probing as he whispered in her ear, "Who's my good girl?"

The slight throbbing she'd been feeling in her clit turned into a full-blown aching need as he slowly fucked his fingers into her pussy. They slid right in, too, as wet as she was.

"I'm *your* good girl, Daddy." She leaned her head back against the seat and struggled to keep her eyes focused on him.

Every thrust of his fingers slid along her clit, teasing her.

"I think," he said, "I could sit here all day and do this to you until you come."

She whimpered. "Yes, Sir."

"Ooh." With his free hand, he grabbed one of her hands and placed it on the front of his slacks. Her palm and fingers molded around his stiff cock. "I won't deny when we're like this"—he pressed her hand hard against his cock—"you calling me Sir turns me right the hell on faster than anything."

"Yes, Sir."

He let go of her hand and took hold of her left nipple through the sundress. He hadn't let her put on a bra, either. She whimpered again as he pinched her nipple.

In her pussy, his hand worked harder, faster, thrusting, fucking her.

Owning her.

Her breathing grew faster, almost in time with his thrusts, until she was nearly ready to come, so close—

She let out a cry as he stopped, withdrawing his fingers from her cunt and pressing them against her lips. "Clean them off."

Without hesitation she opened her mouth and sucked.

"Aw, my poor girl. You look so preciously desperate right now."

"Mmm." Which meant, *Why the* hell *did you* stop?

Once she'd sucked her juices off his fingers, he let go of her nipple and sat back. He had her put her dress down, and pulled her hand from his cock, putting it back in her lap.

"Keep your legs spread all the way home, sweetheart." She'd kill for that evilly playful smile he now wore.

Hell, she'd let him fuck her right there on the hood of the car, in the middle of the parking lot.

That shocked her a little to realize, and shocked her even more to realize she didn't care if he did it.

"Yes, Sir."

She could barely think, much less talk, on the short drive home. He pulled the car into the garage and once the door was down, he made her wait. He got out, walked around to her side, and opened the door for her. Then he held her hand as she got out and led her over to the hood of the car.

After placing his own palm on the warm hood, to check to see how hot it was, he pushed her forward. "Hands flat on the hood. Legs spread. Don't move."

She immediately complied, her heart racing.

Behind her, he raised the hem of her dress, gathering it onto her back. She felt him step between her legs, followed by the sound of him unfastening his belt and undoing his zipper.

Then the feel of his slacks pressing against the backs of her thighs, his feet forcing hers out a little wider, one hand on her waist, the other between her legs.

"Who's my good girl?"

"I'm your good girl, Sir."

"That's right. Does my good girl want to be fucked?"

"*Please* fuck your good girl, Sir."

He chuckled. "Do I sense a little desperation in your tone?"

"Yes, Sir!"

He rubbed the head of his cock up and down through the juices now coating not only her pussy, but her inner thighs. "Do you want my cock inside you?"

"Yes, Sir!"

He stopped. "I beg your pardon?"

Mind racing, she guessed. "Your good girl wants your cock inside her. Please!"

He thrust, hard and deep and fast and shoving her against the car.

She let out a gasp of shock and pleasure.

"Fuck, that was the sexiest goddamned thing I've ever heard," he said, his voice hoarse. His other hand settled on her waist and he started fucking her, hard, fast, deep.

And from her position, all she could do was lie there and take it.

And she loved it.

"Are you going to come for me?" he asked.

"I want to, Sir."

He slowed down, pacing himself. "I plan on fucking you all day, sweetheart," he said, his voice now strained from the effort of holding back. Her nipples chafed against the fabric of her dress, and combined with the heat from the engine under the hood, it all felt deliciously, evilly sexy.

"When I'm done fucking you here, you can keep that dress on. I want you to feel my cum running down your legs until I'm ready to let you clean up. After I fuck you a few more times and make sure that pussy's nice and full, I'm going to start playing with your ass. By the time we go to sleep tonight, I'm going to come in that sweet ass of yours. Understand?"

Hell, she wanted him to do it right that moment. "Yes, Sir!"

He stopped, lightly slapping her ass. "What was that?"

"Yes, Sir, I want you to please fuck your good girl's ass."

He leaned forward, his weight pressing her against the hood. "Such a good girl." With his cock buried all the way inside her, he reached around and found her clit and tweaked it, lightly pinching. "I want you to come for me, sweetheart. Come hard."

She did, crying out, her pussy clamping around the stiff cock now deep inside her.

"That's my good girl." He started fucking her again, hard and fast, slamming her thighs against the front of the car. She suspected she'd have bruises on the fronts of her thighs the next morning.

She was good with that.

When he finally caught up and exploded, falling still with his cock buried all the way inside her, pulsing and beginning the start of his promise as his balls emptied his cum into her, he let out a content sigh. "That's number one."

She tried to laugh, but couldn't, still catching her breath. It came out as breathless, soundless chuckles.

Then he bit the back of her shoulder, hard, making her cry out again, and starting her clit throbbing once more.

"I wasn't kidding, sweetheart," he said. He sat up enough he could slide a hand between them, and, without pulling out his cock, worked a finger inside the seam of her ass, finding her rim.

He didn't press forward. "I bought a couple of tubes of lube, sweetheart, and some condoms," he said. "The next step of your training is going to start tonight. I'm going to get you used to having my cock in one place, a nice big dildo or butt plug in the other, and you coming for me as many times as I want you to." He laughed. "Of course, I really like what Tony does, using a butt plug, a dildo, and then having Shay suck him off."

She let out a little gasp that froze him. He leaned in once more. "Did I just feel your pussy squeeze my cock, sweetheart?"

There wasn't any use lying to him about it. "Yes, Sir."

"You liked that idea, didn't you?"

"Yes, Sir."

He pulled her up off the hood and wrapped both arms around her, cupping her breasts in his hands, rolling her nipples between his fingers. "Then I think our next goal will be for the party at Tony's on Friday night. You're going to get tied down to the bench, stuffed full in your pussy and your ass with a dildo and butt plug, and you're going to suck my cock while I use a Hitachi on your clit. Is that what you want? Out in the open so everyone can see you take it?"

She had to swallow to form spit, her pussy greedily grabbing at his cock, which had started swelling and growing hard again. "Please train your good girl to take a butt plug so you can tie her to the bench, stuff her full, and she can suck your cock."

"In front of everyone at Tony's party?" He'd done forced orgasm play on her before at the private parties, and even some at the club. But he'd never taken it to that step at any of the private parties before, of fucking her or having her suck him off. Not out in the open like that.

She belonged to him. Among their friends, she didn't care who knew it. Their play barely bumped a seismograph reading compared to how some of their friends played. "Your good girl wants you to do it at Tony's party in front of everyone," she whispered.

He chuckled, his cock now hard inside her once more. He pushed her back down onto the hood. "Such a good girl you are. Let's go for number two, shall we?"

THE END

WWW.TYMBERDALTON.COM

ABOUT THE AUTHOR

Tymber Dalton lives in the Tampa Bay region of Florida with her husband (aka "The World's Best Husband™") and too many pets. Not only is she active in the BDSM lifestyle, the two-time EPIC winner is also the bestselling author of over fifty books, such as *The Reluctant Dom*, *The Denim Dom*, *Cardinal's Rule*, the Love Slave for Two series, the Triple Trouble series, the Coffeeshop Coven series, the Good Will Ghost Hunting series, and many more.

She loves to hear from readers! Please feel free to drop by her website and sign up for her newsletter to keep abreast of the latest news, views, snarkage, and releases. (Don't forget to look up her writing alter egos Lesli Richardson, Tessa Monroe, and Macy Largo.)

www.tymberdalton.com
www.facebook.com/tymberdalton
www.twitter.com/TymberDalton

For all titles by Tymber Dalton, please visit
www.bookstrand.com/tymber-dalton

For titles by Tymber Dalton writing as
Tessa Monroe, please visit
www.bookstrand.com/tessa-monroe

For titles by Tymber Dalton writing as
Macy Largo, please visit
www.bookstrand.com/macy-largo

For titles by Tymber Dalton writing as
Lesli Richardson, please visit
www.bookstrand.com/lesli-richardson

Siren Publishing, Inc.
www.SirenPublishing.com